Sun & Water

a novel by
CRAIG WALLENBROCK

Teitelbaum Publishing

Sun & Water

This is a work of fiction. Some events, names, characters, and events are a fictitious re-telling based on remembered life experiences and interesting people met along the way.

ISBN - 978-1-7326485-2-4

Teitelbaum Publishing

Cover design by Susan Lee

CHAPTER ONE

Corey hurried to finish packing his car. It wasn't that he was so anxious to get back to college, although it was his senior year. In fact, the prospect of graduation caused more trepidation than excitement, which was why he had changed majors in his junior year. He had told his father the change was because he had come to realize that he loved literature more than the business major, which had been selected by his father when Corey first went away to school. Corey's primary reason for the change was he hoped by changing majors, he could gain an extra year of student deferment from the draft. In the process, he learned he truly loved literature.

His father helped him pack, but the two did not speak to one another unless it was his father asking Corey where he wanted something placed in the car. Actually, they seldom talked with each other since Corey began college; now they only argued. Earlier that morning, the argument was over the length of Corey's hair — which Corey wore long because it was the preferred style of his peer group, and most importantly because Karen, his girlfriend, liked it that way. To his father, Frank Jameson, Corey's hair length represented the hippie, anti-war sentiment that he despised so much.

Their relationship had not always been as troublesome as it was in the present. There was a time, not all that long ago, when Corey considered his dad his best friend. Back during Corey's high school days, he and his father would sit for hours and discuss a multitude of subjects ... when they openly shared their deepest emotions. Corey knew that like himself, his dad had been an outstanding high school football player who had earned a scholarship to Nebraska, whose football team was the pride of his father's native state. A broken leg his freshman year of college, then the bombing of Pearl Harbor, put an end to those dreams. Corey understood why his dad lived vicariously through Corey's successes, but Corey did not care, for he was proud of his father's accomplishments. In fact, he respected the sacrifices Frank Jameson's generation made during that horrific war.

Instead of spending the last night with his parents, Corey stayed out late visiting with an old high school buddy and some of his friend's new college comrades. They had a few beers, passed around a joint, and as intelligently as their altered state would allow, denounced the war, their parents' materialistic values, and the establishment in general. To be sure his parents would be asleep when he got home, he talked his friends into a few more beers, another joint, and listening to the latest Bob Dylan album while trying to decipher deeper meanings implied in the lyrics. By the time he got home, his mind was racing in a myriad of directions, none of which led to any meaningful resolution.

He was tired, but the minute his head hit the pillow, his mind began racing. He closed his bedroom door and opened a window next to his bed. He searched his already-packed bags until he reached a small locked box near the bottom of his travel bag, where he had stashed a roach. He lit up at the window, inhaling and holding the smoke as long as he could. He took two long hits, closed the window, and lay back on his bed. He concentrated on how heavy his body felt, hoping to drift into sleep, but more thoughts randomly crept into his consciousness. The first memories were pleasant ones of his first years of high school. Those good recollections ended November of 1963, during his senior year.

The beginning of his senior year started as perfect and idyllic as any seventeen-year-old boy could hope it would be. He was captain of his school's football team, the returning star running back. He expected to be captain of the baseball team as well. He liked baseball more than football and had been excited by several colleges which had contacted him over the summer regarding a possible baseball scholarship. Corey was quite popular, having been junior class president and, to his father's delight, also president of the Young Republicans, the most powerful club on campus in his conservative San Marino community.

Yes, going into his senior year, "the world was his oyster." He knew nothing of Vietnam, nor thought his generation would experience war like his father's generation had endured.

Probably the only unpleasant thing he had experienced in four years of high school was the election of the brash young Democrat, Jack Kennedy. Although Corey experienced no personal change in his lifestyle, his father and all his father's friends insisted that four years under JFK would bring about the demise of democracy and the start of socialism in America. He trusted his father's judgment, even though he secretly thought Kennedy a much more pleasant man than the stiff, shifty-eyed Nixon. Corey, to please his father, dutifully repeated all his father's beliefs at the meetings of the Young Republicans Club.

On November 22, 1963, Corey walked into his ten o'clock American history class, taught by Marshall Qualak, who was also the varsity football coach. Mr. Qualak was a short, yet powerfully built man. He had a large head that looked more rectangular than round, which was accentuated by his short crew-cut hair, a seemingly mandatory haircut for both the coaches and football team. Coach always wore a clean, white, heavily starched short-sleeved dress shirt with a blue tie. Blue and white, of course, were the school colors. Protruding from the short-sleeved shirt were intimidating Popeye forearms about as hairy as Corey had ever seen. Whenever Mr. Qualak spoke, he used many hand and arms gestures that seemed to accentuate the strength in those big hairy arms. That morning, Mr. Qualak was more animated than usual as he discussed media image and its importance in the last half of the twentieth century.

"Had you listened to the Nixon/Kennedy debates on the radio, rather than watch them on TV, the boob tube, you would have thought Nixon to be a clear winner as he was more logical and far better prepared in his research on the issues. However, the youthful, charismatic Mr. Kennedy mesmerized the nation. You all know the results," Mr. Qualak said, clenching his fist in disapproval. He squeezed so tight, Corey thought some of those hairs would pop out like porcupine quills. Suddenly the door burst open and one of Corey's classmates, who had been absent that day, walked into the room. The boy wore a soiled-looking night-robe over dirty pajamas. His eyes were red and watery. The gaze in his eyes looked more like a person in shock than someone who was sick.

"President Kennedy was assassinated at a parade in Dallas," he said, his voice cracking with emotion. "I was alone. I had to tell someone; our president is dead." The class collectively froze in disbelief, but the boy's eyes and voice were more convincing than his words.

Mr. Qualak looked at the boy with calm disdain. "If you come late to class, you are not permitted entry without a yellow slip from the attendance office. I don't see any slip, and of course your attire is improper."

The boy, whose head was drooped toward the floor to hide his eyes, suddenly snapped a look at the teacher. "The president is dead," he repeated, as if maybe Mr. Qualak hadn't heard him. “Don’t you understand? I was home alone and sick and our president was murdered.”

Undaunted, Qualak looked at the class as if he were going to continue his lesson plan. “When a tragedy, a national catastrophe occurs, which by the way has not been confirmed,” he added glancing at the boy, “it is imperative that we maintain order and proper procedure, or let chaos reign over reason.” He raised one of his massive forearms and pointed a finger to the sky, as if he believed his words had come from divine inspiration. His eyes fixed on the class and his hand remained up, as if he expected applause for his words of wisdom.

Receiving none, he turned back to the frightened student. “You will return home, properly dress, and come back with the correct yellow slip. Tomorrow you will apologize to the class for this intrusion.”

Corey stood up and walked over to the boy. “Return to your seat, Mr. Jameson,” Qualak shouted. Corey wheeled around, looked Qualak in the eye, and just stared at him for several long seconds.

Corey replied to the command in a firm but soft voice. “Sometimes rules and what you think is proper procedure don't apply. You have to put them aside temporarily.”

Corey turned back to his scared classmate and put his arm around his shoulder. “It’s okay,” he whispered. “Let’s go to the nurse’s office.”

“You step out the door and you face expulsion,” Qualak said, his anger becoming more intense.

"Our president was just assassinated," Corey shouted and walked the young man toward the door.

"Get back in here this minute," Qualak yelled as if he were shouting at his players during practice. Then something happened that Corey did not, nor could not, have understood then. It was as if he was suddenly possessed by some external force which entered his body. The foreign spirit even disguised its voice to sound like Corey's. The voice shouted back something Corey would never say to anyone in a position of authority, particularly not a coach. "Fuck you!" the spirit yelled. Immediately Corey began to tremble as he realized what the voice had uttered, but it was too late. Embarrassed, he hurried his classmate out the door and to the nurse's office. The realization of what had just happened suddenly hit him. He knew the moment he stood up he was out of line and his perfectly wonderful high school days would never be the same. He thought, "I just jeopardized the football season, probably any chance at a baseball scholarship," yet for some reason he didn't care. A faint smile crossed his face.

"Thanks," his classmate said weakly, almost apologetically. "I was alone. I was scared — I'm sorry."

"Any one of us would have reacted the same," Corey said as nonchalantly as he could.

Years later, thinking back on the incident, Corey realized that the person who wanted to remain seated, to not speak out, was the extension of his father's will. It was not only his father's will, but also that of the community in which he had been raised and whose values were so embedded in his mindset that he unquestionably accepted them as his own. Those words "the president has been assassinated," coupled with Qualak's reaction, was like an electrical shock, a lightning bolt that struck and broke free Corey's innate spirit. He tasted freedom for the first time and had not known what it was, or how to control it. He only knew for some unexplained reason, it felt good.

While Corey was in the nurse's office, she received a call and informed Corey he was to go to the principal's office, where he was told to remain seated in the waiting room until his father arrived. From the outer office, he heard familiar voices coming from within the principal's office. He recognized Principal Landal's and Coach Qualak's voices. Although he could not make out what they were saying, he knew he was the topic and would have to wait to hear his punishment, which Corey was quite sure would be expulsion.

Frank Jameson's office was in a neighboring community, and it only took him about fifteen minutes to get to the school. As he entered the office, he looked at Corey with a confused expression. Corey knew his father's sympathies were with the coach and the principal, and his father would support their judgment, but Corey also detected a look of affection that his father had for his son. Corey acknowledged his father's glance with an appearance of apology, which he truly felt at the time.

Principal Landal spoke first. "Ordinarily a student who curses at a teacher and defies their orders would be expelled for a minimum of two weeks, but you are very lucky to have

Mr. Qualak as your coach, teacher, and, whether or not you know it, your friend." He paused and nodded toward the coach, who picked up the conversation.

"This Friday our football team, league champions for the first time in ten years, will be playing in the CIF championship playoffs. You are probably our most valuable player, an honor that you will not receive because of your actions today. Nevertheless, not letting you play would not be fair to your teammates who have worked just as hard as you to make this season successful."

"Son, you had better play the game of your life," his father added, still appearing bewildered.

Landal then stated, "I want you to understand you will be punished. You have six hours detention each Saturday for ten weekends starting the first weekend upon the conclusion of the season."

"I assure you there will be further discipline at home," his father quickly added. "Now I think you should apologize to Coach Qualak and thank him for standing up on your behalf."

Corey looked at the principal and then at Coach Qualak, but he avoided eye contact with his father. "In light of what's just happened, do you guys really think that we should be playing this Friday?"

"Is there somewhere I can speak to my son privately?" Mr. Jameson snapped.

"We'll leave you two to talk in here," Principal Landal answered. He and Coach Qualak immediately exited the room. No sooner had the door clicked shut when his father stood up, walked over, and slapped Corey in the face. "What kind of remark was that? You should have been apologizing out your ass and thanking them for their more than fair decision," his father said, trying to sound under control despite his confusion over the incident.

As Corey jumped to his feet and stood before his father, he felt the demon resurface.

Although Corey had passed his father's height the year before, he had never thought of his dad as being shorter, but at that moment he realized he was taller than his father.

Mr. Jameson raised his hand to strike again.

"Don't!" Corey commended. "Not now or ever again." He looked his father straight in the eyes. Corey did not remember his father's words; he just knew his dad's lips moved. He looked at his father as if he were some insignificant bit player in a bad movie. Mr. Jameson fell silent and sank into his chair.

"Son," he spoke softly, then paused a long while. Corey sat, but never took his eyes off his father. "I don't know what to think. I'm as confused as you are." His father paused again. He looked as if he was no longer looking at Corey but into his own mind. "Sometimes a father loses sight of the fact that his son has his own ideas, his own ambitions. He believes he will always be the one leading his son into manhood without realizing when his son has arrived. I never thought what happened today would happen in my lifetime. I'm sure that we'll soon learn that the Russians are behind this. If, as a nation, we allow a tragedy such as this to break down the very essence of our beliefs, then our enemies will think we are weak, and who knows what will happen next. If we carry on as normal, I'm sure they will think we are a strong and resilient people.

The expression on his father's face told Corey his father was now speaking to him as a peer, but still, Corey did not think his dad could understand why Corey acted as he did. Corey was not sure himself, but he felt he did the right thing and should apologize to no one.

"I'm sure Coach Qualak is a very unique teacher," his father continued. "He cares about his players and students beyond the field and classroom. He wants you to be a better person all your life. I think you owe him an apology as I owe you one. I should have never slapped you. I'm sorry."

"I think there needs to be a lot of reflecting on this day," Corey answered. "There should be a lot of apologies."

Most of the team did not want to play that Friday — it was too soon after the assassination. Their opponents, the children of a blue-collar working community and from a much poorer school district, were eager to play. They were from a predominately Democratic city and their president had been killed. They wanted revenge, and although that vengeance was misdirected, they wanted to beat the Republican-dominant San Marino team to give them a sense of vindication.

After much discussion at governmental and theological levels, both statewide and local, the decision was made by most schools for Friday night playoff games to go on as scheduled. Corey did play. He set the school's single game rushing record, but they still lost. The moment the game started he knew what the result would be. He saw it in his own teammates eyes as compared to the focus of purpose, heightened by anger, in the eyes of their opponents.

Upon returning to the school, Corey's defeated teammates sat, confused, on the bus. Some cried, some cursed the administration for allowing the game to go on. Most vented that if game had been played a week later, they would have “kicked their redneck asses.” Corey said nothing other than he would catch up with his teammates later. He waited for the locker room to empty, then knocked on the coaches' office door.

Qualak opened the door. Seeing Corey was alone, he stepped out and closed the door so the other coaches would not hear their conversation.

“You played a great game. Too bad some of your teammates could not find the courage to play as hard as you. I'm proud of you, son.”

“That's why I needed to talk with you, Coach. I need you and everyone else to understand, I played that game for myself ... not for the school, not for my father, and certainly not for you. I'll serve the detention. I'll apologize as instructed but only because I have to. But make no mistake, I played that game for myself.”

Qualak's face turned red, but he disguised his anger with laughter. “Well, I guess I really pissed you off. You don't realize it yet, but I had everything to do with your performance tonight.” Then he put his hand on Corey's shoulder, saying,

"There has been a lot of rumblings about a place called Vietnam. I'm afraid it's going to escalate, maybe lead to another war. What you did tonight, or what some other players do in the future, really does not matter. What matters is that if you or any other young men I coach or teach might have to go to war, God forbid, then the lessons of duty, of courage, that old Coach Qualak taught his boys will help make your parents, your country, and especially me proud of my boys. What you showed on that field tonight is confirmation that I have guided you well."

Corey stepped away from his coach. "You really believe that, don't you? Knowing what happened in your classroom, and the punishment I must serve — I'd do it again in a heartbeat. If you think you are in any way responsible for my game tonight, then you are one pitiful son of a bitch."

Coach Qualak's anger returned. He turned his back on Corey and walked into his office, slamming the door behind him.

His father finally spoke as they put the last of Corey's belongings in the car. "You got in pretty late last night. I thought you might get home a little early — spend your last evening talking with your mom and me."

"We wouldn't have talked. We'd have continued arguing about my hair or something else."

"Well, since you brought it up, when you come home for Christmas break, you will have a haircut, or don't come home," Frank Jameson commanded.

Corey shot an angry glance toward his father but said

nothing. He walked back into the house to say goodbye to his mother.

Emily Jameson was seated at the breakfast table working a crossword puzzle in the morning paper. She alternated sips of coffee with her morning Bloody Mary. She looked tired.

"Bye, Mom," he said, and bent over to kiss her. She did not turn her head; her gaze remained fixed on the crossword puzzle. He kissed her cheek which, like the rest of her skin, was the color of an undercooked chicken breast. Corey knew her fixation on the puzzle was because she no longer knew how to show her emotions — even to her own son. "I love you," he said, and kissed her again.

"Luv ya too," she acknowledged without looking up at him.

That duty done, he hastily shook his father's hand. "See you both at Christmas, maybe?"

Nothing else was said. Corey got in his car and began backing out of the driveway. He glanced back and waved at his father. Although Corey was still angry from their arguments about his long hair, among numerous subjects, he noticed sadness in his father's eyes. He knew both his mom and dad still longed for the way things used to be, or maybe he wanted to believe that and was just projecting his own feelings upon them. It was not his hair, he was sure of that. It was because of the goddamn war ... or maybe it was just Corey's time to move on.

CHAPTER TWO

COREY MADE ONE LAST STOP BEFORE RETURNING TO school, and it was the same stop he had been making for the three previous years. At the bottom of his block lived an elderly couple named Hank and Millie Victor, his surrogate parents, or more aptly the grandparents he would have selected if the matter was left to choice, not genetics.

Corey's friendship with the Victors began when Corey was seven years old and his parents first moved to their current home. He was then old enough to explore a territory no larger than the street on which he lived, so he relied on valuable information volunteered by other neighborhood kids concerning their street. So through the rumor mill, he became aware of an older couple who lived in a house on the south corner of their neighborhood, a home with a particularly large backyard. His new friends further volunteered that the couple did not have any children of their own, probably because "Mr. Victor is a full-blooded Apache Indian ... and Indian and white blood doesn't mix well, kind of like why dogs can't mate with cats," or so the neighborhood kids said and shared with young Corey.

Corey immediately went down to the house. He had seen many Indians on movie westerns, but he had never seen one in real life. The only person he saw on that first visit was a lady watering her roses in the front of the house. Corey saw no Indian, so he began hanging around the place as much as possible hoping to see the Indian ... only to be met with disappointment after disappointment, as no Indian ever appeared. The lady was nice and was always offering lemonade and fresh-baked cookies to the neighborhood kids. However, the only man he saw wore a coat and tie and went to work each day. He looked just like all the other fathers, only older. Corey thought that maybe the man was Mrs. Victor's brother and maybe the Indian lived in a wigwam in the backyard.

Corey's curiosity became so overwhelming he sneaked into their backyard. To the seven- year-old boy, the yard seemed like a small forest of various kinds of plants and trees, mostly fruit trees. There was one section with rows of many different colors of flowers with fragrances sweeter than a candy store — but unlike natural woods, these trees and flowers were in perfect columns, well cared for and neatly trimmed. There were plenty of places to hide, but unfortunately the yard could also hide someone from him.

"Well, look who's visiting — the new boy," he heard Mrs. Victor say. She was kneeling while working behind a leafy bush, which had prevented Corey from seeing her. Corey was so frightened he began to tremble and even cry. She came over and hugged him. "There, there, I didn't mean to scare you. Come inside, I'll give you some cookies and milk," she said as she led him toward the house.

The man he saw go to work each day heard them talking and came outside.

"We have a visitor, Hank," Millie said.

Corey, still embarrassed at being caught in the yard, tried to explain his presence, although the Victors weren't at all upset about him being there; in fact, they encouraged neighborhood kids to play in their yard ... even pick an orange or other ripe fruit.

"The other kids played a trick on me ... because I'm new... I guess. They said you were married to an Indian. I just wanted to see the Indian."

"You are seeing him," the man said. He and Millie began laughing as if they were sharing a joke with a friend. It made young Corey feel at ease. "I am a full-blooded Apache Indian," the man continued, "born on an Arizona Indian reservation. When I left the reservation, I changed my name from Henry Victorio to Hank Victor." He extended his hand to Corey, who hesitated, then meekly shook the man's hand.

"Come with me. I'll show you."

He led Corey into the house and down a hallway into a

den with walls decorated with Indian relics and pictures of Indians, the kind the boy envisioned.

"These are my parents," Hank said, pointing to a black-and-white photo of two Indians in traditional Indian clothes. "They believed in the old ways and wanted me to do likewise. I left at eighteen. I wanted to be part of the modern white world, not theirs."

The boy forgot his fears and became enchanted as Hank talked about the shields, medicine bows, and blankets that adorned the walls. He told Corey how those objects represented magical powers of the spirit world and animal world that shared the land with the Indians. Since spirits and other worlds exist in the imagination of a seven-year-old, his discomfort gave way to curiosity, and that curiosity led to an enduring friendship that manifested itself into camping trips into the High Sierras with Corey, his friends, and other neighborhood kids. Maybe it was because the Victors had no children of their own, or maybe because Hank just loved the outdoors, but as Corey grew, he realized those trips were as much for Hank as they were for the boys. What counted most was that Hank became young Corey's mentor and teacher.

At that first meeting, the Victors were in their fifties, which seemed really old to the boy who compared their age to those of his own parents, but by the time Corey reached college age, the Victors were growing older, and visibly showing it. During the past year, Hank suffered several minor strokes as the arteries in his legs hardened. His doctor wanted to operate, but Hank was reluctant, partially from a fear of modern science, and partially from the Indian ways taught him by him father that remained in his subconscious.

"This will be your senior year, won't it?" the old man asked without looking at Corey nor caring if he answered right away. He was preoccupied with the far more important task of pouring his favorite drink — Seagram's VO — carefully over a glass filled with crystal-clear ice. He filled the glass three-quarters full without a splash or losing a drop. Then, using a silver swivel stick, he stirred it three times. He held the crystal glass up to the sunlight streaming in through a large arch-shaped picture window. As if touched by the philosopher's stone, the amber liquid blazed sparkling gold as the sunlight filtered through it. He was not satisfied, so he gave it a few more swirls and repeated the sunlight inspection. He then looked content. Hank's eyes brightened as he took a small sip, gently swishing it in his mouth before swallowing. He savored the aroma for several seconds before exhaling in a way to stimulate every olfactory nerve, and then he set his glass on the coffee table and looked Corey in the eye.

"I'll bet your old man is going crazy over your hair," he said.

"He's pretty convinced that long hair makes you a pot-smoking anti-establishment revolutionary."

"Well, is he correct?" Hank asked.

"Not a revolutionary," Corey answered with an impish smile.

Hank took another sip of whiskey. He set the glass down

and gave Corey a confused stare. "Don't let this old Indian get drunk. My mind plays enough tricks on me at my age, and the firewater might make me hallucinate. Then I might think you're General Yellow-Haired Custer and try and scalp you."

"Your mind is already foggy. It was the Sioux that got Custer, not the Apaches, but if you're right about firewater and Indians ... you ought to try pot. That's probably what your ancestor's smoked in those peace pipes."

"It had to be some kind of potent weed for them to keep believing those stupid white man's treaties," Hank answered.

"We did try some marijuana about three years ago," Millie confessed. "Remember Hank?"

Corey gasped. "Did you really?"

Millie nodded yes. "I have a nephew going to Berkeley. He and his girlfriend visited us after coming home that summer. They talked us into trying some."

"Well? What did you think?" Corey pursued.

"It made me silly," Millie said, laughing at the memory.

"Made my heart race. Scared the hell out me," Hank said, then took another sip of the VO. "Each generation has to do their own thing," he said, lifting his glass in a toast to nothing in particular except maybe just living life to the fullest. "This is mine."

The word 'generation' struck a chord with Corey. His parents were always talking about the 'generation gap,' the buzz phrase of the media that they used to explain Corey's rebellion. Millie and Hank were older than his parents, yet he felt like he was talking with his college buddies. That was it; they talked *with* him, not at him like his parents did — lecture versus casual conversation — the kind you have sitting on your porch talking with friends on a lazy summer's night.

Once, when Corey was fourteen — it was probably the second to last camping trip before Hank's health started deteriorating — they awoke to a beautiful High Sierra sunrise. They were camped at about nine thousand feet elevation. The sky was as clear a turquoise blue he had ever seen and contrasted even more with a few cirrus clouds, whose pure-white wispy filaments seem like brushstrokes on a painter's canvas.

The wind, slightly cool, blew over their encampment, covering the dew-wet mountain grass with a sweet nectar-like aroma that stimulated their mountain-high senses even more. The whole scene seemed to be musically scored by the lamenting cry of a hunting hawk, chipmunks nervously chattering as they scurried for safety. In the background, aspen leaves rustled like soft castanets, and the stream brushed the submerged rocks like a drummer gently tapping out the rhythm for the whole song.

"People are always complaining — if they only were a little richer, taller, better looking, or a thousand more 'ifs.' Then you wake to a morning like this and realize that somehow this tiny little planet got blessed with just the right amount of heat and water that makes us unique from what we know of the rest of the universe. On a morning like this I have to ask myself, 'What else do you need?' Just nothing but sun and water," he said, then took a deep breath as if he were trying to inhale the beauty of the sweet nectar produced by ancient gods.

Corey didn't know why he thought about that morning until now. Maybe it was because one of those other "ifs" that people shouldn't be too concerned about was the length of someone else's hair. Hank and Millie sure weren't. He could talk with them, even kid about pot and other fads of his generation. Talking with them was as peaceful and easy as that High Sierra morning.

"It's the war. That's what my dad and I are really fighting over. You know that, don't you?" Corey said.

Hank smiled. He took another sip and looked at the sunlight penetrating the window. "It's your patriotic duty to serve in Vietnam. Better to fight on foreign soil than on our own shores ... I guess you don't buy into that, huh?"

Corey nodded yes. "You and I have never talked about the war, but if you don't mind, I'd like to talk about it now. I just don't believe in the domino theory like my father does ... least not concerning Vietnam. I think it's a civil war in which we have no business being involved."

Hank paused a long while before answering. "What war? I keep reading the politicians call this a police action and say our position as the free world leader makes us world policemen."

"Do you believe that? My father says we need to be there to stop the spread of communism.

Most people in this town would agree with him, but at school most kids think all war is immoral."

"And you're stuck in the middle between what you've always been taught and the anti-war position of your peers," Hank said.

"I sure don't think Vietnam is part of any communist master plan. So many things I believed as a kid I now know aren't true. When I was younger and someone disagreed with me, it pissed me off — I was ready to fight them. Now I realize they might have been looking at things from a perspective I never thought of ... might even have been closer to the truth than I was. I'm even embarrassed by some things I was adamant about in the past. Because of that, I guess I'm afraid to believe too strongly in anything now."

"I think you're experiencing a strong case of doubt, which comes with maturity." Hank lifted his glass toward Corey. "I now propose a toast. To Corey, whose doubt has embarked him onto the path of wisdom."

Corey looked puzzled by Hank's toast. The old man saw it and smiled. "That doesn't answer your question, does it? Don't think I can, cuz you're asking the kind of a question a man has to ask of himself, only to discover the right answer he can never explain with words ... It's just something he knows by intuition, not logic."

"Out of respect, I'm asking for your opinion now."

Hank looked hard at Corey. "That ain't right neither. You want to replace your father's views with mine. Growing into your own man means asking questions that sometimes make you wish some truths were lies, but only you can determine that by refining the quality of questions you ask of yourself."

Corey sighed. "I'm not sure I know what you mean."

This time Hank looked a little lost. He gazed at his drink, then slowly took another sip. "You read much about the Nuremberg trials? It seems to me that what we told our allies and enemies alike is there are higher laws than laws of man or any countries. Because of those higher laws, you can't be absolved of personal responsibility by pledging your allegiance to your government. That's how my generation justified punishing the Germans for committing atrocities beyond our — and most of the rest of the world's — ideas on morality. In so doing, we established and accentuated the notion of a conscientious objector."

Now our government has to label the Vietnam conflict a police action, not a war," Corey said.

Hank nodded. "So what are you going to do about the draft?"

Millie sensed Corey was getting quite uncomfortable. "I'm tired of hearing about Vietnam," she interjected. "How about some fresh lemonade? Picked the lemons this morning and baked an apple pie. Both the lemons and the apples are fresh from our trees."

"I'm trying to get Corey to ask himself questions he should be asking himself and you want to talk about lemonade?"

"Can I oppose the war and still love my country?" Corey

said, then smiled. "I think I should mull over that question with some real American standards like fresh-squeezed lemonade and apple pie."

"Millie's right in interrupting, as she usually is," Hank said. "It's better to digest pie than to try and digest the morality of war. In the past you've figured things out pretty well on your own. I'm confident you'll do the right thing when it's time to do so again."

Millie added, "I think every generation has to solve its own problems, whether or not they are responsible for them. All us old folks can to do is feed 'em well and remind them of the pleasant things in life. So I'll get the food, and when I return I want to hear about that girlfriend of yours."

Millie left the room. Hank waited until she was out of earshot. "So what do you think you're going to do?" he said.

"I don't know. I changed my major hoping to get an extra year of deferment. At least I can delay it for a while, give myself a chance to think on it some more. Funny thing is I found I like my lit classes a lot more than the business classes my dad insisted I take," Corey answered, then stared out the window for few seconds. "To be honest, I don't know if it is because of the war or from the inspiration from reading the great authors, but I somehow feel more alive than I've ever felt before."

"Funny how fear or tragedy does that to us," Hank said, then added, "If you get that extension, maybe you should take that girl of yours camping in the Sierras. Living at the beach, you might be getting too much water on the brain. You need some of that good, clean mountain air to clear your head."

"Take who into the mountains?" Millie said, coming back into the room carrying a serving table with three slices of pie and two glasses of lemonade.

"Karen, Corey's girlfriend. We took your advice and we're talking about her."

"Good. Have you asked her to marry you yet?" Millie asked.

"Boy, let's talk about the war again." They all laughed before Corey answered. "Yes, but there is one big obstacle. She's afraid if she marries me, we'll have children right away. She's not sure she wants kids at all. She's committed to becoming a professional photographer, which means a lot of travel and is not conducive to staying at home and raising kids. I told her I didn't care. She said, 'Sure you say that now, but I know you want a family with children, and I know you'd make a great father.'"

"Well, do you feel that way?" Millie asked.

"The two of you never had kids. Did it matter? You seem to have made the most of it without them."

"That was because my guys swim in circles," Hank said, "not because we didn't want any. We thought about adopting though, but with you and the other kids on the block — turns out we have more children than it would have been healthy for Millie to bear, as strong as she is," Hank said and squeezed her arm. He then looked at Corey and added, "Kinda like what you said about the war. We took a bad thing and made it into something positive."

"Sure, I think both of us wanted children," Millie chimed in. "But like Hank said, the neighborhood children sort of became ours. Hank and I traveled more and had more time with each other, which could have strained our relationship or strengthened it ... and fortunately it was the latter."

Hank winked at her, then patted her hand. Corey took his last swallow of lemonade then said, "I suppose if I get drafted, she might marry me out of pity. I hear that kind of thing often happens during war. I'm not so sure it wasn't the case with my parents. But that's not a topic for now. It's getting late and I better hit the road. I promise to call you regularly."

Millie got up and walked Corey to his car. Outside, he took her hands and looked her directly in the eye. "Tell me honestly, how's he doing?"

"His leg circulation is real bad — hardening of the arteries. There's some doctor down in Texas who is doing remarkable things. Somehow he replaces worn-out arteries with some kind of artificial plastic. Hank says it is too expensive. When he goes, he wants to make sure I have no financial worries. I can't convince him that he is my life, and I want him here as long as possible, no matter what the cost."

"You know how I feel about the both of you. These are tough times for me, and I need your guidance more than ever. I'll talk to Hank. You both have to attend my wedding when Karen finally decides to say yes." He kissed her on the cheek and gave her a hug. "We'll get that old goat to get that operation ... I promise."

As he got in the car, he saw Hank waving from the picture window.

Corey felt a rush of emotion that made him want to go back and talk with them a little longer. "This is the way I should feel when I leave my parents," he thought as he pulled away from the curb.

CHAPTER THREE

Corey tensed as he drove out of LA. It wasn't until he neared Red Hill Road, the exit to get to Laguna Beach, that he began to relax. It was here the city sprawl ended and homes gave way to orange groves and strawberry fields, the gritty smog stench of LA air changing into the sweet smell of fresh fruit. Soon the air would be further purified by the prevailing breezes blowing the moist clean air from the Pacific Ocean. "I'll see the ocean in about fifteen minutes," he thought as he turned on the radio.

"General Westmoreland advised Congress today that there were not enough troops in Vietnam to maintain and protect the necessary ground to ensure victory," the voice from the radio said. "Westmoreland suggested an additional seventy-five thousand troops be added to the four hundred and eighty-five thousand currently stationed there. Without the increase, the war could last another ten years, Westmoreland told Congress.

"In related news, military intelligence reports heavy enemy troop buildup along the Ho Chi Minh Trail. The buildup is centered around the city of Khe Sanh where a major offensive action is expected this winter. Early this morning outside of Khe Sanh, US forces reported killing two hundred and fifteen Vietcong. Forty-seven US soldiers were killed in what's being called 'a major assault.'"

"I guess that means we won two hundred fifteen to forty-seven," Corey shouted back at the radio, angered that the reality of the war interrupted his pleasant memories of the past, which had been evoked by the sensuous fragrances. He quickly changed the station. The raspy voice of Bob Dylan came over the new station.

I met a young child beside a dead pony.

I met a white man who walked a black dog.

I met a young woman whose body was burning.

Corey envisioned the cover of a recent *Life* magazine photo of a little Vietnamese girl fleeing her just-bombed village. She was naked and crying, her body scalded by napalm burns.

Corey changed the station again. All the stations these days, it seemed, played nothing but war protest songs or tunes crying for action against other social injustices. He turned the radio off as he reached Capistrano Beach. Dana Point and the ocean would soon come into view. He eased his foot off the gas and moved to the right lane as he neared San Clemente, where he could more easily see the familiar sights that magically conjured memories of happier times of past summers spent at his parents' beach house in San Clemente. He could not drive by the quaint beach town without reliving the events that summoned recollections of those good times, and even the presence of the busy Marine base at Camp Pendleton could not diminish the memories of those wonderful pre-war summers which he and his family so enjoyed.

Corey saw the cliffs of Dana Point. Big waves and swells pounded into the rocks. Instantly he thought, "Trestles will be breaking." In his mind, he was sixteen again. There was no war ... he didn't even know where Vietnam was. His father was still one of his best friends and he wasn't aware his mother had begun drinking too much. Good waves and beach volleyball were his immediate concerns.

Because the Jamesons spent their summer in San Clemente, Corey had been exposed to surfing at an early age. He'd gotten his first surfboard at age eleven, and being athletic, he had become an accomplished surfer by the time he was fourteen. His surfing ability became the key that unlocked a door Corey had been only remotely aware existed.

San Clemente was the summer resort town of a good many San Marino residents who, like Corey's parents, either owned a beach house or rented homes for summer vacations at the oceanfront community. The San Marino people stayed together as they frequented the same beach area, sat with each other on the beach, ate at each other's homes, and when not at the beach, played golf, tennis, or cards together. In effect, they formed a San Marino clique that excluded the local residents. The older San Clemente residents tolerated the aloof out-of-towners, as they needed the summer tourism for their own income, and the affluent San Marino group spent more than other tourists. The teenage and younger town residents resented the San Marino snobs because the summer tourist invasion infringed on their personal lifestyle. They directed their anger at tourists in general, but particularly the arrogant San Marino bunch.

"Tourists Go Home" warnings were spray-painted on walls and road signs. The T-Street train overpass was one of the more popular beach areas. Each summer, the sign, posting beach regulations, was spray-painted "Death to Tourists," and no matter how many times it was erased and no matter what form of surveillance, the threat was repainted within a few days.

Apart from the aloof way in which the San Marinians behaved, the San Clemente kids had another reason for hating the children of the tourists. The "locals," as they referred to themselves, were board surfers, while the tourists were rafters and body surfers. T-Street provided one of the better breaks during the frequent southern swells of summer, but T-Street was closed from ten a.m. to six p.m. to board surfing and strictly enforced by the lifeguards who could arbitrarily extend the no board surfing regulations even longer depending on the crowd, which often stayed until dark, thus preventing the locals from board surfing altogether.

As a result of the territorial conflict, the locals tended to congregate in two places. One was south of T-Street, a place called the Riviera District, and then just below the San Clemente pier, which was north of the tourist hangouts. These two areas became off-limits to the tourists' kids save one — Corey. Being a board surfer, and a good one at that, Corey overcame the territorial and class boundary. He often joined forces with the locals in taunting the lifeguards when they chose to keep the beach closed to board surfing past six. He spent much of the day at the Riviera, where board surfing was allowed all day. When he wasn't surfing, he played volleyball with the locals instead of frisbee or touch football, the recreation of preference of the summer visitors. Corey also associated with his hometown group, thus placing his truce with the locals close to the edge. Had they not respected his surfing, he probably would have been treated as a typical tourist.

One of the local surfers, and one of their leaders, was a big, rugged-looking lad of Irish descent, and proud of it. Bob McGwire was six foot three, narrow waisted, and built like a triangle turned upside down. His narrow hips expanded to a strong chest, chiseled from hours spent paddling after waves. He had dark black hair, which hung shoulder length even before that hairstyle became popular. They called him "Hot," which Corey thought was because of Bob's habit of shrieking a drawn-out yell of "Hot" whenever one of his friends got a particularly good ride. Later Corey learned the nickname came from Bob's basketball skills. It was said he went on scoring streaks that made him a one-man show and evoked the chant of "Hot, Hot, Hot" from his cheering classmates.

He and Corey were cordial as they respected each other as surfers and athletes, but nothing beyond that until one July morning. On that morning, a hurricane off the southern tip of Mexico produced a larger than usual swell along the California coast. Riviera became packed with local surfers, which included Hot and Corey. They stood in a small circle and studied the big waves. They discussed where best to paddle out and the best entry spot for catching the wave.

They were about to enter the water when two younger boys, about fourteen, walked down the beach from the direction of T-Street. They carried expensive new boards and wore trunks that were bought at a high-class men's store, the kind that catered to San Marino incomes. "Hey, Hot," someone said, drawing attention to the boys. "A couple of kooks, huh?"

Corey knew "kooks" was the local word for an unskilled inland surfboarder. He also knew that "kooks" were asking for trouble when they tried to mingle with locals. And worst of all, he recognized one of them as the younger brother of a girl in Corey's class, a girl he liked and sometimes dated.

The boys hesitated as the locals stared at them. The younger of the two, the one Corey recognized, stopped and said something to his friend. Corey thought he said, "Let's go back to T-Street and body surf." The older-looking boy gave the locals an imperious glance and continued to swagger forward. "This is a public beach," Corey heard him say.

"Are you queers gonna try surfboarding?" someone said with a sinister tone.

The haughty-looking one ignored the comment. He set his board down and pulled from his pocket a new bar of scented, colored surfboard wax. He began waxing his board as the other boy stood behind him and uneasily watched the local crowd.

"You guys belong at T Street. Now get the hell out of here!" Hot shouted.

The arrogant one looked up defiantly and said, "We can surf here if we want."

The locals laughed, then closed their ranks and whispered among themselves, which was followed by mischievous laughter. Both boys began growing uneasy. The younger one whispered, "Let's leave."

"All right, you can surf here," a skinny, blond-headed surfer said, emerging from the group. "But this is not a public beach. It's a pubic beach," the blonde surfer said, mimicking the boy's early-pubescent voice. The others laughed when he said pubic, so he continued. "It's kind of an initiation ... your first wave you ride naked."

The locals quickly surrounded the boys, cutting off any retreat. "Strip," Hot said.

The boys stood next to each other and both looked scared. The younger boy, the girl's brother, looked toward Corey, who was trying to hide from the congregation, hoping the boy wouldn't see him and compromise his neutrality.

Corey felt sorry for the girl's little brother, but didn't care what they might do to the other one. He pretended he had not seen the boy and let the locals do whatever they might do. The kids, he figured, would just learn a lesson in judgment.

"Yeah, I've always heard rich kids have small peckers. That's why they need money to get girls," someone else yelled, eliciting more laughter.

"Leave us alone. We'll leave," the younger-looking boy pleaded, his voice cracking in mid- sentence, drawing even more snickers.

"Maybe they can't make a pubic appearance 'cause they haven't got any pubes yet," someone said.

"Doesn't matter. Their trunks are coming off anyway," Hot said, and the group rushed the boys.

"Corey! Help!" the boy screamed in panic.

Corey didn't know what to do. He was angry that the two kids had showed up, and at the same time felt sorry for the little brother. "Hold it," he shouted. "I don't care what you do to that one," he said, pointing at the pompous one, "but I date the squeaker's sister every once in a while. Why don't you just take his towel and that pretty wax, then let him go crying back to T-Street."

"Towels and trunks from both of them," Hot said, looking at Corey to make sure Corey understood who was in charge.

"Look," Corey said. "Why don't you just pants the smart-ass. Let the other one go."

"Both of them need to be taught a lesson," Hot said even louder, now facing Corey.

Corey walked to the boys. He took their towels and the

wax and gave them to Hot. He turned to the boys. "Now get out of here or I'll see to it your first year in high school will be hell."

Hot threw the towels down and came up close to Corey's face. He stared at him with the kind of look boxers give each other just before a fight. Suddenly, he shoved Corey and the fight was on. Hot's height and longer arms gave him a slight advantage, but Corey was just as strong and a little quicker. They exchanged several blows, each drawing blood. It was apparent they were evenly matched and it could be a long fight. Hot threw a punch that hit fairly solid on the side of Corey's head, but Corey hardly flinched and quickly retaliated with a jab to Hot's nose that drew more blood. With all the attention turned to the fight, the two San Marino boys fled with trunks, boards, and towels.

The fight continued another five minutes with neither Hot nor Corey establishing dominance. Without warning, Hot stepped back and started laughing. He held out his open hands, gesturing enough.

"This is stupid," he said, still chuckling. "I really don't care about seeing a couple of kids' peckers. Besides, San Marino kids ain't got dicks big enough to be proud of."

Corey smiled back and dropped his fists. "Probably bigger than yours," he said. "Those kids?" Hot said.

"Sure, that's why you would rather fight than fuck," Corey answered.

"Don't you believe that one," Hot said, still smiling. Then he added, "Let's surf."

"I think I'll surf naked," Corey said. "But of course, I don't expect any of you pencil dicks will do the same."

What happened next became a part of San Clemente surfing folklore. On a big south swell on a sunny summer morning, about fifteen surfers entered the water wearing their trunks around their necks. They surfed naked for almost a half hour before a lifeguard in a patrol jeep spotted them and threatened to call the police if they didn't put their trunks on immediately. For Corey and Hot, that day was the start of a friendship that resulted in them being roommates in college.

The memory of that morning momentarily erased Corey's thoughts of Vietnam. He drove through San Clemente seeing more dreams than town. He realized he was almost to Baseline Road, the far northern entrance to Camp Pendleton Marine base, where, with the proper identification, the entrance to the San Onofre Surfing Park. He pulled off onto the ramp, then slowly left the pavement onto the dirt shoulder and got out of the car.

From the off-ramp he had a clear view of one of his favorite surfing spots, the infamous Trestles. Trestles was actually on the Marine base, and it was illegal to get there by crossing government land. A surfer either had to sneak across the well-patrolled beach or paddle a long way from either San Clemente's Cotton Point or the San Onofre Beach Club. No matter how you got there, if you lost your board and the wave carried it to the shore before you could retrieve it, the Marines would confiscate it and arrest the surfer for trespassing. Even parking at the overlook off the ramp was only temporary. He knew that an MP jeep would soon show up and order him to move. He decided to watch the waves and the few surfers in the water enjoying them. If the memories of San Clemente were wonderful, so were those of San Onofre. Soon, Corey slipped back into his private sanctuary of recollection. The club itself was picturesquely located near the northern end of the Marine base, just below a segment of sheer cliff that had been carved by erosion and tides and now looked like a miniature replica of the walls of the Grand Canyon. San Onofre was the only chartered surf club in California with a private beach and water access on government land.

Corey had become a member in 1961, at age fourteen. He did so with the help of a San Clemente neighbor who had taken a liking to him. Harold Blackman had been an LA businessman who got tired of the LA rat race. He spent three years going to night school to get a teaching credential and finally moved to San Clemente, where he got a job as a math teacher at the local high school. Since Frank Jameson did not surf, Mr. Blackman frequently took Corey with him when he went surfing at the club. Technically, Corey was too young to be a member, and a junior membership was only granted to the relatives of an adult member. Harold, a surfer all his life, was a charter member of the club and was personally involved in all those early political battles it took for the club to get the charter. Because of Harold's status in the club, no one questioned him when he said Corey was his nephew and sponsored him for a junior membership and the opportunity to be a full member when Corey turned eighteen.

To Corey, San Onofre was more than just a surfing club. It was a unique and mysterious place where people enjoyed the outdoors and the camaraderie around the evening campfires. It was the kind of place he thought Hank would have enjoyed if Hank had been more of a beach person rather than a mountaineer. It was the fireside conversations that made him think of Hank. On one of his camping trips with Hank, as they sat around their campfire, Corey mentioned how boring he thought school was. Hank told him that he thought the principal weakness with school learning was that it was regimented by the clock on the wall.

"Sometimes an hour is an eternity. Other times, it's only a fleeting moment. It all depends on your level of interest, or on the teacher's ability to motivate," Hank said as they sat around the campfire that night. "For example, right now. You're feeling pretty comfortable. The campfire has cast its hypnotic spell where you sort of sit outside of yourself ... time stops. You don't try, or even care about impressing anyone. Your imagination is the only thing piqued. If each community had a park and once or twice a week had town meetings, with everyone invited, and they held those meetings around a couple of good fires, you might learn more in a couple hours than you would in a year at school."

At the time, Hank did not elaborate on his theory because it wasn't a theory at all, just a passing thought, the kind that comes from sitting around campfires. But as Corey got older and had come to spend quite a few nights around San Onofre fires, he too developed similar thoughts.

The club members were a diversified group, both in age and background. Surfing was their only common bond, and the only restriction on membership. A typical summer's day for the members meant arriving at sunrise and getting into the water as soon as there was enough light to see the waves. You surfed until you were bone weary, then returned to the beach for a brief rest and light snack and then got back into the water. If the wind became too strong, you stayed on the shore and played volleyball, or if your hair was a little gray and your midsection had begun to soften, then bocce ball or horseshoes. By evening, the wind always died and you were back in the water surfing until dark. When you finally returned to the beach, the women had fires going in the fire rings and charcoal in portable barbecues was glowing and the smell of hamburger, fish, and sometimes even steak cooking on the grill soon permeated the air.

After dinner, people gathered in small groups around the fire rings. With a full stomach, a tired body, and the mesmerizing dance of the flames, you soon shared thoughts with one another.

Most always someone had a guitar, so you sang a few songs, then storytelling began. The older members taught the new ones the history of the club and passed down tales of surfing legends and myths. Soon everyone shared ideas on a multitude of topics. Without realizing how, when, or why, you might find yourself contemplating man's purpose in the universe, or how to make a good steak marinade, both seeming equally important. What impressed Corey most about those evenings was the way people shared both ideas and emotions unguarded by ego. The only clock was the sun and a Marine siren that sounded at ten p.m. as a signal that the beach was now closed and the members had to go home.

As Corey looked back, what amazed him was all that he remembered without being forced to memorize it. Without realizing it, the lessons learned were ones he would never have studied intentionally at school — things like philosophy, religion, history, and most of all, lessons of human nature.

As he stood next to his car, Corey observed that the waves were adequate and the surfers pretty good. He glanced around and saw no military police jeep in the vicinity, so he decided to watch a while longer and dream a little more. He recalled a campfire conversation about the origin of the name San Onofre.

In some of the writings of the early Capistrano Mission priest, the name was mentioned.

The name also appeared in the Santa Margarita land grant papers written in 1886, but nothing of its origin was revealed. The San Clemente library had a special section on the history of the area, but they had no facts as to the origin of San Onofre. Some people thought it might have been a derivation of an Indian word passed down from a long-extinct tribe. Maybe it was something sacred that the early Spaniards converted to a name they could easily pronounce in their native tongue.

"San Onofre has no Mexican translation," an older member said one night as the club's history was being retold.

The club member who spoke was an English professor at UCLA. He was a fanatic on ancient myths and legends. He claimed there was an Egyptian goddess named Onuphrius. This gave rise to speculation that ancient Egyptian explorers were much better sailors and navigators than history gave credit, and maybe they discovered America long before Columbus landed in the West Indies. It was possible they landed exactly where the club was today. Maybe they named their landing place Onuphrius in honor of their protecting goddess.

If the history behind the name was a mystery, the rest of the club's background was just the opposite. Corey could no longer recite the preamble to the Constitution, nor the Gettysburg Address, or anything else he had been forced to memorize, but he knew the history of the club as if by osmosis.

Duke Kahanamoko was a famous Hawaiian swimmer who won a gold medal in the Stockholm Olympics of 1912. He was also an early surfer who stopped at the Southern California coast on his way back from the Olympics. He brought with him the old, long, wooden boards used in the early surfing days. Body surfers of that decade watched the "Duke" ride waves on his board and were anxious to try it themselves. Duke left a board with some California friends, and soon the more adventurous beachgoers began making crude boards modeled after the one left by the Hawaiian gold medalist.

Soon the new breed of board surfers began exploring the coast for places with wave configurations conducive for their boards. About 1920, they discovered good waves about sixty miles south of Los Angeles, at an old railroad siding identified as "San Onofre." Other places, depending on the time of the year and the size of the swell, had better waves, but no place was as consistent year-round as San Onofre.

About the same time the surfers discovered the beach at San Onofre, surf fisherman also began using the same beach for their sport. The camp became so popular by the mid-thirties that land was leased from Rancho Santa Margarita. A Texaco gas station, a small restaurant, several cabins for rental purposes, and a few crude toilet and shower facilities were erected to accommodate the influx of sportsmen. A charge of twenty-five cents for day use and fifty cents for overnight camping was levied to cover maintenance costs. Surfers didn't like the fishing

lines, with their sharp hooks, being pulled through the same waters they paddled to reach waves or retrieve lost boards. On the other hand, the fishermen didn't like the idea of a bunch of surfers splashing around and scaring off the fish. Civil war broke out between the two sportsman factions, with skirmishes lasting until 1943, when war of a different kind settled the beach access question for a while.

When World War II broke out, the government bought most of Rancho San Margarita to form a Marine base called Camp Pendleton. Gas rationing, shortages of surfboard materials, and the military draft temporarily wiped out surfing all along the coast, including San Onofre.

During the war, the beach area, as well as the ranch, were off-limits to civilians, but with the war ending, the surfers returned to their beaches. The Marines, no longer needing the beach area at the north end of the camp, willingly gave permits for public beach use. With the end of the war, there was a festive mood, even with the peacetime Marines who, on their days off, began watching the surfers and trying the sport themselves. The number of surfers skyrocketed. Among the returning servicemen was a soon-to-be licensed dentist by the name of Barney Wilkes. He opened his practice in San Clemente so after hours and on weekends, he could pursue his favorite pastime, surfing. Being a respected professional and war veteran, Barney became the spokesman for a group of surfers who were successful in gaining a beach access permit from the Marine Corps.

The club was officially formed on April 24, 1952. Members paid dues, established a budget and banking, and issued membership cards and a decal logo for car windshields. The Marines built a guard gate at the San Onofre entrance, and only cars bearing the decal and whose occupants held membership cards were allowed to pass.

Then in 1955, the Marine Corps decided they liked the cozy camp built by the club members, so they canceled the access grant and took the facility over for their own recreational use, as well as opened it to the general public. The Marines said they would take responsibility for the trash pickup and toilet cleaning. The result was an unkempt beach with wild parties, whose participants, most of whom had no past, present, or future concern about the club and the area, abused the land horribly.

The grass shack, the symbol of the club, was torched. The wooden train trestle across the estuary, just below from where Corey now stood, was burned badly, the result of a careless brush fire. A passenger train was nearly derailed as a result of that fire. Dressing rooms and road signs were torn down and used for campfire wood. In short, the club and the use of the land were almost destroyed.

Finally, in 1958, the camp's commanding officer decided that control of that section of the beach be restored to the club. However, during the chaotic period, membership had drastically dropped, so one hundred fifty new members were allowed in to rebuild it to the desired five- hundred-member number established by the original club members.

The club suffered one loss through the troubled fifties. The best waves were in front of the old railroad trestle. The Marines had built their own facility just south of "Trestle" Beach, so everything north became off-limits. However, the surfers would park their cars at the extreme south end of San Clemente, sneak through the heavy brush and tall grass that grew on the base at that region, and then sprint across the open beach to the safety of the water. Sometimes, they would paddle an hour or more from San Clemente in order to reach Trestle by sea.

The Marines patrolled the area both on foot and in jeeps.

Chases and confrontations were frequent. Horror tales were told about surfers who were captured while sneaking into the "Trestle" area. Supposedly, their boards were confiscated before they were beaten up by the MP, then turned over to the San Clemente police, who issued them trespassing citations with accompanying fines.

Once in the water, a surfer was safe since the heavy military uniform was prohibitive for swimming. But even then, stories were told of them firing wax bullets at surfers, bullets that stung like a wasp sting when you were hit. Corey never saw the firing of wax bullets, but he had been chased. Also, he witnessed Marines waiting on the beach for a surfer to wipe out and not be able to retrieve his board before a succeeding wave washed it up to the shoreline. They would smash the board with rocks. Once he saw a surfer come in to protect his board. He saw the surfer beaten and taken away in handcuffs.

As a reaction to the Marine policy at "Trestles," frequently off-duty Marines visiting San Clemente were forced into fights, and groups of surfers plotted destructive tactics against Marine equipment. Corey had taken part in one such operation when he was angered when one of his friends had his board confiscated.

For revenge, a couple of surfers chided a couple of MPs by coming onto the shoreline and challenging them to a fight. The Marines got out of their jeep and hurried down to the water's edge to oblige. The surfers ran, and the MPs gave chase on foot. Meanwhile, Corey hurried to the abandoned jeep, unscrewed the gas cap, and stuffed as much sand into the gas tank as he could before the Marines gave up the chase. He was joined by the other two surfers, who acted as the decoys, and together they watched and laughed as the MPs struggled with the awful-sounding engine.

"No parking on the off-ramp shoulder. Move it, or we'll have the highway patrol here in minutes," a gruff voice said, interrupting Corey's remembrances.

Lost in thought, Corey had not seen the MP approach. He apologized, got back in the car, and pulled onto the ramp. Just before reentering the freeway, he honked his horn to draw the MP's attention. When he looked up, Corey waved his middle finger at him, then accelerated onto the freeway for his final hour drive to Mission Beach.

CHAPTER FOUR

A BOY, NO MORE THAN THIRTEEN YEARS OLD, EMERGED from one of the sidewalks that separated the rows of small cottage-like houses on the ocean side of Mission Beach Boulevard. He moved with cat-like agility between two parked cars, crossed hurriedly in front of oncoming traffic, came to an abrupt stop on the narrow island that separated the north-south flow of traffic, then waited for the busy rush of cars on the far side to subside. He brushed his long blond hair from his eyes as he waited. Someone from a passing car shouted, "Hey, Joey!"

"Hey," he yelled back, flashing them the peace symbol as he squinted in the midday sun, trying to recognize the caller. The traffic passed, and he darted the rest of the way to the far side of the street and down another sidewalk.

A college-aged boy and girl were talking with one another

on a patch of grass yard in front of one of the small cottages. The boy, like Joey, had long blond hair. He was shirtless and wore blue denim bell-bottom trousers. The girl, whose hair was darker but long and windblown, wore a cotton blouse with a flower cluster design. She had on a bikini bottom, which revealed her long tan legs. They turned toward the boy as he raced by. "Joey, where's the action tonight?" the girl shouted.

Joey turned and faced them while still moving gracefully, although now running backwards. "Party at the Surf Rider about five. Everyone's back 'cept Corey, and he should be here this afternoon." Joey answered as he cut sideways between two houses.

In the direction the boy moved, you could hear the electric guitar music of a Jimi Hendrix album. The music muffled a repetitious scratching sound.

When the boy reached the next court, he saw another young man, only this one was in his mid-twenties. He was sanding a white Styrofoam surfboard blank. The blank laid across two sawhorses whose beams were covered with heavy but clean pieces of carpet. The front door was open, and two speakers were pulled out onto the front porch. They had been placed so that they both faced the young man as he worked.

"Turk," the boy yelled.

Turk turned. He had on a surgical mask, which he pulled down, revealing a big grin. White flakes of Styrofoam dust speckled his frizzy, dark-brown hair. The whiteness complimented the pearly white teeth exposed when he grinned. He lifted the newly shaped blank and held it out for the boy to inspect. "Righteous, isn't it?" he said. His eyes sparkled the way the sunlight reflects off morning ocean water.

"Righteous," the boy echoed, then asked, "Who you makin' it for?"

"For me," Turk answered, setting the blank back down. He tracked his hand along the rail of the board as if he were feeling the soft skin of a newborn baby.

"State of the art," he said. "Created for both cutting and banking off California coast waves." He motioned for Joey to feel the rails. Joey approached the board even more cautiously than Turk. He pressed softly at first, then harder as he felt the firm texture of the rails. He felt no bumps or nicks.

"I need to make a few finishing touches before I glass it. Why don't you go in and get me a beer? You can have one too, if you like. Put on a new album also. This one's about over."

Joey slid by the speakers and into the house. From the inside, it appeared more like an adjoining guest room, as a partition cut off about a quarter of the space. The partition was made from rows of turquoise beads that dangled from fishing line attached to a wooden beam that Turk had affixed to the ceiling. On the far side of the beads was a breakfast table that stood before the kitchen door. The kitchen itself was about as big as a service porch. Every appliance was unusually small in order to fit in the room.

The beads knocked against one another as Joey pushed through them. They made a noise like marbles striking each other. Before entering the kitchen, Joey noticed several beer cans on the table. Two were partially crushed. The third had moisture on its surface. He felt it. It was cool and half full. He took it into the kitchen with him and placed it back in the refrigerator, which was really a half refrigerator, the kind many hotels have in guest rooms. There were three full beers remaining from a twelve pack. Joey took just one.

He searched the counter for a can opener. He saw a stack of dirty dishes in the sink and even more strewn over the counter. A slow but steady dripping of water came from the faucet. It had leaked ever since Joey had met Turk. The porcelain sink was now water stained by the leak, just as Turk had been blemished by the war. He found the can opener among the dirty dishes that he had to move to reach it. The movement freed trapped odors of stale and decaying food that probably amounted to a full week of meals. He glanced at the wastebasket next to the counter. It was full too, mostly with empty beer cans and one glass jug of cheap wine.

"If only it was as easy to cleanse Turk's memory of the war as it would be to clean the dirty kitchen," the boy thought as he turned to take Turk his beer. It was then he noticed the only clean object in the kitchen, maybe the entire house. It was a photograph of five soldiers sitting at a bar table. They had their arms looped around each other's shoulders, and they all wore silly grins as if they were trying to appear sober. In faded ink, in the upper left-hand corner was written "The Ferocious Five, Saigon '64." One of the five was a short-haired and slightly younger-looking Turk. Joey had seen the picture many times before. What caught his eye was that the picture was crooked. The boy knew that when Turk was both really depressed and drunk, or stoned on top of that, he often took the picture down and stared at it — sometimes crying softly to himself until he fell asleep. Joey straightened it before leaving.

As he came back into the front room, the music stopped and he remembered he was supposed to change the record. He turned toward the record rack Turk had built from wood on which he had carved Asian-looking designs. The stand was next to Turk's waterbed, which was propped against the wall in the corner of the room. The top shelf of the rack, was a resting place for a lamp, a water pipe, a stash box, and an incense burner instead of records. There was a recently burned incense stick protruding from the hand-carved holder. Although, when burning, it produced a pleasant, perfumery aroma, now the pungent odor of marijuana commingled in the air, giving the room the smell of decaying moss from a drying marsh pond. In Turks' house, grass burned more frequently than incense. The odor had seeped into the pores of wood and fibers of every cloth, becoming a permanent fixture of the room, much the same way the briny smell of the ocean hovers over the beach sands on a still day.

There were about fifty record albums on the second shelf of the two-shelf case. Another twenty record jackets or so were scattered on the floor and bed. All the music was contemporary rock or folk. Turk was a big fan of Bob Dylan. He had every album Dylan had recorded. On the wall above the case was a poster of Dylan's silhouette, only instead of the profile being in traditional black, his wavy hair was streaked with psychedelic colors. Joey put on Dylan's *Freewheelin* album. He returned the Hendrix record to its cover and then placed it with all the scattered albums back on the shelf.

Turk had just finished shaping when the boy returned. He had just taken off the filter mask and he turned toward Joey and took the beer. "Hey! You didn't get one for yourself. You want me to drink alone?" he said and smiled at the boy.

"Nah. I'm going surfing this afternoon. Besides I don't like the taste of beer. I really came by just to say hi, and tell you they're throwing a big party at the Surf Rider tonight to celebrate everybody getting back."

Turk took one big gulp, finishing half the beer in one swig. He again smiled at the boy. Turk's grin, when directed at the boy or when he talked surfing, was always warm and genuine looking, but when he smiled around his peers, the same smile changed to a haunting, or even maniacal expression. The latter smile scared most of the girls and even some of the guys among the Surf Rider clan.

Joey had talked to Corey and Hot about Turk's smile just at the end of last school year. They agreed it wasn't the smile that was different as much as it was his eyes. When Turk smiled at the boy, his eyes were bright and happy ... they were the same eyes as those captured in the picture of Turk with his buddies in the Saigon bar. But when Turk was with people his own age or older, those bright eyes dimmed the way stage lights fade to create a more reflective mood, only it seemed that Turk was seeing something sinister or frightening.

Corey thought that maybe because Turk had been through so much in the war, his eyes expressed a deeper wisdom than the others could know.

Hot said, “Maybe when you’ve looked in the face of a terrifying monster and survived, you get that look. You know you’re safe now, but you also know that the monster is real, and it’s still out there somewhere.”

Turk put his strong hand on the boy’s shoulder. He led him back into his house. “Come on in for a second. I’ve got a few things I want to show you.”

He led Joey over to the stash box next to the water pipe. Turk opened it and showed the boy four plastic baggies with an ounce of grass in each.

“I went down to Mexico yesterday,” he said while lifting one of the bags from the box. He carefully peeled open the bag and lifted it toward his nose. “Primo stuff ... Acapulco gold.”

He offered a whiff to the boy, who breathed in the aroma with the identical mannerisms of Turk. Turk took a small amount and stuffed it into the stock of the water pipe.

“A hit or two will help your surfing. It will mellow out your style,” he said and winked at the boy.

“Okay. Just a couple,” Joey whispered.

They took two drags a piece. The water cooled the hot smoke so they could take longer, deeper drags.

After the second hit, Joey said, “Maybe one more.”

“No!” Turk said. “This is pretty powerful shit. It hits you slow, but it’s real spacey.”

Turk was right, the boy thought. Almost immediately after he asked for the third drag, he began to feel a slight numbing sensation in his hands and feet. Soon his whole body tingled, then his vision became myopic.

"The rest of what I want to show you is in the back room," Turk said.

The back room of the house was supposed to be a bedroom, but Turk, by making another partition of beads, turned it into two rooms, which he used for his various ways of making money. On one half stood two more sawhorses that rested on a heavily resin-stained, thick layer of painter's drop cloth. From the ceiling hung a long and bright fluorescent light. Turk frequently both shaped and glassed surfboards, which he sold at under-average retail prices. Most of the Mission Beach locals felt Turk was one of the best shape designers in Southern California, yet, despite offers from companies like Hobie and Challenge, he preferred to work for himself and sell by word of mouth.

But Turk's primary income came from a jewelry-making business. As a surfer who was always on the beach, Turk collected shells and rocks both from tide pools and those washed up on shore. He polished and cut them, then made necklaces, rings, earrings, and occasional special pieces which he sold at craft shows and, again, by reputation and referral. The second half of the back room was fixed up so that it could be entirely devoted to that line of work. He had built, what looked like an architect's flat workbench with a flexible lamp that he could adjust to various angles. There was a small box containing chisels, emery boards, tumblers, and the other equipment needed for cutting and polishing. In larger boxes stacked next to the table were his collections of shells and rocks, and next to them were the leather strings and metal used as settings for different pieces.

During the summer months when the wealthier summer vacationers inhabited the apartments and houses, replacing the college students, Turk's business escalated and his prices doubled. This past summer, he had employed Joey as his helper, paying him little, but diligently teaching him the trade both from the craftsmanship side and the sales side.

Turk sat the boy down at the workbench. He pulled a burlap bag from under it, from which he pulled several abalone shells.

"I got these in Mexico too. Tell me what you see in them."

By then, Joey's eyes felt like two periscopes. Turk had already polished the inside portion. The silver-white interior, called mother-of-pearl, glistened like the silver lining around the edge of a dark cloud that momentarily covers the sun. Amidst the translucent silver-white were trapped opaque swirls of pink, green, yellow, and blue that changed in intensity depending on how you held the shell to the light. But it was not a description of the color or the identification of the kind of shell that Turk sought from the boy. It was a work lesson testing Joey on what he had learned.

"With the college dudes, ab shell peace symbols are real popular and easy to make. They also like the whole shell filled with wax and made into candles, but you can't get much money for those. I'd go with the peace signs. Girls dig ab earrings too. I'd make a few of those," Joey answered.

"Good boy! Remember, whatever you look at, not only see it for what it is, but what it can become," Turk said with the warm smile he reserved for the boy.

Suddenly, Joey felt more stoned. He did not want to be inside for fear Turk would want to smoke again, then work more on the shells. Turk liked to work at his jewelry business only when he was stoned. He said it helped him focus more.

Joey got to his feet. "I've got to split. I told Hot I'd drop by Karen's and tell her what to bring for the party."

"I'll see you at the evening glass off," Turk said. "You know what I'll contribute — I might even make them into brownies."

Joey found himself at Mission Beach Boulevard waiting for another break in traffic. He did not remember leaving Turk's house. He suddenly was at the street curb. It seemed like the traffic was never-ending. He became almost hypnotized by the parade of faces in the cars, and it was as if their occupants were all staring at him. He was thinking he wished he had not smoked, then he realized the street was clear and had been for several seconds. He hurried across, then sort of ambled along the way to Karen's apartment. It was as if his feet were leading him and working faster than his mind.

He reached Karen's before he knew it. Spotting her place was like finding a dollar on the street. It was a pleasant, unexpected surprise, even though that was his destination. He definitely was high, more than he wanted to be, and paranoia was setting in. He needed a safe sanctuary.

The door was partially ajar. He could hear someone moving about inside. “Hello,” he yelled.

“Joey!” Karen shouted as she came to the door. She grabbed him and gave him a tight hug, then surprised him by kissing him on the lips.

“Look at you, dude. You must have grown a foot over the summer,” she said as she stepped back and examined him from head to toe. Her examination became fixed on his legs.

She gasped, “Oh my God!”

“What’s wrong?” he asked, somewhat alarmed. He looked down at his legs, thinking maybe he had cut himself on a rock while surfing that morning. He saw nothing out of the ordinary.

“What’s wrong?” he repeated.

“Well look, you’re getting tiny little white hairs popping out all over. When I was in junior high, I remember this boy I liked, and he started getting hairs like that. It turned me on. I thought it was so sexy.”

She reached down to pet his leg, but he jumped back.

“You’re getting a little fuzzy over your lip too. I do believe our flower child is starting to bloom. I better be careful about letting you in my place. Corey will think I’ve got another man in the house.”

“You’re so full of it,” Joey said. “It’s just the sun bleaches the fuzz I’ve always had.”

She reached and grabbed his arm and pulled him into the room. Inside, she tried to lift his arms. "I'll bet you're getting armpit hair too."

Joey pushed her away, almost knocking her down. She dropped to one knee and reached for his legs. Laughing, she said," It's the white hair that turns me on so."

He grabbed her and tried to push her back. His hand slipped from her wrist and landed flush against her breast. She suddenly looked as embarrassed as he felt. Seeing her so startled, he jumped back. She began laughing harder. "Oh my! I bet that was intentional."

"It was an accident," he protested. "Honest." Then his embarrassed look turned mischievous. "It's kind of nice to get it any way you can though."

"That does it," Karen yelled and ran over and tackled him. For several minutes the two of them wrestled on the floor, laughing all the while. Karen finally was able to pin him down. She sat with her pelvis pressed against his midsection, her knees holding his arms at his side. She tried to lift his arm again, saying she wanted to see if he was getting any armpit hair, when suddenly both stopped struggling and momentarily look red-faced at each other. During the tussle, Joey got an erection, and she felt it.

Karen practically sprang off the boy, then smiled. "You are growing up, aren't you?"

Joey was as confused as he was ashamed. He did not know where to look or what to say. He sat up and looked blankly at the wall.

"Hey," she said, trying to sound like nothing had happened. "It's good to see you again. I really did miss you. I think of you as my little brother, and I'm stoked to see you are growing up. Can I get you a lemonade or soft drink?"

Joey's throat was dry from the pot and all the running around. "Lemonade sounds really good," he answered.

When she left the room, he glanced at the pictures she had been hanging when he arrived. Most were blowups of her own work. On the surface, each photo appeared to be of one simple eye-appealing object. But the more you studied the photos, you realized she had captured a number of small but significant details in the background.

One was a new picture of a very majestic-looking seagull perched on a rock. In the background was a perfectly formed translucent-blue wave. The wave's transparency reflected the sunlight in a way that formed a yellow aura around the bird's head.

Just as you were admiring the beauty of the bird, you noticed on the rock at the bird's feet was a freshly killed and partially mutilated fish. From the bird's beak, a small piece of bloody gut hung dangling in the wind.

That contrast of the ugliness of life next to the beauty was a reoccurring theme of her work. Joey asked her about it once. She told him that many artists, be they painters, sculptors, or photographers, try to capture beauty as if it can be frozen and immortal, but real beauty is fleeting and must be recognized through contrast.

Karen returned with the lemonade, which he gulped down, then thanked her.

"I'm pumped having everybody back," he said. "As much as I like summer vacation, I miss you guys, especially you and Corey. You're so much cooler than the goonie summer tourists."

"Missed you too and am really glad to see you. Sorry if I embarrassed you a little," Karen said.

A wry smile appeared on Joey's face.

"Sorry I got a hard-on," he said, then bolted for the door.

"Get out of here, you brat. Tell Corey and Hot I'll be there about five."

Once outside he hurried along the boardwalk toward the Surf Rider apartments. Out of view from Karen's place, he paused and glanced down at his legs. He smiled, then hurried on his way.

CHAPTER FIVE

Corey turned off the freeway at Pacific Beach Boulevard, drove due west until he hit Mission Beach Boulevand, and turned south to the Surf Rider. On the ocean side of the boulevard were mostly modest homes and only a few apartment buildings, while across the street on the bay side, there were smaller cottage-like houses and more two-story dwellings with rarely more than four units per complex. There was an alley on the ocean side that paralleled the dwellings. Parking in Mission Beach was at a premium, which made the Surf Rider a more desirable habitat, because not only was it on the beach, but there was a carport under the back row of the second-story units.

The owner and landlord of the Surf Rider, Eric Svenhard, was in his fifties. His slender frame, year-round tan, and bleached blond hair gave the appearance of someone much younger. Only up close did the weathered wrinkles of many years of exposure to beach sun and wind give his age away. Most of the tenants thought Eric's name to be a pseudonym chosen to fit his desired self-image. His persona was further revealed in the layout and landscaping of the Surf Rider. In the center courtyard, Eric had built a large brick barbecue with a grill that could hold enough food to cook for twenty people at one time. There were three large wooden picnic tables and a dozen or so chairs surrounding a fire ring next to the barbecue. An assortment of tropical plants bordered the complex. Next to the garage entrance was a small fountain that flowed continuously from the statue of a small, naked boy pissing in the pond.

According to Eric, the statue was a replica of one sculpted by a Dutch artist named Jerome Duquesnoy. According to legend, he sculpted the statue for a wealthy tourist whose young son went missing while they were visiting the countryside outside of Brussels. After searching all day and near hysteria as it grew dark in the evening, the search party heard a tinkling sound coming from a small garden pond, where they found the boy happily urinating away. The merchant left the statue as a gift of gratitude to the locals who helped him find his son.

Eric was single and sought to convey the image of a Renaissance man of old combined with an activist and environmentalist of the modern day. He lived alone in one of the small cottages across the street from the Surf Rider. At one time or another, his tenants, who were all males, surfers, and college students, had been invited to have lunch or dinner at his home, where they found Eric's preferred motif to be that of an exotic Hawaiian beach hut. Inside was a collection of hand-carved Hawaiian fertility gods. Some were six feet tall, others small enough to fit on the windowsill. Large or small, the commonality was the large disproportionate mask, usually the image of some kind of a bird, that fit over the head of each man's naked body. Each statue had an even more disproportionate penis in full erection. Some were just decorations, but on others, depending on their size and placement in his home, he hung jackets, umbrellas, towels, or most anything that needed hanging.

Despite his self-deception, the whole macho Scandinavian look, the pissing boy, and the fertility gods made everyone think, as Hot said, "Eric is as queer as a three-dollar bill." No one cared though, for Eric was not only a fair landlord, but he was a photographer for a popular surf magazine who, from time to time, would use pictures of the Surf Rider clan in the magazine. His strong anti-war sentiments, as well as his activism on environmental issues, particularly when they concerned the preservation of the beautiful California coast, made him somewhat of a local hero and anti-establishment spokesman for Corey's generation. So what if he encouraged nude surfing on remote beaches in Mexico? Naked surfing was an "in" thing they often did anyway.

Eric never approached any of them, and again as Hot explained, "It's cool. Besides, it's probably some kind of hormone imbalance he can't control."

Corey had not heard Spook walk up while he was unpacking his car. People rarely heard Spook come in or leave any gathering. He just sort of appeared, which along with his tall, thin, skeletal frame, sun-bleached blond hair, and skin that never tanned, earned him the nickname of "Spook." His real name was Ed Hawkins and, next to Hot, he was Corey's next closest friend.

Spook was a journalism major who, like Corey, had aspirations of someday being a writer. They met while Corey was still in his campus jock phase, and like his friendship with Hot, their first meeting was something less than amicable ... actually adversarial.

The meeting occurred during their sophomore year when Spook was a writer for the school paper. He was a liberal and always fighting with the teacher advisers who edited some of Spook's strongest anti-war articles. Eventually he was assigned sports reporting, the adviser thinking that would prevent Ed's outspoken political views from being espoused. Of course Spook tried to depict competitive sports as a form of war training and the young athletes as pawns of the mighty military industrial complex.

Corey was familiar with Ed Hawkins' writing and did not like the athlete being portrayed as a brainwashed future war monger, so when Ed interviewed him, Corey was curt and very guarded in his answers. Ed asked if Corey thought there was too much emphasis on winning, to which Corey surprised him by answering, "I think that is more a coaches and press thing. Me and most of my teammates are in it for the love of the game. As long as I play up to my personal standards, winning and losing are secondary."

"You mean you don't get a vicarious thrill out of beating the other team?" Ed pursued. "I don't know if you have ever surfed, but in the ocean you really don't compete against other surfers. You surf with them, not against them, getting stoked by good waves alone. The better the waves and the better the surfers you hang with, the more fun it is. You are competing against other surfers, but in a way that helps you push the limits of your own ability. I think I play baseball with the same attitude I surf."

Ed offered his hand to Corey. "My surfing buddies call me Spook. When would you like to go surfing with us?" The friendship formed that day and became even stronger when Corey quit baseball and changed his major to English Literature, a move suggested by Spook after Corey confessed he was only a business major to please his dad. Corey introduced Spook to the Surf Rider, which happened to have one vacant unit available that Ed snatched up immediately.

Surfing allowed them to overcome their political differences and was the vehicle that introduced Spook to his current roommate, "Weirdness," a choice even more bizarre than his friendship with a jock. He was known as Glen Holdridge before he got the nickname "Weirdness." Glen had been born into money — old La Jolla money from his mom's side of the family. His father, a career military man, married late and fathered Glen while in his forties. He retired when

Glen started high school and, with nothing else to do, was a full-time father and commander to Glen.

Glen did not start out at State. He attended the more prestigious University of California at San Diego. He had been a business major, wore the military crew-cut style haircut, and had been a member of the school's ROTC program. Glen's political views, as described by Hot, were "something right of the John Birch Society." Ed only tolerated the clan because of his love for surfing. The way Corey and Hot viewed it, his love of surfing meant Glen had to have at least one redeeming quality. He was a decent enough surfer despite his rigid, hurky-jerky style, which Spook described as what a goose-stepping Nazi would look like on a surfboard. His short hair had more butch wax than his board contained surf wax. He stood out like a pelican flying among a flock of seagulls.

The beach break in front of the Surf Rider was one of the better beach breaks in North Mission and attracted more than just the local residents who were cordial to outsiders. Glen wanted to gain their friendship because he admired their style of surfing so much, particularly Corey's. Once Spook discovered Glen's political views, which he was already suspicious of because of Glen's appearance, he wanted nothing to do with him. When Corey invited Glen to join them on one of their surfing expeditions into Mexico, Spook became enraged. Corey calmed Spook down by saying, "Anyone who loves surfing as much as Glen must be salvageable, and if not, we can make him so miserable he won't want to hang with us anymore."

The particular weekend Glen joined them, they were also joined by a Huntington Beach surfer named David Harakowa, who was a West Coast surfing legend and often the cover picture on *Surfer* magazine. David was Glen's ultimate surfing idol, although his style was the complete opposite of Glen's. David was smooth, as he seemed to move in slow motion on even the fastest waves.

The first night, they sat around the campfire — everyone high on pot or tequila, and usually both, except for Glen, who watched them with both disdain and a preconceived fear of how marijuana would make you do crazy things. Corey wasn't sure if maybe Glen also was a little envious at being left out, even though it was by Glen's own choice. David looked at Glen and said, "You surf like you have a broomstick stuck up your ass. But don't take offense; you could be pretty good if you let me help you."

Glen was startled, but quickly said, "Okay!"

The next morning David and Glen walked down to the shoreline until David stopped and sat cross-legged, posed like a Buddha statue with his palms up resting on his knees. David was so flexible his knees lay flush against the sand, his back straight. Glen tried to mimic David's position, but Glen's rigidness made his knees point up like a vertical letter *V*, while his back hunched forward.

"The first thing you must do is think of the ocean as a living organism that is not your enemy. You must think of yourself as a particle connected to all particles in the universe, not just living things, but inanimate ones as well. Sit and dwell on your inner connectedness."

David sat quietly for about fifteen minutes, intently studying the swell and its break. Then he pulled out a joint and lit it, took a deep hit, and passed it to Glen.

"I don't do drugs," Glen said meekly.

"This isn't a drug. It is a key to unlocking yourself from your useless notion that you are a separate being unique from the rest of the universe. Take a deep hit and hold it until you count slowly to five, then exhale as slow as you can."

David demonstrated again, then passed the joint to Glen, who hesitated at first, but then tried to copy his surfing god — David.

David counted slowly. At five, Glen expelled the smoke with a hacking cough. "Relax and take another hit." Glen obeyed.

Soon Glen giggled. "Let's surf," he said through a Cheshire cat smile.

"No, not yet. I want you to think about the female salmon. Somewhere out at sea she begins a journey that instinctively drives her to return to her spawning grounds. She braves both sea and land predators to get there. She not only fights natural obstacles like storms, tides, and river currents, but often she must overcome man-made hazards like dams and fishing nets. She braves it all driven by a force greater than regard for own life. She intrinsically knows she must make that journey in order to give birth to her offspring, which will perpetuate her species. She dies after that final battle.

"A wave is just like the salmon. Somewhere it is formed by melting snows of fresh water reaching warmer ocean water, or maybe winds produced by climate change, or maybe something as simple as a child throwing a rock to create a ripple. Whatever the impetus, the motion begins the journey whose final destination reaches a sacred place like this. A beautiful wave is her death dance, and the beginning of a blissful moment for you.

"You are nothing but a small fish living in waters and playing in waves so mysteriously created that you have no understanding of how infinitesimally small and unimportant you are in the grand scheme of things, but still the entire universe can still be at your disposal. Now take off your wet suit and trunks and surf," David instructed.

Glen hesitated. "The water is freezing this time of year!" he protested.

"I just told you the wave is like the pregnant salmon ... it is feminine. When you enter her hollow tube you become a fetus in her womb to be delivered to a joyous world as her final act before she dies at the shore. All infants are born naked, so too shall you. Having been born once, you are reborn to a new and greater awareness than any experience you've had before."

A miracle occurred. Although Glen did not walk on water, he did surf far smoother than anyone had ever seen him surf before. When he did wipe out, he did not become angry and curse the wave or blame other surfers as he often had before, but now he laughed, childlike, and hurried back for more.

After an hour of surfing, they returned to the beach. Glen's body was blue from the cold. But like a child who had just come in from playing in the snow, he was having too much fun to notice his chill. He laughed as he described rides, both good and bad, while complimenting others on rides he watched them take. It didn't even bother him that much that they wouldn't tell him where they buried his trunks and wet suit for another twenty minutes.

Later, in discussing what happened, Hot reasoned that Glen had always seen things as black or white. Pot of course was black, but David was white. Nothing had changed in Glen's beliefs — there still was no gray area — so what changed were Glen's perception of what was black and white, and since David was white, well ... by the end of the year Glen dropped out of UC, enrolled as a sociology major at state, grew his hair long, and became a full-blown pot-smoking hippie. Banned from his parents' palatial home, he took shelter as Spook's roommate and new friend — "Weirdness."

Spook helped Corey unload his belongings. Just as they finished, they heard a noise at the front door and Hot's familiar greeting. "HOT MAN is here!" Hot came in giving Corey a big bear hug. Behind him was Weirdness and two other tenants, Dougie and Aaron, who had been at the Surf Rider since their sophomore year.

After their hellos and welcome backs, they helped in the unpacking. Someone suggested they check out the surf in front of the apartments. They said there had been a nice swell that morning, but it was spoiled by strong winds that were just then beginning to shift and were now blowing offshore, enhancing the waves' shape.

"By the time you finish unpacking, the waves should be smokin'," Dougie said.

"That'll give us time to set up for a party we were planning tonight," Hot said. "Hey, hey, hey!" a boyish voice said from behind the group.

"Joey." Corey turned and saw the boy. "You're growing like a wild weed," he exclaimed.

Joey smiled. "I just left Karen's. She'll be over in about an hour. She's made salad and Turk is making his special brownies. You guys are supposed to get burgers and buns."

"Let's go to the market now. The surf should be even more perfect when we get back," Hot suggested.

As they piled into Hot's van, Corey thought "perfect' was more than just the right word to describe the surf, but also the right word for what he felt. He was away from all the tension at his parents' house. He was with friends who shared the same views of the world as they traveled down similar roads on their journey into the future. It was something else too — he felt the same sense of innocence he had at San Onofre before the war when he still thought of his father as his best friend.

CHAPTER SIX

When they got back, they found the surf as good as Mission Beach could get in early September. They hurriedly waxed their boards and paddled out. Surfing was unlike any sport Corey had ever tried. Hot, having also been a high school jock, agreed that surfing was unique. In most other sports, your competitors' moves are predictable, there are field dimensions, a clock that governs time, and an explicit scoring regulation. In surfing, the real competition was against the wave, not another team or individual. Sometimes waves changed their appearance or velocity without warning. At times you would have to wait twenty or thirty minutes between good sets.

You could surf for hours and come away feeling exhilarated for simply having gotten one good tube ride that lasted maybe three seconds ... your average ride being no more than eight seconds. Sure there were surfing contests in which judges scored the quality of rides, but only rides taken within an allotted time frame. Still, there was no objective point system, and competitive surfers knew who amongst them rode best that day, regardless of the judges' scores. Most surfers who Corey respected surfed for the same reason. Some called it being locked in the moment, while others labeled it as being trapped in suspended animation ... a mystical out-of-body experience. To Corey, it seemed that all his senses became so elevated that his body ceased to be. The force of the wave and the energy he felt were one and the same, so for an instant it was a taste of immortality.

One night he and Hot were talking about their high school athletic days. Corey told Hot what he had said to Spook in the interview several years before. "I never felt that winning or losing was all that important. If the team lost, but I played well, I felt good about myself. If we won, but if I played shitty, then I was stoked for my teammates, but it was a hollow victory for myself. Surfing was not about victories or losses, nor even judgments — just the gift of existence."

"Duh," Hot answered. "I'll bet you anything that the coaches who stress winning like it's a matter of life or death were probably losers as players. I always felt good if I knew I gave it my best. In fact, playing my ass off was what it was all about for me. Keeping score was what old folks did when they couldn't play anymore. When you surf, it doesn't matter if you wipe out or get the tube of your life, you're just stoked to be surfing, and if you're surfing with good friends, ah ... nirvana."

The more Corey thought about it, the more he thought Hot was right. He thought about the first time he played Little League baseball and about the first home run he hit. He could not remember the score of the game or whether his team had won or lost; all he could remember was the adrenaline rush. Even before he watched the flight of the ball going over the fence, he knew at contact the ball was gone. Then too, like in surfing, his mind left his body and became one with the achievement. Unfortunately, that kind of exhilaration faded from baseball the higher level he played. Although he still loved the game, by the time he was on scholarship playing for State, the fun was gone and only the grind remained. In the present, every wave he surfed held a little bit of that first home run. Even the wipeouts were fun, especially if you did it while trying to pull off some impossible maneuver. Like Hot once said, "In surfing there is no difference between what's possible and what isn't. It's the doing, not the result."

Watching Joey surf brought back memories of himself at that age. Corey knew the boy would someday be a better surfer than him, and maybe already was. Joey just didn't have the strength that maturity would bring. He was aware also that the boy studied every one of Corey's maneuvers and tried not only to copy them, but to execute them even better than Corey, who was considered by the rest of the clan to be the best surfer. He would have to teach the boy that surfing was not about proving you were better than someone else, but always striving to be better than you are at the present.

"Rankings," as Hot said, cutting right to the chase, "Don't mean shit to a tree." These were Corey's thoughts as he paddled out to surf with friends once again. Good waves, sunshine, and surfing with friends was all he wanted to think about for a while.

"Hoooooot," Hot shouted as Dougie caught the first wave and got a little tube. His cry was a universal prayer of celebration among surfing buddies and upon hearing it, Corey thought, "The world is far from perfect, but there are flawless moments, and this was one."

They had surfed for nearly two hours, oblivious to time, until someone spotted smoke from the Surf Rider barbecue pit. They decided to ride one more wave each. Nearly everyone returned to the shore, leaving Corey and Joey the last rides. Corey went first. The surf was five to six feet. Corey caught the wave as close to the crest as possible. Dropping in fast, he angled his board under the crashing lip and made a quick bottom turn just barely in front of the spiraling tube. At maximum speed, he shot out in front of the curling crest and shot back up the face to the very lip of the wave as it was about to break, turning a full three hundred and sixty degrees, banking off the crest and back to the bottom of its face. He maintained his balance by squatting and holding the rail with his hand. He became submerged under the tube, barely visible except for the nose of his board. He came out from the tube and milked the white water to the shore.

Everyone on the beach howled or hooted the signature surfer cry of supreme approval — "Righteous." Corey lifted his fist in acknowledgment, then turned to watch Joey's final ride.

Just as he turned, he saw Joey taking off on a similar wave. The boy attempted to repeat Corey's three sixty. It looked like he was going to do it, but at the top of the crest, the lip seemed to spit out further and knocked the boy off his board. The wave victoriously washed the boy's empty board onto the sand at water's edge, where Corey retrieved it and waited for Joey to swim to shore.

Joey looked frustrated as he yanked his board from Corey and mumbled a hollow "Thanks." "That was awesome, little man. That wave was bigger and gnarlier than the one I caught, only your size held you back, but the way you're growing that won't be a problem much longer. In another year you'll be doing three sixties with ease. You do know you will be better than me?"

The boy said nothing as he hauled his board back to the Surf Rider. But for the second time that day, he felt older than thirteen.

Karen and Dawn were in Corey's and Hot's kitchen making hamburger patties. Their apartment was closest to the barbecue pit, so their kitchen was the workshop for the party, as it was for most Surf Rider gatherings.

Corey kissed Karen's cheek. "What can I do to help, babe?"

"Get the fire ring lit," she answered, and handed him a book of matches along with a few pages from the morning paper to be used as a starter.

Outside, Eric had arrived and was tuning his guitar when two unfamiliar faces appeared in the courtyard. Two girls with sunburned faces walked toward the firepit.

"Christy, Jan," Hot said and raced toward the girls. He put his arm around Christy, who snuggled under his arm. She fit under his shoulder like the missing piece of a jigsaw puzzle. Jan stepped back. "Watch it, I'm really sunburned," she warned.

"Hey, everybody, meet Christy and Jan. They recently moved into those apartments just south of the Surf Rider. They're from Olmsteadville, New York. I think that's somewhere in the Adirondack Mountains," Hot said.

"It sure is," Dougie said. "Aaron and I are from Montauk."

"Yikes! Rich guys from Staten Island. We're just a couple of poor, naive mountain girls," Christy said, smiling.

"For those Californians unfamiliar with our state, Olmsteadville is about as conservative a town as there is in the nation. Except for maybe San Marino," Dougie said, getting in a dig at Corey.

Everyone stepped forward and introduced themselves to the new girls.

"This Surf Rider clan is not very conservative, I'll warn you," Eric said as he met the girls. "That's okay. The reason we left is we found out the city leaders were hiding from the town's populace that Rutherford B. Hayes was no longer president," Christy retorted.

Christy did almost all the talking outside of Jan's occasional polite "pleased to meet you."

They learned from Christy that Jan had a twin sister, Debbie, who ran away about two years ago. The last they heard she was somewhere in California.

Jan volunteered something besides "please to meet you." "Run away? My parents kicked her out."

"Hope you find her. Sounds like she would fit in nicely with this group," Weirdness said. "We were looking for her down here, fell in love with San Diego, enrolled in State, and here we are," Christy continued.

Turk then stepped forward. "I brought some appetizers. Most appetizers fill you up, but these are groovy cuz they make you hungry," he said as he pulled two tightly rolled joints from his pocket. He lit both and took a hit from each, then passed them on.

"No, thank you; I don't smoke," Jan said as Dougie offered her a hit.

"Old Rutherford would be proud of you," Turk said, smiling.

"How about a glass of wine?" Karen quickly suggested. "That I'll take," Jan answered.

"Bacchus would be prouder," Hot said, making everyone, including Jan, laugh. She took a sip of wine as Hot lifted his glass and said, "To both our old and new friends, and of course to Bacchus."

Jan was about to take another sip when she noticed that Joey was handed one of the joints and took a deep drag. Jan involuntarily gasped. Her eyes skirted the crowd; no one paid the boy any mind. Only Karen, with her photographer's eye for small details, noticed Jan's apprehension. She casually approached Jan.

"Say, I could use a little help in the kitchen. Would you mind?: she said.

"I'd love to", Jan practically blurted out and quickly followed her into the kitchen.

Once inside, Karen said, "Let's sit down for a few minutes. They won't be ready to eat until they finish the joints." She paused a few seconds, then said, "I'm not sure if you were as ready to leave home as much as your friend."

Jan, who was fidgeting nervously, said, "Christy, her name is Christy ... she's my sister's best friend. She is helping me find her."

"That doesn't answer my question, and you don't have to if you don't want, but Helen Keller could see how uncomfortable you are."

"How old is that little boy? He seemed pretty used to smoking pot."

Karen laughed. "Don't worry about Joey. He's thirteen going on twenty. To fill you in on Joey, I can tell you what most of the rest of us have come to learn over the past few years. Joey 's mom got pregnant while she was still in high school. The father whom none of us, including Joey, know anything about, split a year or so later. They never heard from him again. His mom works as a cocktail waitress at a notorious pickup bar, where she is hoping some Prince Charming will come along and solve all her woes and disappointments. She does some extra work for an escort service, or in other words, to be blunt, she's a whore. Joey is in the way when she brings her lovers home, so when that happens Joey stays with me, Corey, Turk, or any other college friends whom all have adopted him as kind of our universal flower child. You'll soon see, despite his background, he's a really neat kid. Somehow, his heart is always in the right spot. It kinda makes us all realize you can overcome some pretty bad stuff and turn out okay." Karen paused. "You've never tried weed have you?" she continued. "It doesn't matter. This group is pretty laid back when it comes to judging other people as long as they don't judge us too harshly in return. You can try weed whenever you're ready, or not at all; it's all cool. Now unless there is anything else you want to ask, help me take these burgers out to the barbecue."

"I have no more questions now, but thanks for this," Jan said.

"Well, anytime I can help, feel free to ask. You'll find, with maybe a few exceptions, this is really a groovy group. If you relax, you're going to be in for a good time."

After the meal, Eric picked up his guitar and strummed a few chords. He enjoyed playing for the young crowd and took his guitar and music books with him whenever they invited him to their parties or surfing safaris to Mexico. Eric played quite well and complimented his playing with a very pleasant voice that reminded Corey of a less harsh sounding Phil Ochs. Eric wrote some of his own songs, but neither Corey, Karen, or Hot cared much for them. They were too personal. Eric's lyrics implied that Eric's perceptions were the only ones that were worth consideration. Corey tried to tell Eric that what he thought made a song great was when the lyrics had universal appeal without coming off as didactic. Corey felt that when Eric sang his own songs, he came off as being superior to his audience. Eric either missed the point or chose to ignore it, yet always seemed surprised when everyone requested popular cover songs over his own.

“I learned this song over the summer,” Eric said. “It just might be the best anti-war song I've ever heard. It was written by a young, very talented singer-songwriter named Buffy Saint Marie. It's entitled 'The Universal Soldier.'”

“Hey, Eric, how about doing that one a little later? I think everyone is in party mode and pretty happy to be back and together again. I know I'm stoked and don't want to think about the goddamn war right now. Why don't you do some happy music, or love songs,” Corey said as he gave Karen a hug.

“Yah!” Hot added. “I've just introduced everyone to the two new hot babes that are now our neighbors. It's time for celebration.”

“You can't bury you heads in the sand forever. We've got to end this war, and songs like this might be more potent than marches,” Eric said as he readied himself to play.

“How about doing a request first? Last year you did your version of 'The Times They Are a Changin',' which was about the best I've ever heard it sung,” Karen said.

Dougie started to put another log on the fire before Eric could respond.

"Hold on," Corey said, picking up a stick. "You should have spent more time in the Adirondacks where, if you weren't lucky enough to meet a couple of good-lookin' chicks like Christy and Jan, at least you might have learned some useful campfire knowledge." Corey pushed around the remaining burning logs. As he rolled one log over, they heard a hiss as a thin blue flame rose like a burning exclamation point. "Campfires are an art. You see how long you can make a couple of logs burn before you add more," Corey continued. "See the logs? They are a changin' both color and intensity as gases and unburnt wood are released. The times, like the logs, they are a changin', aren't they, Eric?"

"I'd rather have a big fire," Dougie said.

Corey laughed. "There's an old man who lives on my street. I've talked about him before, but for you newcomers, his name is Hank, and he's a full-blood Apache. He says, 'Indians build small fires and sit close together near the fire where they can speak softly to one another. White men build big fires, consume more wood, and speak loudly.'"

"What difference does how loud you talk matter?" Dougie asked.

"Hank says that truth is usually spoken in quiet whispers. When people shout out their beliefs, they are trying to convince themselves more than others."

"You sure that old man was telling the truth about that being an Indian belief?" Spook inquired.

"He might have been lying. I think some of Hank's stories take liberties with the truth, but that didn't bother me none since his lies seemed to clarify the truth even more," Corey answered. "What else did the old man teach you?" Hot said, almost whispering as he moved closer to the fire.

Corey held up the stick he had used to turn the logs. "When we sat around the campfires, it seemed everyone wanted to talk at the same time, so we passed around a stick like this. Whoever held the stick was the only one who could speak. When you said your piece, you passed the stick to the person of your choice. I say we choose songs by the passing of this stick." He passed the stick to Karen. "You're first, my luv."

"I already made my choice: 'The Times They Are a Changin'."

Eric reluctantly did the song. When he finished, Corey took the stick from Karen and pushed the fire around, releasing some more trapped gas in a piece of wood. This time a horizontal green flame raced low across the full length of the log. He then gave it to Hot.

Hot put his arm around Christy. "I chose 'Love the One You're With.' If you don't know it, I think we all do. If you can, just strum the melody."

Eric, who had seemed a little hurt at first, probably because he had rehearsed a series of anti- war songs, was still the center of attraction. "Just because I'm over thirty doesn't mean I don't know a good song when I hear it. That's one of my favorite Crosby, Stills and Nash songs." He happily played Hots' request.

Turk took the stick next. "Everyone's nice and stoned like

the Tambourine man. Take us disappearing down the smoke rings of our minds." Everyone laughed, and Eric played the song.

Turk passed the stick to Corey. "It seems kind of funny to me, almost everyone thinks that song is about smokin' pot. I sorta think it's more about finding time to just get away from everything for a while ... like the last line of the song says. 'Let me forget about today until tomorrow.'" Corey handed the stick to Eric. "Thank you, Eric. Now it's your turn. Just no war songs or the stick is going up your ass."

Eric smiled at the group. "Okay, why don't we do one we all know. It's one of my all-time favorite songs ... 'Amazing Grace.' It was written by Captain John Newton, who was a slave trader, on his way back from Africa with a full cargo of slaves. He heard their moans and cries of sorrow over the grinding of their chains. He turned the boat around and sailed back to Africa and freed the intended slaves. He lost his captains license and served a little prison time, where he wrote this song of redemption out of his sense of personal guilt for his part in perpetuating slavery. Pete Seeger wrote an additional verse that you guys and gals have never heard. It's so hard to admit your own guilt. It's hard to change course once you're committed to another direction."

"You gonna sing or give history lesson?" Hot said.

"I'm going to sing, but you all have to join in until the last verse, then listen carefully. Come on. Let's all move closer to Corey's puny fire." Eric began playing "Amazing Grace." Most everyone sang with him until he reached the last verse, which Eric sang alone.

> *"Shall I be wafted to the skies On flowery beds of ease*
> *While others strive to win the prize And sail on*
> *bloody seas*
> *Amazing grace how sweet the sound, that saved a*
> *wretch like me."*

Toward the end of the evening, Joey came over to Corey. "With this swell, I'll bet the waves at New Break are piping hot. Can I crash on your couch so we can go there first thing in the morning? Unless you're going to spend the night with Karen, of course?"

"You don't have to sleep on the couch. Use my bed. I'll be back from Karen's early and will take you to down to New Break. It's my favorite spot too, and it's especially good when you surf it with one of your best friends."

CHAPTER SEVEN

THE NEXT MORNING, DOUGIE AWOKE EARLY AND WALKED into the front room where he could look out the window and observe the surf. He found Aaron dressed only in a T-shirt, sitting on the sofa rubbing cold cream on his dick.

"It serves you right, "Dougie said.

Aaron looked up as he continued to gingerly apply the cream. "Fuck you," he muttered, then added, "Just wait. I'll get even with that bitch."

Dougie walked over to the windows and looked out at the ocean. The swell had come up a little more during the night. An offshore breeze helped the shape.

"I'm serious," Aaron said as he slowly eased his trunks up. "She knew I was only kidding around. You wait, I'll get even big time."

Dougie turned, shaking his head in frustration. "No you won't. You'll apologize."

"She threw that hot coffee right on my crotch," Aaron protested.

Dougie ignored him as he turned to gaze at the ocean once more. "Everybody was going to go to New Break, but I think everybody slept in; too much party last night. The waves out front have great shape and the cool water will feel good on your nuts. We'll surf for a while, then we can go buy some flowers or chocolates for you to give to Dawn when you apologize."

"Why can't anyone understand it was just a joke?" Aaron said, still pleading his case.

"What did you expect her to do? She goes into the bathroom and as soon as she turns on the light, some naked guy pulls back the shower curtain and jumps toward her."

"She could see it was me."

"So what? after all the crazy things you've done, I would have not known what to expect either ... I'd have thrown hot coffee on your cock too."

Aaron started to say more, but Dougie stopped him. "I'm tired of always defending you after one of your pranks. We've had this conversation a million times before. Sure, I know how crappy your childhood was ... I understand that and that's why I try to help, but that shitty childhood story only goes so far. These people are willing to be your friend — that's why they've tolerated you as long as they have — but they've got to see you make some kind of effort to change. Screw your past. Don't you see you really have a chance with these guys to change for the better?"

"Bullshit! You know Corey and Hot would love to beat me to a pulp," Aaron said. "They don't only because of you."

"That's because you pick on Joey so much and he's too young to defend himself."

"Hey! When younger kids hang around with older kids, they have to expect to be a target."

"Think first next time. Think of consequences. Think how you would feel being on the butt end of one of your pranks," Dougie exclaimed.

"Those guys kid around with Joey too! Don't tell me you haven't seen that."

"Kid yes, all in fun, but your practical jokes are cruel ... Can't you see the difference?"

Aaron's eyes became watery. "You know, I really wish I could be different than I am; I really do. You know my background, but you don't know what it was like to see hatred in your own father's eyes every time he looked at you," he said and began to sob.

"It's okay," Dougie said as he walked over and gave Aaron a hug. "No, I knew my parents loved me even when we argued or fought over something. What I do know is that somewhere under all that hurt, all that undeserved pain, there is a good person locked inside you. Remember, I was small for my age and a late bloomer on top of that. I was an easy target, but you became my bodyguard instead of joining in on the hazing. Where you are now is not with your asshole father but with people who are willing to take you in as a friend. They are willing to help unlock that good person I know is in there. Treat people the way you wanted to be treated and they will gladly help you set it free. Let's start by cooling off in some good surf, then I'll help you pick out some flowers for Dawn."

At New Break, the rising sun on the eastern horizon slowly crept dim morning light westward, revealing the silhouettes of a young man and a boy as they stood motionless on the shoreline, sizing up the now visible waves.

"Listen," Corey said. "What do you hear?" "Just the ocean," Joey answered.

"Right. Nothing else — no voices, no music, no traffic sounds — just the howling wind against crashing waves. Makes you feel like it's the first morning after creation. I'm glad no one else got up early, although I wish Turk could have joined us."

The boy shrugged his shoulders. "Eric just had to get you guys talking about the war. He shouldn't do it in front of Turk."

"Eric thinks he's doing the right thing. I'm sure as a kid he was different from other kids.

What he's doing now ... I guess he's sort of relishing his local popularity as an activist since I'm pretty sure he wasn't taken too seriously as a child or teenager," Corey answered.

"Do you guys really like him? I think he's a dick," Joey said.

"He's harmless, and he tries to fit in by saying all the right things on issues that young people believe in today. I think in a way he's glad there's a war going on so he can be a rally leader against it. You know how people want to align themselves with a sports team or club or something like that? I think they do that in order to feel bigger, or more important than they really are. Not only does he feel accepted now, but I think, in his mind, it gives him the recognition he never had when he was our age," Corey reasoned, then added, "But you're right, most people think he's strange."

"Just the same, Eric has to know that Turk was in the war and it messed up his head. He's trying to put the pieces back together by forgetting the war altogether."

Corey began waxing his board. "A big step in putting things back together is being able to deal with the Erics of the world, because there will always be somebody or something to remind you of what you are hoping to forget." Corey paused, then intentionally changed the subject. "You fell asleep and missed the excitement last night. Aaron hid naked in Spook's shower. Dawn went in to use the head and Aaron jumped out naked. She had a hot cup of coffee in her hand and threw it at his cock."

"Good," Joey said. "I hope she burned his balls off."

"Not a bad idea; sterilizing Aaron would improve the gene pool."

"It's weird, but as screwed up as he is, I still feel sorry for him," Joey confessed. "Dougie told me that when Aaron was about two, he ran out in the street, not seeing an oncoming car. His mom ran out after him and pushed him out of the way, but she was hit and killed. He said Aaron's father never was the same after that .... He couldn't show him any love. He didn't even want his own kid to live with him, so he passed him around to various relatives who cared for him a while. Dougie said Aaron's father was rich so he paid for boarding schools and stuff like that. He said he gave Aaron everything but love."

"Sounds like his old man needed castration too," Corey said as he finished waxing his board and flipped the wax to Joey. "You haven't had the most ideal life either ... How come you're not more like Aaron?"

Joey looked totally perplexed. "What do you mean? I live year-round at the beach and have great friends like you and the rest of the Surf Rider clan. You guys always take me on surfing trips that other kids my age have never been on. Turk's taught me how to shape surfboards and make jewelry from rocks and seashells. I have it great."

"I suppose you do," Corey said, smiling at the boy. "I guess what I'm trying to say ... Well, when I was a kid, younger than yourself, after it rained or if it was summer and people were watering their lawns, the gutter next to the curb would fill with water that rushed down to a drain at the bottom of the street. We used to put twigs, or better yet popsicle sticks, in the water and watch them race toward the drain. We'd hurry ahead and create obstacles to block both water and our small vessels. You know what I mean; we'd dump some dirt or clump of grass to build a dam. It would slow the water temporarily, but while the water would eddy for a moment, it would always find a way to change course or build up enough pressure to break through the crude edifice so the stick could continue its journey. Sometimes our small craft would get stuck and remain there as the water pressure waned. It would never reach our intended destination. That's Aaron; he's stuck on something in his past. What happened to him was wrong, not even his fault, but life is filled with injustices, and like the water, you just have to keep flowing and find a way to get past whatever it is that fucked you up for a while."

"You talk to me like I was one of your college friends and I like that ... It makes me feel older."

"Well I like talking to you because it makes me feel like I'm still a kid, and I had a great childhood despite a few bumps along the way."

"I don't see how it could have been better than mine. That's why I don't understand why you say I had it rough like asshole Aaron," Joey said.

"I mean you never had a father around, and your mom seems pretty stressed by the way her life is playing out, but you're not angry like Aaron," Corey replied.

"Like I said, what could be better than to live at the beach year-round and surf anytime you want? Even if my mom's a little different than the other kids' moms, it doesn't matter, cuz friends like you and Turk turn me onto things other kids my age don't even know exist."

"I guess you're right. See? You've stayed floating on the water and haven't got hung up on obstacles that might have gotten in your way. You're way cool, little man, way cool," Corey said, then added, "I guess there is a time for talkin' and time for surfin', and right now we ought to get in the water before too many other surfers get here."

Joey pushed Corey backward then quickly grabbed his own board and sprinted toward the water. "Betcha I get the first ride," he said, laughing while he ran.

CHAPTER EIGHT

THE YEAR BEFORE, WHEN COREY CHANGED HIS MAJOR TO English Literature, he was introduced to a Professor Vanderhoof, who eventually became his favorite teacher. Vanderhoof had a subtle way of getting his students interested in whichever author they studied. He accomplished this by reading passages from their work that brought out the essence of that particular author's beliefs.

Corey had signed up for a class taught by Professor Vanderhoof which focused on two of the most notable nineteenth-century American writers — Mark Twain and Herman Melville. In an American literature class Corey had taken the year before, he was introduced to Twain. He loved Twain's ability to combine humor with pathos, or more aptly, explore moral issues amorally.

Vanderhoof's class was held in a small amphitheater also

used by the drama department for staging short plays. The architecture of the room was modeled after the ancient Greek Amphitheaters, so upon entering the room, you felt as if you had traveled back in time. The professor entered the room after all the students arrived. He did not look at any of them until he had surveyed the pillars and carvings around the doors and ceiling. He glanced around the class, peering at each student individually, then stated, "I love this classroom" as his eyes drifted to the architecture once more. Many of the students took their eyes off the professor and looked around the room, following his lead. The professor wore thick glasses that magnified his eyes, making them look abnormally large, and the room lights refracted their rays off the lenses of his glasses, which made them sparkle as his head moved. The room seemed to fill with an uneasy quiet as if the professor had forgotten the class and was enjoying the ambiance.

He finally spoke. "I think that when great writers, or great men for that matter, die, their thoughts live and hover in the ether until someone, such as this class, gather to study their works. We become mediums who awaken their souls so they live again through us. It will be my goal, and hopefully yours if you expect a good grade, to roust the spirits of Misters Clemens and Melville and bring their presence to this very classroom.

He opened his briefcase, which looked much older than him. He then took out a pamphlet and laid it open on the podium and began to read. His usual soft-spoken tone changed to that of an almost boisterous Shakespearean thespian.

> *"It was a time of great and exalting excitement. The country was up in arms, the war was on. In every breast burned the holy fire of patriotism."*

He stopped reading and closed the pamphlet. He held it up for the class to see the cover. "This is *The War Prayer* by Mister Clemens, also known by his literary name, Mark Twain. You can find copies of these in the bookstore, and when I hand out our reading list for the Semester, you will be expected to purchase each work individually, or, as I would suggest, buy the complete works of each of our authors. You might find enjoyment in reading beyond that which is required. By Friday, I want you to have read *The War Prayer* and write an essay on its social relevancy in today's world. I don't care how long the essay is, or if you feel very creative, even a poem would suffice, as long as it is your subjective thoughts. I'm going to dismiss the class early as I know you are all anxious to get started."

Corey waited for the room to clear, then walked up to the podium where Professor Vanderhoof was putting his materials back in his tattered briefcase.

"Professor Vanderhoof, I don't know if you recognize me, but I took a class from you last year. I'm ..."

"Mr. Jameson," the professor said without looking up. "You showed promise as a thinker.

I'm glad to have you back this year."

"Thank you, sir, but I want to ask you a question."

"It's obvious it is not one pertinent for the entire class or you would have asked it earlier," the professor said, looking up and smiling at Corey.

Corey hesitated, then said, "I read *The War Prayer* this summer, among much of Twain's work. I did this because I fell in love with Twain's work after taking your class last semester. Of all the works I read, I thought the *Prayer* was one of his weakest pieces."

The professor's smile widened. "It's good to know one of my students kept his brain working over the summer. So why did you not like that piece?"

"It's a sermon. If you're predisposed to be against the war, then hallelujah, a great sermon. If not, it just pisses you off, and you'll defend your own views with even with more intensity," Corey answered.

"Let's see now. If I recall, you are the ex-jock turned English major, so let us drop locker room language, like pissed off, and say —"

"Provoked, I should have used provoked. My apologies."

"Aw! A much better choice of a word, but vocabulary aside, you've made an interesting observation about human nature. Now, do you disagree with the views advocated in the *Prayer*?"

Professor Vanderhoof reopened his briefcase and pulled out a large book. Corey could read the title: *The Complete Mark Twain*. Vanderhoof thumbed through the pages. He found what he wanted and laid the book open on the podium. "Copy this phrase please."

Corey pulled out his notebook and wrote as the professor read:

> *"'A killing of strangers, against whom you feel no personal animosity.'*

This is a line from one of Twain's short stores entitled, "A Private History of a Campaign That Failed." Mr. Jameson, I want you to compare and contrast *War Prayer* with the "Campaign That Failed," in particular the words I just read. I'm looking most forward to reading your paper."

Corey let out an angry grunt, then mumbled, "Okay."

"What! Do you think you are being punished for challenging me; that you have been given a harder assignment for asking a question?"

"Well ... sort of."

"If you want to look at it that way you can, but I would prefer you look at it as if I were rewarding you for your thoughtful question. The best kind of learning evokes more questions than answers, and good questions have greater intrinsic rewards, as they evoke even more provocative questions. Reading between the lines, I think what you are after is intellectual growth. Am I correct?"

"I'm not sure I know what I'm seeking," Corey quickly answered. "I just felt *The War Prayer* was not one of Twain's better efforts."

"Good, I'm anxious to see what you think of the other work."

"What was that other Twain piece?" Corey asked.

"'A Private History of a Campaign That Failed,'" Professor Vanderhoof answered. Corey gathered his notebook and walked away. Just as his hand touched the doorknob,

Professor Vanderhoof called out.

"Mr. Jameson, incidentally, I also think *The War Prayer* was one of Twain's weakest efforts," he said, and winked at Corey.

CHAPTER NINE

On Wednesday morning, Corey arrived at Vanderhoof's class a few minutes early. The professor was at his desk reading. Corey laid his paper in front of him.

"You know this is not due until Friday."

"I know, but I thought when I reached college putting an apple on the teacher's desk was childish. I thought turning in an assignment early was more fitting."

Vanderhoof gave him a wry smile as he picked up the paper and began to read. Corey went to his seat as the professor continued to read. Even after the rest of the class arrived the professor continued reading Corey's paper, occasionally underlining a few places. After what seemed like a long time to Corey, Vanderhoof walked to the blackboard and wrote "Moral sense."

He turned and faced the class. "'Moral sense' is the

common thread that binds not only Mark Twain's fiction, but also his personal writings to friends and associates. He expresses it many ways, often humorously like 'nothing needs mending more than your neighbor's morals' or through ethical dilemmas such as those Huck Finn faced in helping his runaway slave friend, Jim, escape to freedom."

Vanderhoof returned to the blackboard and wrote "Easy believer."

"Mr. Melville wrote a letter to a close friend stating that there was nothing he despised more than an easy believer. He went on to say that Ahab was such a memorable character because it was the easy believer he wanted to slay, not the whale."

He walked over to his desk and picked up Corey's paper.

"I'd like to read an excerpt written by a noted Twain scholar. Hopefully this might help you with your current assignment."

"*The War Prayer* is uncompromising and absolute in its denunciation of war. It depicts both the soldier and the zealot patriot as one and the same, just Satan by different names.

"Anytime one takes a dogmatic stand and uses the nomenclature popular with that belief, he can galvanize support for that position through blind faith followers. Oh! If only all bad guys wore black and the good guys wore white. The sermon of the 'Prayer' does nothing more than reinforce what anti-war advocates are predisposed to believe.

"In my opinion, a far superior work is *A Private History of a Campaign That Failed*, in which Mr. Clemens relates his personal experience in war. In his unique style, he makes the story as pleasant as an old-fashioned hayride, dressing it with humor and his renowned sarcastic wit. You have no idea that there is a devastating moral dilemma along on this pleasant ride. But events unfold, and the reader, without persuasion or consciousness, is blindsided.

> *"And it seemed an epitome of war that all war must be just that –the killing of strangers against whom you feel no personal animosity strangers, whom, in other circumstances you would help if you found them in trouble, and who would help you if you needed. My campaign was spoiled."*

"Now I know I did not assign the latter work, but I would suggest you read it for your own enlightenment. Near the end of this essay, our critic" — Vanderhoof lifted Corey's paper–"asks the question, 'Would you prefer to be swayed by some gifted orator's euphemistic words, or draw conclusions from examining your own personal experience?'

"Melville believed that the majority are 'easy believers' because they tacitly accept the beliefs and laws of their leaders and heroes, and by doing so, absolve themselves of personal responsibility.

"When you read the works of these two writers, keep their respective notion 'easy believer' and 'moral sense' forefront in your mind. You know it will appear on some test," he said and winked at the class.

Vanderhoof spoke more on the two writers until about ten minutes before period ending. "Nothing wrong with dismissing the class early," he said, glancing at his watch.

As they began to file out, the professor said, "Mr. Jameson, may I speak to you for a moment?"

Corey went to the professor's desk.

"Did you know I have a son just a few years younger than yourself? He was a freshman at Columbia last year. Over the summer, he marched in a peace rally. Things got ugly, and police tried to break up the crowd and lined up to quell a riot. My son was clubbed in the head, resulting in his brain working slower now, and his speech has a slight slur. The doctor feels he will fully recover, but for now he has had to drop out of school." "I'm very sorry, sir; I had no idea."

The professor waved his hand as if to say no apology necessary.

"I was impressed with your paper and even more so with how quickly you were motivated. You did try to sound unnaturally intellectual, maybe because you are still trying to lose your jock image." The professor smiled. "Leave it be. It's part of your charm. Nevertheless, the thought struck me as I read your paper — how would you like to base your entire grade on just one term paper? If you answer yes, you'll be challenged as much, if not more, than trying to drive in the tying run with two outs in the bottom of the ninth."

"Depends on the assignment, sir."

"Let's preface it by saying that when I was fourteen, I wanted to be a baseball player, not an English teacher. I grew up in the Boston area, where my father would, whenever he could afford to on his meager blue-collar wages, take me to Red Sox games. One night, before the game began, an usher wheeled out a hopelessly crippled young boy. They placed the wheelchair about ten feet in front of home plate and gave the boy a ball for the ceremonial throwing out of the first pitch, which he ineffectively bounced toward the catcher. The boy was the poster boy for whatever crippling disease he had — I don't remember now. My father, like all the fans, cheered the feeble throw and said he thought it was great that the Boston organization gave that unfortunate lad that opportunity. I remembered thinking as we drove home that night, why would God allow such an innocent child to suffer so much?

"After what has happened to my own son, I've rekindled my own questions about the existence of God. I think those doubts are the same that Melville and Twain had when they wrote about 'easy believers' and 'moral sense.' Ahab is as obsessed with finding the whale as Huck is intent on getting his friend Jim to freedom. Both quests are the way they explored their personal questions about the existence of God. Rather than do the regular assignment, I would like you to compare and contrast the moral conflicts that Ahab and Huck confronted in their respective journeys. You can draw on any other of their works you care to read."

Corey looked the professor straight in the eye. For a few minutes, the professor stared straight back, then lowered his eyes.

"Would I be doing this assignment for my own education,

or are you using me to explore questions that you are having trouble answering yourself?" Corey asked.

"Both," the professor said as he looked up at Corey, then added, "But I suspect you are having some difficult moral conflicts yourself. I wished I had asked better questions when I was your age."

Corey said, "You know I feel more comfortable in the locker room than in the classroom. I might not be able to find the answers you are looking for ... I might not ask the right questions either."

"Whether it was curiosity or imagination that compelled you to read for pleasure over the summer is unimportant. Your doing so revealed your essence, Mr. Jameson. Remember, I just read your paper. You were moved by Mr. Twain's short story because you share with him something most people say they have, but don't — passion for the human condition. Never lose that, my friend."

The professor extended his right hand. "Do we have a deal?"

Corey hesitated, then shook his hand. "I'll give it my best shot," he said, then added, "People have tried to civilize before, but it wern't much good."

The professor smiled. "That's good. Like Twain, hide your pain with humor."

CHAPTER TEN

It was nearing the end of September. Corey and the rest of the clan were back to their routines. To Corey's surprise and liking, there had not been much talk about the war, probably because the draft was no longer several years away, but right around the corner, which made surfing and partying more an escape from the encroaching reality of Vietnam than a recreation. He and Hot had just returned from school that Friday and were about to go surfing when the phone rang.

Hot answered. "It's for you, your friend Millie."

Corey answered the phone nervously. In the past, a call from Hank or Millie was looked forward to, but with Hank's current condition —

"I was going to call you earlier in the week, but Hank didn't want you to worry. Besides, you couldn't have visited him anyway — He had a stroke and was in the hospital until today, when he's feeling much better so the doctor let me bring him home, so I figured with the weekend —"

Corey had never heard Millie ramble on so fast. "I'll leave now," he said before she could finish.

He explained to Hot what happened, then called Karen and let her know he had to leave for the weekend.

Millie greeted Corey at the door and immediately began telling him how much better Hank was since the first of the week. "So much so that the doctor thought it was a good idea to go home. He said he would recuperate faster in familiar surroundings."

"I'm sure he's getting better; he was probably becoming ornery and they wanted to get rid of him," Corey said, smiling. He put his arm around her and gave her a hug. "I'm sure he is getting a lot better. The doctor wouldn't have let him go home if he didn't think so too."

She looked embarrassed for a few seconds, smiled sheepishly, then led him down the hall toward the bedroom. Near the end of the hall, Corey smelled the artificial flower aroma from an aerosol can Millie had probably used to try cover the stale body odor of Hank's bedridden confinement. As he entered the room, before he saw Hank he saw his nightstand filled with bottles of medication, a glass of water, tissue, and a sky-blue can labeled "Garden Flowers."

Hank was propped up in a sitting position with several

pillows stacked behind his back. He tried to smile when Corey entered, but the left side of his face drooped and saliva trickled from the left side of his mouth. Millie quickly grabbed a tissue and cleaned the drool. Hank's hands were folded in his lap. Corey glanced at Hank's fingers. His fingernails were a sallow yellow, like dying grass. The old man saw that Corey looked at his hands. Quickly with his right hand, he dragged his left hand under the covers, then placed the right one next to it.

Corey felt guilty for looking at the aging, wrinkled hands before he looked Hank in the eye or said hello. "You look better than I expected. You'll probably be mowing the lawn by next week," he said quickly.

"Liar," the old man said, his voice sounding like someone trying to talk with marbles in their mouth.

"Don't he look good?" Millie chimed in. "He even lifted himself when I stacked the pillows. He's doing a lot of things for himself now," she said, trying to sound reassuring as she wiped his mouth once again as more saliva trickled out when Hank spoke.

"Show Corey how well you can smile. Give us a big grin."

Hank attempted to obey, but only the right side of his lips responded.

"Isn't that good?" she said. "Now blink. Watch how he can blink."

Again, the old man labored to please his wife. His face twitched erratically and his right eye closed several times before he managed a slight flutter of the left lid.

"That's great, honey," she said as convincingly as possible. "Now one more. Wiggle your fingers for Corey."

Hank glanced at Corey. His fatigued, tired eyes came to life with a mischievous childlike sparkle. He lifted his right hand from under the covers and waved.

"No, silly. You know what I mean."

Hank's expression grew serious. With the help of his good hand, he lifted his left hand into the air, the back of his hand facing Millie. He labored, obviously in pain, but he managed to curl all his fingers down except for the middle one, which he somehow held erect. Corey broke up laughing.

"You brat," Millie said, then gave a demurring little laugh. Her face blushed. "

When he starts acting like that, you know he's getting better," Corey said.

"I told you he was, and I can take a hint too. I'll leave you two men alone for a while."

"Nag, nag, nag," Hank said with a warm appreciative smile directed toward her as she left the room. His voice still sounded weak. The effort seemed to exhaust him, so he lay quiet for almost a minute.

"That was great," Corey said. "I think I told you that I switched my major to literature, so if I ever become a writer, that episode is somehow going in my book."

"You switched majors to avoid the draft," Hank said, having caught his breath.

"Well, that too, but I still think I might want to write someday."

Hank pointed toward his dresser. "An envelope is up there. Grab it for me."

Corey found the envelope. It was old and soiled, and time had turned it the same color yellow as the old man's fingernails. It was postmarked from Arizona and was dated nineteen thirty-something. The ink had smeared, obliterating the last number.

He handed Hank the letter. Hank fumbled trying to open the unsealed flap. He could not do it with one hand, so he handed it to back to Corey.

"Open the damn thing," he commanded.

Corey pulled out a well-worn newspaper clipping. Its texture had turned tissue thin so he took great care not to tear it as he unfolded it. The article was dated June 5, 1937. The headline read, "Mystery Surrounds Chief's Death."

"Go ahead and read it," Hank said.

Corey obeyed and started reading the clipping to himself.

"The remains of tribal Chief Thomas Victorio were found Friday one week after his disappearance from the reservation's infirmary. He had been under intensive care since early May. Federal Indian agent Willard Christian told reporters that Victorio had fought his hospitalization, saying that he wanted to die in accordance to the custom of his ancestors. (Victorio had dedicated his life to the preservation of tribal traditions.)

"Christian said, 'We knew he was earnest, but we felt

his condition far more serious than he was aware. We felt he would be better off under professional care provided by the reservation hospital. In the morning, his bed was found empty. An extensive search of the reservation was carried out by federal authorities without finding a trace as to the chief's whereabouts.'

"Friday morning, two young Indian men approached Christian and said they would lead him to Victorio's body and led the agent to the northern outskirts of the reservation to a previously unknown hidden canyon. The body was found clothed in full chieftain's regalia and wrapped in a tribal burial blanket.

"Agent Christian explained that the area was very rugged and hard to reach, which was why they had not searched the region before. They figured there was no way a man in Victorio's condition could get there by himself. Tribal members denied anyone assisted the chief.

"'The area itself was rich with archaeological finds,' said Christian. 'Rock paintings and ancient artifacts were everywhere.' Authorities from Arizona's historical society will begin an extensive study of the find.

"Thomas Victorio may have been the last of the tribe's true fundamentalist. He is survived by his wife Helen, and their three sons, William, Raymond,

and Henry. The former two sons still reside on the reservation along with their mother. The third son, Henry, resides in the Los Angeles area."

Corey never knew much about Hank's earlier life. He knew Hank had rejected reservation life and left when he was seventeen. He was aware, through some of Hank's stories, that although Hank disagreed with his father's traditional beliefs, he had not completely disregarded them. On many occasions, Hank had explained to Corey how he felt the Indian reservation was not much more than a prison, and his people were wards of the state, which provided them with just enough comfort to keep them from leaving and trying to make it in the modern white man's world. Yet in the next breath he would explain how he was grateful to his father for teaching him his appreciation of nature and the outdoors. "Big city dwelling puts us out of touch with the everyday lessons revealed by nature. That's why I love the High Sierras so much," Hank would say. "I understand my father's romanticizing the old ways, for life was much simpler then, but those days are gone for good. I feel many of my father's, and my peoples' beliefs, if they have intrinsic value we should allow ourselves to be assimilated into the white man's society where we can share them, and if they truly are universal verities, they would flourish and strengthen both races."

Corey carefully folded the article and was about to replace it when Hank said, "There should be a handwritten letter in there. Read that also."

Corey opened the envelope and found a letter so thin and tightly folded that he had missed it before. He pulled it out and was surprised to see how neat and well written it was. Corey still had a mental picture of Hank's father as some wild, uneducated, television-type Indian.

Dear Henry,

I am writing you after all these years because I am about to die, and there are things I never told you that are now relevant. It is my duty as your father and as an Apache tribal leader.

You have chosen to live as a white man, a decision I loathed for years. But now, I know it must have been the right thing, for I recognize you are happy. You would have returned long ago if you were not. I still hope the early lessons I taught you have added quality to your life. Maybe that thought is just a foolish notion that all fathers want to believe when they get old and know that their progeny will soon be on their own. I still have one more lesson I wish to convey, if you would oblige this old man.

In the white man's world you have chosen, death is probably some abstract notion you don't even think about, as I did not when I was your age. You think you will live forever ... now forever does not seem long enough. What I know of the white man's world is they worship youth so much that they do not respect their elders and ancestors the way the Apache does. In fact, they are so uncertain about death, it frightens them too much to dwell upon. Their society removes the family of any responsibility for the old and dying. They put their old in homes removed from the family and hire morticians to carry out funeral arrangements. The dead are buried in public cemeteries where graves are maintained by paid caretakers. The dying, like some cancer, are removed before you see the inevitable decaying process.

I will tell you about an old oak tree on the reservation. The tree has survived lightning strikes and powerful windstorms. The trunk was scarred and its branches gnarled and twisted. That tree has been my friend ever since I was a small boy. I have climbed its branches for fun, and I've learned about birds, squirrels, and other small creatures that have nested there for generations. It has given me cool shade in the summer and protection from rain in the winter. I have even made love with your mother under its branches ... more than once. There have been times when I have felt lonely and forsaken, yet simply by sitting with my back against its strong trunk I have been energized. Mostly the tree has taught me endurance of spirit, of the life force that abounds on this planet. Now what others see as the decay of time I see as a reminder of the perseverance of life. What I once thought were wounds and scars embedded in the tree's aging bark, I now see as badges of honor, collected from prevailing in life's inevitable struggles.

They say our earth is unique because all the rest of the known universe is dead.

Why our planet was chosen for life, I do not know. But as a leader of my people, and equally important as a father, I know this: responsibility for the things I cherish most I must bequeath on those I love the most. I know the full weight of that responsibility has worn me down and scarred like the old oak, which is now dead. Yet I have received so much solace from that oak, from knowing that its seeds have given birth to many more trees ... and even when it died, its lumber produced wood for many a warm fire. Even its decaying leaves provided fertilizer for its seedlings. Most of all, it taught me that there is one undying spirit and even the inanimate materials from which they are made, as they pass, will be absorbed back into the original life force, which in turn makes the universal spirit perpetually grow stronger by the death of the generations that came before. There are certain places on the earth where the first spirit comes to gather once more the life force from its aging creations. It is important that you find your death spot and die on your terms. The tree told me mine, and I will go there when the time comes. It is where my fragile body will grow as strong as the trunk of that old oak, as I am returned to the whole body of the life force.

Your modern world will make it harder for you to understand this. Therefore, I tell you this now so that in the back of your mind you will always be conscious of the signs that will reveal your place to you.

Love,
Your Father

Many thoughts raced through Corey's mind, but eventually one emerged. "You have chosen a spot, haven't you?"

"Yes."

"What if you are too weak to get there?"

"I'll need help!"

"I know your spot, don't I?" The old man nodded.

"Well, someday I'll help you get there. But I still think you've got a lot of living to do, and I'm not about to lose my mentor for a while, you hear me?"

The old man seemed exhausted and dozed off. Corey thought he was faking it, and that was Hank's way of saying the conversation was done. He quietly left the room.

He talked briefly with Millie before he left. He told her he would help convince Hank to have that operation she mentioned. She thanked him.

As Corey left he turned and said, “Look, you two are my best friends. I need to have the both of you around awhile longe — a long while.”

CHAPTER ELEVEN

After Hank's stroke, it seemed as if something out of the ordinary happened every day, whether it be extremely good or extremely bad. First, Corey heard from his draft board granting him an extension on his student deferment. This meant he would not be faced with being drafted in June, which gave him breathing room to delay his decision as to what he would do if asked to fight in a war he felt the United States did not belong. Further good news came when Millie called and said that Hank agreed to go down to Texas and consult with a Dr. DeBakey, whom Millie had previously told Corey was doing a remarkable new kind of bypass surgery for blocked arteries in the neck, legs, and heart. All the good news made his apprehensive senior year seem less stressful than it had during the beginning of the year. That was until he heard a knock at the door shortly after Hot, Turk, and he had just returned from a great morning of surfing before leaving for school.

The minute he opened the door and saw the expression on Spook's and Dawn's faces, he knew something was horribly wrong.

"Did you hear the news about the massacre in Vietnam?" Spook said, his head lowering as if he wanted to pray.

Dawn squeezed Spook's hand then continued with the news. "It was in a remote jungle village named My Lai. The report said the village was of little strategic value and had not much of a population. A young army lieutenant by the name of William Calley led a hundred and fifty US soldiers into the village and slaughtered five hundred unarmed civilians — men, women, and children. Many were tortured before execution and their bodies mutilated before being thrown into shallow mass graves."

"Here's the clincher," Spook said, looking up to reveal eyes that fought back tears. "The massacre happened over a year ago and was covered up until now. The government would still be hiding it if it wasn't for the work of an honest reporter." Spook and Dawn began to relate more details when the door burst open and Dougie rushed into the room with an even more intense look than the others.

"This is insane," he cried, his voice sounding childlike while his expression showed a more visceral reaction than the others. To their surprise he looked toward Turk, who stood off in the corner of the room with his head hung down, his face hidden by his long hair, still wet from the ocean. “How could that have happened?” Dougie said accusingly.

Turk 's head jerked up. “Why are you asking me?”

“Supposedly Lieutenant Calley saw a baby crawling out of the ditch. He grabbed the baby, threw it back in the ditch, then shot it with his machine gun,” Dougie screamed. “How could that happen?”

Before Turk could answer, Spook cried, “He means you were over there, man. How could something like that happen?” There was more anger in Spook's voice than Corey had ever heard in his friend's voice before. No one, not even Eric, had ever talked so accusingly to Turk.

Turk looked around the room. His eyes rested upon Corey. Corey saw in Turk's expression something different from anything Corey had seen in him before. He looked like a small child who, in unfamiliar territory, had lost sight of his parents. “You guys know how I feel about the war. I'm probably more opposed to it than any of you, and for reasons you wouldn't be able to understand unless you were there.” He spoke soft and apologetically. “There's no such thing as a friendly side, a sanctuary where you can escape from the war, even for just a short while. Can any of you imagine no such thing as a line between friend or foe? There is just endless jungle that all looks the same, just like all the people look just the same. To us, a civilian was someone who'd work for us during the day and then slipped into Viet Cong pajamas at night and would try to slit our throats while we slept.”

“Did little babies fight for the Cong too? Is that why they

slaughtered children?" Christy, who arrived shortly after Dougie, asked.

"Yes! Awfully young children were forced to. That's why the war is so wrong. It's more awful than you can imagine," Turk replied, then bolted for the door. He stopped just before exiting and shifted his eyes from each clan member to the next. "I'm sorry," he whispered. "I'm sorry for each of you and pray none of you will ever have to witness the things I've seen, but if you do, then you'll understand why I feel equally sorry for that young lieutenant. I'm so sorry," he repeated, then left.

Corey was overcome with the same feeling he had the morning he learned of President Kennedy's death. This doesn't happen in America — we are the good guys — we are the champions for the oppressed. The image of John Wayne kickin' some bad guy's ass symbolized America — not machine-gunning little babies — That's what the bad guys did, the kind of evil people John Wayne killed. Corey was numb and so was everyone in the room. There was dead silence. They must have collectively been thinking the same thing until Hot finally broke the silence.

"Fuck! I know you guys never thought I was serious about movin' to Canada. Now, who wants to join me?"

Gradually their conversation returned to condemning war on a less emotional level, which turned into another morality discussion of all wars. Corey just heard noise, for the whole concept of morality had become extremely confusing since delving into Vanderhoof's assignment. Corey wanted to bring up his paper, but he felt awkward doing so. He found himself saying instead, "Is war inevitable?" The question escaped as if someone else had asked it.

"Only because people think it is," Dawn snapped, still angry from the news of My Lai.

Corey thought of Twain and Melville ... the moral sense. He tried to think of a good definition of morality. He had looked up "morality" in the dictionary when he first started thinking about his assignment: "a code of conduct or principals of right and wrong."

"If you look at the animal world, their day consists of finding food while trying not to be food for other predators," Corey said.

"So what's that got to do with the morality of war?" Dawn responded.

"That just seems to be the way life is — a constant struggle for survival," Corey answered. "Some things just are."

"Then what elevates us from that animal world? Doesn't our superiority come from our ability to reason, to develop compassion, make laws governing conduct?" Spook said, answering his own rhetorical question. He gave Dawn a hug, then added, "We were given a brain that enables us to control our own destiny. We don't have to live like animals. We are capable of morality. Aren't all religions about attaining salvation through living a good life by respecting the lives of others?"

"A moral sense," Corey replied.

"Yes," Dawn shouted. "It's our moral duty to oppose war."

Corey became overwhelmed by a feeling of impotence. He

couldn't think of a way to express his confusion because it was just that ... his whole value foundation was now in disarray. The only thing he was sure of was that My Lai would put the clan back to a state of uncertainty and trepidation brought about from the omnipresent war. When the discussion faded into a collective introspective silence, Corey broke the quiet by saying, “I think it's time to take a trip to Hector’s. Let's go next weekend.”

Everyone looked surprised, yet relieved. “Yes!” the clan answered together. The sound in their voices was as if Corey had uttered a catharsis.

The summer between their freshman and sophomore years, Corey, Hot, and Spook crewed on a sailboat that entered a race from Newport Beach to Cabo San Lucas. The boat belonged to the father of one of Spook’s high school buddies. It turned out that the father was more kid than his son. He had absolutely no interest in winning the race. In the forties and early fifties, he was part of the California surfing scene, and a self-proclaimed hell-raiser. He didn’t even care if they finished the race. To him the event was an excuse to bond with his son and friends, swap surf stories, and drink a lot of beer.

As a favor to the boys, he maneuvered the boat close to shore whenever they spotted what looked to be a good surfing spot so the boys could sight landmarks to go with the coastal maps they studied. They hoped that at a future date, they could drive down the coast and find a secret surfing spot — every surfer’s dream. One such place was about eight miles below a known location named Rincon de Baja. There they spotted a small house in the middle of nowhere.

The next fall the clan headed south on the paved road until they found a dirt road peeling off toward the place for which they were searching. About ten miles later they saw the lone house, which was surrounded by a rusted barbed wire fence. They found a crude rusted wire gate latched to a weather-beaten pole looped around an adjoining pole. They drove to the house and met its owner, Hector. Spook spoke Spanish, so they befriended the farmer and his wife and six young children. Hector, they learned, ran a pig ranch that allowed him to eke out a living by selling pork to restaurants in the neighboring cities of Ensenada and Santa Tomas.

Hector led them to another crude fence on the west side of his farm, where they had access to the beach. They paid him a dollar per person and promised him two bottles of tequila each visit. They suggested that he keep their arrangement secret, because he wouldn't want a lot of traffic going through his property, maybe scaring the pigs or even running over one. They even helped him put a no trespassing sign on the roadside gate.

Corey was successful. The morality of war discussion gave way to planning a trip to their private surfing getaway the next weekend.

"My God, would you look at that sand," Jan said as she emerged from Dougie's van.

They knew exactly what she meant, for they had the same reaction on their first visit to their secret surfing spot. The sand on California beaches was pockmarked by human footprints, or as Eric had once written, "Earth's skin at our beaches is scarred by cancerous-looking lesions left wherever modern man has tread." There were no billboards of advertisement or discarded trash litter. The sands at Hector's were pristine. The prevailing winds rippled the sands with mirror images of those that were wind formed on the surface of the water.

"That's what surfing is all about. The hippies stole our creed: 'Travel light and often, and don't leave footprints behind,'" Hot said.

They caught the evening surf, started a campfire, and began cooking dinner. Turk opened a bottle of tequila, a rare tequila he had been saving for a special occasion. It was tequila made from mescal cactus, with the worm still in the bottom of the bottle. He took a healthy swig then passed the bottle around. When it reached Joey, Turk took the bottle from him and gave him a beer.

"You're too young to be drinking this stuff. It'll stunt your growth. Stick with a few beers for now."

Turk then took another big swig. He had started drinking heavily after the news of the My Lai massacre. His drinking that night was nothing more than a continuation from the beginning of last week. The clan, sensing the possibility of a binge drinking episode, began talking about past surfing trips, hoping to get Turk's mind out of the bottle and into surfing. They began speculating about tomorrow's waves, which had begun to rise that evening. By nightfall they could hear a more powerful crashing than the waves made when they had first arrived. Karen and the other girls dished bowls of stew from the simmering pot that hung over the fire.

Turk said he wasn't hungry and opened another bottle of tequila. He already had been taking two shots for every one the others drank. By the time he opened the second bottle, the rest of their group had either quit drinking or sipped on beer. "No one wants to surf big waves hung over," Hot said, declining Turk's offer for another shot. Turk sat back and drank by himself.

After dinner, Jan, who was becoming more vocal as she became comfortable with the clan, said, "It almost seems wrong that we are down here in such a beautiful and peaceful place while most of the people I know are at demonstrations at Balboa Park, protesting the My Lai cover-up."

Turk chuckled to himself and took one more gulp of tequila.

"Protesting the war," he said. "Morality - morality," he said cynically as he looked at the bottle of tequila and at the worm on the bottom. "Hello, Mr. Morality," he said to the worm.

Everyone grew quiet. There was a collective uneasiness. Joey got up and walked over to Turk and sat next to him.

Turk glanced at him and smiled.

"I was an eighteen-year-old high school fuck up when I joined the army, a loner with no strong beliefs or principals other than to have a good time. 'Come on baby let the good times roll,'" he sang, then laughed.

"I joined the army because up to that point I hadn't done one worthwhile thing in my life. I thought maybe, like the recruiter said, the army could make me into a man, teach me a vocation while I served my country. Humph!" he sighed. "I didn't even know there was a country called Vietnam, nor did most of the guys enlisting. They were all pretty much the same as me — a bunch of aimless fuckups ... That's who they were sending over to fight for our country ... to defend our nation from communism," he said, his voice sounding more sarcastic the more he spoke.

Turk paused, his eyes passing slowly from each member of the clan to the next, and although he looked toward them, it seemed as if he were staring at something much more distant until he lowered his gaze to the fire.

"First, in boot camp, they stripped us of what little self-esteem we had. They found even the strongest among us had vulnerabilities, and they attacked them and broke us down to a single body, a unit who responded unobstructed by reason. We reacted to every command as quick as your knee jerks from the tap of a doctor's hammer.

"I was strong. I was good. I was tough. And for the first time in my life, I was going to do something worthwhile. I was going to protect my country by kicking some commie's ass." He paused. "But you know what else? I had friends. Yeah, buddies who went through the same shit I did. I'd never had such a sense of camaraderie. Together we were going to do something good." He sniffled. "A lot of us felt that we were really doing something right for the first time in our lives. Those guys became the best friends I had ever had. Not only had we gone through hell together, but we trusted each other. I never trusted anyone until I met those boot camp buddies. I shared intimate thoughts with them, and them with me. I wasn't a loser. I, we, could make something worthwhile of our lives."

Turk took another sip of tequila. Corey got up and started toward Turk. Joey instinctively knew Corey was going to try to take the bottle from Turk.

"No," he whispered and motioned Corey to sit back down. Turk looked at Corey. There was both anger and disdain in Turk's expression.

"I was one mean soldier. We were one ferocious unit. But something happened while I was fighting those battles — people died. I was drenched in the blood of both friends and enemies and the blood felt and looked the same. The people we were fighting for looked just like the people we were fighting against. But what was worse, the Vietnam and the Vietcong looked at us the same way. We were intruders on their homeland.

"After a while I forgot why we were fighting at all. I was just plain scared and wanted to go home. My enemies became anyone who kept me there. That's not even true. Because there was no true or false, right or wrong. It was just staying alive anyway you could. If you had to kill, you did, and you hoped there was a God to sort it all out later."

Turk started breathing like he was in deep pain, like a woman in childbirth, another being inside him kicking, clawing, trying to get out but at the same time wanting to stay.

"All four of my closest friends were killed in Vietnam. The last friend to die was Ed Riker.

We were in the jungle. We could hear the gooks. We knew there would be fighting. We just didn't know when it would begin.

"You know what we did? We started whispering to each other about the first thing we would do when we got home. We decided we would go to Bob's Big Boy and have the greasiest burger they could make, smothered with onions, and a large side of fries.

"Ed laughed, then said, 'And a chocolate malt.' Then I heard him make a gurgling sound like he was using a straw to suck up the last malt at the bottom of the glass.

"I looked at him, laughing to myself, and started to pretend I was sucking up the last of my drink also." Turk quivered, then groaned. "His head was twisted in the most grotesque way. A dark figure behind him had slipped piano wire around his neck and his head was almost completely decapitated. Blood, not red blood, but dark almost blue-black blood gushed from his neck and was pouring down his torso.

"I heard a noise behind me and turned just as another gook tried to slip a wire around my neck. I fired without aiming. The figure yelled and I heard it crumple to the ground.

"The fighting started then, but I don't remember being in

it. I don't think I fired my rifle again. What I do know is that I had a hunting knife strapped to my boot. I pulled it out and charged the gook who was still twisting the cord below the nearly severed head of Ed. I grabbed the little bastard by his chin and pushed back his head and plunged my knife in his neck just under his left ear and cut through his throat to the right ear. I heard something snap. It wasn't like the crack when you break a dried stick, but more of a crunch, like stepping on a snail. I saw his face then. His eyes bulged. He was maybe sixteen years old. I felt the quiver of every nerve, muscle, and tendon along his throat. I felt the life leave his body just as I knew it had left Ed's."

Turk paused and glanced at Joey. For an instant the terror left his face. He looked back at the group and let out a cry of agony. "That's when I felt the blood. Even though the jungle was hot, the night air suddenly felt cold compared to the hot blood that spurted from his jugular and hit me in the face. I was cold and the blood warm. For an instant I felt good. I was cold and the blood warm."

Turk dropped his head to his chest. His breathing slowed.

"Morality," he whispered. "The night was so fucking cold," he shouted, then began to whimper. "And his blood so hot it burned my skin. Do you understand the blood was hot?"

Joey immediately rose and put his arm around Turk.

"It's okay now, the blood is gone. I cleaned it up," the boy said.

Turk looked at Joey. "I didn't want to kill you, boy ... I had to ... Oh, please forgive me." "It's okay now," Joey repeated.

“You did what you had to do. I forgive you.” He took Turk’s sleeping bag and unzipped it, and he wrapped it around Turk's quivering body. “Here’s your pillow. Lie back; everything is alright now. I cleaned up the blood.”

Turk passed out.

CHAPTER TWELVE

THE NEXT MORNING COREY AWOKE AND FOUND THE WAVES had increased greatly. They were ten to twelve feet with good shape and breaking fast. Yesterday the sea let them play in its smaller gentler side, but today it was going to challenge them.

Corey thought about waking the others, but instead he walked to the shoreline and studied the break. He would not have time to think about the ride. He simply had to catch the wave and race the curl. Instinct, not consciousness, would determine the success of his ride.

Just as he returned to wake the others, he heard someone else getting up. He was surprised to see it was Turk.

"Morning," he said, sounding more asleep than awake. Corey walked over to him and said, "Big waves, huh?"

Turk nodded. "Too big for me the way I feel. I think when the girls get up, I'll take them shopping in Ensenada. They were disappointed we didn't stop on the way down. Christy and Jan have never spent any time in a Mexican city."

"About last night," Corey said.

"Yeah, sorry about that man. I was really drunk and don't remember much. Hope I didn't make too much of an ass of myself."

"I think you do remember last night, but it doesn't matter. You told us about your friends in Vietnam and how they were the only ones you ever trusted to share intimate feelings like those you shared with us last night ... like maybe you've found a new circle of friends ... I mean like the friends you had back then and never thought you would ever have again."

"I did? I hope I didn't insult anyone. I was really drunk," he said and smiled at Corey. "But thanks for listening man."

The others began to move about. The first topic of conversation was the size and speed of the waves. Dougie and Aaron were East Coast surfers, so anything over eight feet elicited awe. Weirdness hadn't been surfing long enough to be comfortable on big waves. Joey would try anything in order to keep pace with Corey, Hot, and Spook, but Corey knew it was false bravado. Overall, there was an uneasy mood throughout the clan, provoked by the ever-increasing waves.

The girls, on the other hand, were delighted by Turk's offer to drive them into Ensenada for some shopping. Karen was the only one who wanted stay. She promised Corey she would try to get some surfing pictures of the big waves and later, she wanted to visit some interesting tide pools to the south of the point in hopes of getting some unusual shots of aquatic life.

It didn't take long for Aaron to give up trying to surf the waves that had grown to a consistent twelve to fourteen feet. Soon, he was joined by Dougie and Weirdness, who were content to watch their better and more experienced surfing buddies get some amazing rides.

Joey tried to keep pace with the older guys and was holding his own until he took a bad wipeout on one of the fastest breaking waves of the morning. As he reached the shore to retrieve his board, he hesitated as he thought about paddling out again.

Karen, who had stopped filming and was preparing to go to the tide pools, saw Joey take the wipeout and noticed the boy's hesitation to return.

"Hey, Joey, come here a second," she yelled. The boy hurried to her.

"I've got some really good pictures of all of you, so I was thinking about walking down to the cove just south of here. There are some really neat tide pools down there, and I thought you might want to explore them with me. Help me find some strange shells and weird sea creatures to photograph. You can surf again later."

Joey looked back at the waves. "The wind is picking up and the tide is going out. You're right; it will probably be better later this afternoon."

In recent years, Joey had not spent much time exploring tide pools as he had done when he was younger. He had come to think of the activity as something for younger kids and older folks who no longer engaged in active water sports. He followed Karen to the pools, pretending he was doing so as a favor to her. He discovered the pools in Hector's bay to be like nothing he had ever seen before. Every few minutes he was yelling "Wow" or "My God," beckoning Karen to come see his latest discovery.

He found numerous sea slugs of enormous size with colors so bright they looked as if their bodies had been painted by some sixties' psychedelic artist. The pools trapped small schools of fish that darted in panic as he approached them. There were diverse species of crabs, many of which who made their homes in a myriad variety of shells.

"We've got to get Turk down here when he gets back. I know he'd want to collect some of these shells," Joey said.

"Come over here!" Karen yelled.

On a rock under about a foot or two of water clung a garden of sea anemone. They looked like underwater sun flowers, only more varied in color and size. Karen broke off a mussel from another rock. She cracked the shell open and gauged out the meat, which she dropped in the center of one of the larger sea anemones. The tentacle-like petals closed as the anemone shrunk to about the size of a golf ball.

"Radical," Joey said, sounding more like the child he once was rather than the budding teenager he was trying to be.

"They call that a cunt fish," a deep male voice said as Aaron unexpectedly came up behind them.

"That's what the Mexican kids call them. Do you know

why?" he said, grinning the way he did when he was up to no good. "That's how they learn about sex when they're too young to have a woman. They stick their cocks in the center of the anemone and when it closes, it gives a little tug that turns on their wanger," he said with a widening, sinister grin.

"Aaron, take your sick mind and go somewhere else," Karen snapped.

"It's true," he said, ignoring her. "Ever since we learned that, we even tried it ourselves.

When we bring a new guy here he has to do it as sort of an initiation. This is your first time here, isn't it?"

"Don't pay any attention to him, Joey. He's lying."

Joey was scared. He couldn't take his eyes off Aaron. He had once too often been the target of one of Aaron's sick practical jokes.

"Your initiation is today. I'll be the witness, unless Karen wants to watch too?" "Get lost now," Karen shouted.

Aaron laughed maniacally. "Drop your trunks and rub your noodle 'til it gets hard."

Joey tried to run, but Aaron grabbed the boy, knocked him down, then pulled his trunks off. "I'm going to rip these in half unless you start screwing a cunt fish."

Karen tried to steal Joey's trunks back from Aaron. He pushed her away hard enough to knock her down. Joey jumped up and took a swing at Aaron, who caught his arm and twisted it until the boy cried out in pain.

"Better screw a small one with that pencil dick and fuzz

nuts you've got." He then let go of Joey and ripped the boy's trunks in half as he laughed.

Karen recovered and charged Aaron, hitting him in the nose. Aaron's nose began to bleed. "You bitch," he said. "I'm going to rip your top off and rub your tits against a sea urchin." He stepped toward her, only to have Joey grab one of his ankles and pull it from under him.

Aaron fell on the slippery rocks. Joey then tried to make his escape, but Aaron caught and pushed the boy toward the submerged rock where the sea anemones clung. Joey's knee hit the rock. He felt a sharp pain where his knee landed against a barnacle. The water turned pink as blood squirted from his knee.

Aaron ignored the boy's pain and pushed his head toward the sea anemone. "See if you can find one that looks cute enough for you."

Suddenly Aaron let out a yell and crumpled into a ball as Karen kicked him in the groin. Joey grabbed a piece of shredded swimsuit which he held it over his privates as he and Karen ran back toward the camp.

They had gone about fifty yards when they heard Aaron gaining on them, cursing them as he ran.

"Keep running," Karen ordered Joey, then turned to face Aaron. She picked up a fist-sized rock and demanded that Aaron stop.

Aaron unexpectedly obeyed. His crazy expression turned friendly. "I was just joking around. You guys overreacted. I was just kidding."

"No you weren't," she heard Hot yell from somewhere behind her.

She turned and saw Corey and Hot running towards them. She dropped the rock as Corey arrived and put his arm around her.

"What happened, babe? You okay?"

Karen started to explain when Aaron interrupted, saying, "It was a joke ... just a misunderstanding." He held up his hands as if surrendering.

Hot stepped forward. "No, it wasn't. You're just a plain asshole and now you are going to get the ass kicking of your life."

"No, Hot," Corey said. "Not here, not at Hector's. Besides, kicking his ass isn't going to change anything." Then he looked at Aaron.

"Go back to camp and get your things together. I'll drive you to Ensenada and put you on a bus to the border where you can hitchhike or take a taxi back to Mission Beach."

"You can't do that," Aaron protested.

"Okay, Hot, he's yours. I'll help carry him back and will still drive him back to Ensenada."

"No, wait. I'll go, but this is a misunderstanding. I didn't mean for anyone to get hurt. I'll apologize to Joey and pay for some new trunks," Aaron pleaded.

"Go get your things. You're leaving," Corey ordered.

Back at camp, Dougie came over to Corey and apologized for Aaron's behavior. "He's really sorry. You know what an awful childhood he had. We need to work with him. I know he wants to be a better person."

"There comes a time when you have to change course. We've been as patient with Aaron as we can be and how's that worked? It's time to move on. Aaron is no longer welcome at any of our functions. If you want to save him, do it on your own, but make sure he understands this: if he ever touches Joey again, or any of my friends for that matter, I'll beat him within an inch of his life." Corey paused. "Where is Joey anyway?"

"He walked up to the point. I think he was crying," Karen said.

"Be ready to go when I get back," Corey said to Aaron, then left to search for the boy. He found Joey sitting on a rock at a small cove about a hundred yards north of the point.

The boy looked toward the sea. There was no discernible expression on his face, other than evidence he had been crying a short while ago. There was a stream of partially coagulated blood running down from the gash on his knee.

Corey said nothing. He walked over to the boy, knelt, and examined the cut on his knee. "He got you good. You might need a couple of stitches."

"I'll be all right," Joey whispered, then asked, "Did you kick his ass?"

"No, it wouldn't do any good. I don't think he'll ever change. No, instead I'm going to drive him to Ensenada, put him on a bus, and send him home. I told him to stay away from the Surf Rider clan for good."

"What about Dougie?"

"He'll just have to deal with that."

Corey then sat on the rock next to the boy. A cormorant was gliding over the water a couple of hundred yards offshore. Every so often it would draw its' wings close to its' body so it resembled a spearhead, then would dive-bomb into the water where it would disappear for several seconds. It was fishing and having no luck. After about four such dives it emerged with a wiggling fish trapped in its beak.

"Finally got one," Joey said.

Corey nodded, then said, "Isn't this a great? Think of all the problems going on in the world and here we are in our own little secluded paradise watching neat sea birds doing their thing, surfing by ourselves, camping out — Doesn't get much better than this."

"I hate that Aaron. I hope he gets drafted, goes to Vietnam, and gets his ass blown off," Joey said.

"That sounds like something Aaron would say. You know, little man, you've had just as rough a start in life as Aaron, maybe tougher, but everyone loves you because you're not like him at all. Makes me think that mankind has a chance despite all the bad shit going on in the world."

For the first time, Joey turned and looked at Corey. Joey's eyes were growing moist again.

He quickly brushed the tears away.

Corey looked at the wound again. "You know what I think? Instead of getting this stitched, you need to let the ocean water clean it out, then I've got some bandages and I'll butterfly the skin together. I've done that several times to myself."

Corey pointed to an old scar on his right ankle. "Got that one a couple of years ago surfing at Cuatro Casas." He then put his hand on Joey's head and ruffled his hair.

Joey returned his gaze toward the open sea. "I'll get over the Aaron thing, but you know there's something else that's been bothering me all year, something I don't know how say."

"Try me," Corey said.

The tears started again as he blurted the words out. "What happens at the end of the year when all you guys graduate? I can take anything Aaron can dish out, but you guys have been my family for four years ... the best family I've ever had. What happens to me when you guys are gone?" Joey tried to rub away the tears.

Corey stood up and found a rock, which he threw into the water, then came back and sat next to Joey once more. "When I graduated from high school, I thought it was going to be tough leaving all my friends, most of whom I'd known since I was six years old. It's only been four years since I left my hometown, yet it seems like another lifetime. I now have new, and I think better friends. There are a few close friends from high school I stay in touch with and hope I always will. The rest are just foggy memories. I'm pretty sure — no I'm positive — Turk, Karen, Hot, and I will be your friend for a long time. I promise you I will."

They sat in silence and watched another cormorant fish.

"If you don't get that cut stitched, it's going to leave a

pretty visible scar. You know what? The more I think about it, that's a good thing. Fifteen years from now, hell, the rest of your life, you'll be glad you have that scar," Corey said.

"Why's that?"

"Because no matter where you are or what you do the rest of your life, when you look at the scar, the pain will be long gone, but you'll find yourself back at Hector's, or at Mission Beach with the Surf Rider clan and think of the good times we had, which will remain as long or longer than the scar."

Corey glanced at Joey's cut. "When I was in the eighth grade I had four close friends. We were inseparable. We often talked about how we were going to take high school by storm. We would make our class legendary. In late July, one of our group, Bob Johann, came to us all upset. His father had been transferred to a better job in Nebraska, and they would be moving in September so Bob and his brother and sister could start school on time at their new location. We came up with all kinds of ideas how Bob wouldn't have to move. He could live with each of us for a while and we'd all graduate from high school together as we had always assumed. When we realized how impossible our schemes were, something strange took place. Instead of enjoying Bob's company as much as we could in the short amount of time we had left with him, instead we began to pick on him. Privately we talked among ourselves about how we never did like Bob as much as we did each other. We spoke of him as an unwanted intruder."

"That old man I've told you about, Hank, somehow sensed what was going on. He suggested we go on one last camping trip. We thought it was a great idea if we didn't have to invite Bob, but Hank made us anyway. As we were hiking along, we came across a tree trunk and Hank gathered us around it. He pointed to the rings. 'See how each year the rings become larger as the tree grows? Each ring is complete unto itself, but each ring is part of the same tree. The smaller inner ones from when the tree was young are just as necessary in the life of the tree as the outer circles become as the tree grows. Although the tree is always in the present, rings past and present will remain as long as the tree lives.'

"That evening we reached a lake where we camped. We didn't have much luck fishing. We wondered if there were any fish in the lake at all. Just before dark, Bob and I climbed a boulder whose outcrop hung over the water. We saw a bug hovering over the lake. Just as it settled on the surface, an enormous trout came from the depths, broke water, and ate the bug. Bob and I let go a collective 'Wow!' We looked at each other and laughed, then hugged, for we knew we would always be best friends, even if we were never to see each other again. Aaron will never have friends like that ... like the ones you have now and will always have."

Joey got up and walked to the water, where he grimaced as he washed his wound. Corey followed him, picked up a couple of flat stones, and handed one to Joey. "Beat this," he said as he skipped the rock six times across the surface. Joey made his skip seven times. He smiled at Core., "I beat ya," Joey said, his voice sounding stronger. "I think I'll stay a little longer; watch some more birds fishing if that's okay with you?"

Corey nodded, then started to leave. He stopped and turned back to the boy. "By the way, Karen was really impressed with the way you stood up to Aaron and tried to defend her."

"I just reacted."

"Oh! She said one other thing." "What was that?"

"She couldn't believe a thirteen-year-old could have a cock that big," Corey said, then hurried away.

"Corey," the boy yelled after him. "I bet it was bigger than yours when you were my age."

Corey laughed and shouted back to the boy, "You must have got hit in the head and are still a little delusional."

CHAPTER THIRTEEN

To Corey's surprise, he returned from Ensenada before Turk and the girls. Joey was back. Hot had put a butterfly bandage on the boy's knee. Although it would be another hour before sunset, the others had a fire going, and everyone was sitting around quietly talking. Only Dougie sat apart from the group. He was near the water's edge and staring toward the open sea.

"Is he okay?" Corey asked.

"He's just sulking over what's happened. How you could remorse over that prick, I'll never know," Hot said.

Corey walked toward the water and sat next to Dougie.

Dougie immediately came to Aaron's defense. "You guys don't know half the story about Aaron. Not only was he rejected and blamed for his mother's death, but he was continuously panned off to other relatives so his dad wouldn't have to raise Aaron himself. I even suspect there might have been some physical abuse."

"Dougie, when I was growing up, my father's best friend had a boy my age. At about eight years old I started a friendship with the kid, mainly because our fathers were always over at one or the other's home, and of course would drag their son along. About the time we entered junior high, his family moved to the same city as us. The kid was arrogant, self-centered, and aloof to other kids, all traits I had overlooked because we had so much history and had shared many good times together. I soon realized most people weren't flawed like him, and although I was liked, they didn't want me around because I would drag him with me. Let me ask you this. Had you met Aaron a week ago, say when he pulled that stunt on Dawn, would you choose him for a friend?"

"But I do know his history, and I think we should be more tolerant and try to help him be a better person. I know he wants to change."

"Aaron hasn't changed since I've met him. You and everyone else in our group has, and I think for the better. He could have seriously hurt Karen or Joey and I can't live with that knowing I allowed him to stay around too long. The Dougie I've come to know I don't think can either." Maybe the shock of losing his only friend will bring the change that you haven't been able to succeed in doing so far."

Dougie didn't respond at first; he looked at the waves for a few seconds, then said, "If I had just met him I probably wouldn't like him either, but Corey, I haven't told you this.

After that prank with Dawn, I sat him down and had a real heart-to-heart talk with him about his behavior. You know what he did? He broke down and started crying and begged me to help him change ... Does that sound like someone incapable of remorse and unable to change?"

"Oh! He cried for you too? How many times has he done that before? I know he's done it with me, Karen, and Spook on separate occasions when we have approached him with the kid gloves method. Besides, when Eric finds out what happened, he'll want him out. He never liked him anyway."

"What will I do for a roommate?"

"We'll help you find someone. There are a lot of good dudes out there who would love to live at the Surf Rider. You'll probably wished you had dropped Aaron years ago."

Just then Turk pulled in with the girls, who piled out of the car, laughing hysterically. "What's so funny?" Corey asked as he and Dougie returned to the group.

"This," Dawn and Christy answered in unison, holding up legal-looking certificates. "We are now certified prostitutes with papers to prove it," Christy said as she giggled louder.

Dawn then explained that when they got to town and the bars opened, Turk needed a little "hair of the dog" after last night. "We had a drink with him at Hassong's Cantina, where we agreed to rendezvous around three. When we didn't show, Turk searched everywhere and finally went to the police station."

"There they were," Turk said. "The desk sergeant spoke English and explained they were three unchaperoned young women dressed in shorts and revealing halter tops, with no bras, obvious solicitors, and would have to go before the judge on Monday."

"Fortunately," Dawn continued, "Turk has a pretty good understanding of how the system works down here. For ten dollars, we could buy prostitute licenses and be set free."

"They're in Spanish, but you can make out what they are. I think I'm going to make shrunken copies to fit on a Christmas card and send them back to certain acquaintances in Olmstedville."

"I'm going to frame mine and put it on the wall," Dawn said, then turned to Spook. "No more free sex. Now you have to pay."

Amid the laughter, Jan spoke up angrily. "You think the whole thing is some big joke. It's blatant corruption. That's what is wrong with this country and why it remains so poor. Weren't you guys humiliated enough, and then having to pay a bribe on top of that?"

"Relax," Turk said. "Nobody got hurt. This is a poor country, and tonight that cop's kids will eat better because of your contributions." "Wrong is wrong," she answered.

"Come on, Jan, lighten up," Christy said. "Why don't you just put your license in a scrapbook? Then years from now you'll pull it out, have a good laugh, and think of your California adventure."

"Sure," Joey said. "It's like this scar I'm going to have on my knee." He proudly held his bandaged knee out for everyone to see. "What happened?" Turk asked.

Karen then filled them in on the details of Joey's and her encounter with Aaron, and how Corey handled it.

"It would have been handled a little differently if I had been here," Turk said.

As they were talking about Aaron, Jan walked over and dropped her license in the fire.

Despite Jan's sulking, the rest of the clan became even more festive upon hearing of Aaron's removal. No one even noticed Jan's feeble act of defiance. They huddled around Joey, the girls hugging him and the guys patting him on the back for being the primary cause of Aaron's departure.

"You should have pantsed him and made him screw the anemone before you took him into town," Dawn said, then walked over to Joey and planted a firm kiss right on his lips.

Joey looked more embarrassed than when Aaron had ripped his trunks off.

Hot handed him a beer, then passed one to everybody. "Let's drink a toast to the clan's littlest but mightiest warrior."

Maybe it was the kicking out of Aaron, maybe it was Turk's confession, or maybe the simple hilarity of the prostitute hiatus, but somehow they all added up to something larger. Corey felt like he — no, all of them — were in the perfect place at the perfect time. The conversation the rest of the evening was mostly recalling all the good times from past parties and surfing excursions.

The evening was about to end when Hot said, "Up until now, the only trip that tops this one was Matachen Bay."

There was silence then among the clan as they thought

about San Blas and Matachen Bay. "Where's that?" Christy asked.

"It's a small fishing village about fifteen hundred miles south of the US border. It's on the mainland side, across from the Baja peninsula."

"We've got to go again this Christmas break," Spook said. "We've got our newcomers and of course, Joey, you're going with us this time."

After a little more talk of San Blas and a bit more reminiscing, Karen whispered in Corey's ear. "Let's grab your sleeping bag and move down the beach away from the others."

She led him about fifty yards away, where they slipped into Corey's bag. There was no moon, and being a long way from any city lights, the black sky was quilted with millions of twinkling stars. It reminded Corey of how much he had loved stargazing during his camping trips with Hank in the High Sierras.

Karen snuggled tighter against him. "Lots of people are afraid of the dark," she began whispering, "but if you think about it, there are many things you see at night that you can't see during the day."

"Like the stars," Corey answered.

"Like the stars," Karen said. "But also in the quiet dark of night, thoughts become clearer too. Small things or passing random comments that seemed so insignificant during the day — maybe they were only seen or heard in the unconscious part of your mind — you suddenly remember them in the darkness and they appear so much more important."

"So what are those magic moments you're recalling?" Corey asked.

"All that has happened the last couple of days. I thought this trip was going to be a bummer and a feeble attempt to forget the news of the massacre in Vietnam. Then came Turk's horrifying confession, followed by Aaron's sick attack on Joey, but somehow, for some obscure reason that I can't put into the right words, and least of all explain, I feel happier and more alive than I've felt in a long, long while."

Corey pulled her on top of his body and softly kissed her. He started to say something, but she smiled and whispered "Shh" as she rolled onto her back, easing his body over hers.

CHAPTER FOURTEEN

"They went off and I got aboard the raft because I knowed very well I had done wrong, and I see it wasn't no use for me to try to learn to do right, a body that don't get started right when he's little ain't got no show – when the pinch comes there ain't nothing to back him up and keep him to his work, and so he gets beat. Then I thought a minute and says to myself, hold on; s'pose you'd done a right and give Jim up, would you felt better than what you do now? No say I. I'd feel bad – I'd feel just the same way I do now.

Well, then says I, what's the use you learning to do right when it's troublesome to do right and ain't no trouble to do wrong, and the wages is just the same? I was stuck, I couldn't answer that. So I'd reckoned I wouldn't bother no more about it, but after this always to do whichever comes handiest at the time."

COREY READ THE PARAGRAPH FROM *HUCKLEBERRY FINN* A second time. Ever since he got back from Hector's, Vanderhoof's assignment gnawed on his conscience like a dog preoccupied with a bone. At times he thought about going into the professor and confessing that he bit off more than he could chew. He thought he would thank his professor for the opportunity to do the unusual assignment but confess that he was just a "jock turned 'surfer dude'; not an academic." But like the dog who has gnawed all the marrow out of one end of the bone and flips it over and begins chomping on the other end, Corey began to think of the assignment as not having anything to do with the class, but rather a lesson in life's continuing struggle, and the professor was a friend who suggested it was time that Corey ask questions of himself that every human should ask of himself. "Where was Huck going and why?" or more aptly put, "Where was Corey going and why?" Those questions both frightened and excited him simultaneously.

Everything Huck had been taught by both church and society said helping a slave escape was not only against the law, but immoral, yet Huck would rather accept damnation than betray a friend. It was that passage which Corey had yellow marked and read, then re-read trying to suck every little piece of meaning he could muster from the words. Then he realized that Huck, like himself, didn't know where he was going, but Huck, unlike Corey, knew exactly where he was and accepted his own decision whether it was approved by his governing society or not.

Corey was thinking to himself, "So where am I?" when Hot came home. Corey immediately explained his assignment to Hot and even read him the passage. To his surprise, Hot didn't seem moved, which disappointed Corey, so he pressed Hot to get more of a reaction that Corey hoped would help him find the answer.

"Don't you see that you're in an identical situation over wanting to go to Canada rather than get drafted and maybe being forced to go to Vietnam?"

"Look, man, don't take this wrong, because I love ya like a brother, but there is one big difference between the two of us — your background. Your upbringing allows you the luxury of philosophizing over things. It's a luxury of the rich. You can enjoy an expensive steak, sip on brandy, and then relax in front of a nice cozy fire in your comfortable den, probably sitting on a plush leather recliner. With me, you have a totally different perspective. Dinner is often SPAM sandwiches, a cheap generic cola to drink, then after dinner, trying to stay warm in front of an electric wall heater which is standard for the low-price tract home my parents lease. Face it, man. You were born with a silver spoon in your mouth and raised in a mansion."

"My folks' place is not a mansion. In fact, it is one of the smaller homes in San Marino," Corey said, sounding annoyed with Hot's response.

"Compared to my folks' place it is. Hell! Your parents own a second home in San Clemente that's still nicer than my folks' place. When things like food, shelter, and clothes are high priority, then things like moral contemplation just don't take up a helluva lot of your time."

"But even living in the harshest conditions, you still have to make decisions about doing right and wrong, don't you?" Corey asked.

"I think that most people you've been around most of your life don't understand why everyone else doesn't see things from the same perspective as theirs. I don't think of my decision to go to Canada as a moral one. My parents sacrificed so much for me to be the first member of either side of their families to graduate from college. I'm not about to let my ass get shot off in some obscure country because leaders that neither you or I voted for expect us to believe that we are saving our nation from communism," Hot answered.

"Could you really give up your citizenship and move to Canada? That could mean never being able to return."

"For a long time I've been thinking I would love to live in Australia permanently. The only reason I won't go there first is because we duped them into helping us fight over in Vietnam.

Canada would be temporary, until the war ends anyway. Who knows, I might learn to love it there, but I think I would miss surfing too much, so then off to Australia the first chance I get."

"I'm just as opposed to the war as you, but I don't think that I could leave the country," Corey said. "With all our problems and faults, this still is the greatest country in the world."

"That sounds like something your dad would say, but that's okay. I understand." "Understand what?" Corey said, raising his voice.

"I understand we're both rebelling against the mess our parents' generation has got us into, but buddy, it's time to fly from the nest. Let's face it, your nest is a lot better than mine, so obviously, you'll want to stay close to yours. I would if I were in your shoes. Besides, you'll find a way to stay out of Vietnam without goin' to prison or leaving the country. People with money always do. As much as you think that your father is against you and your stand on the war, when push comes to shove, he'll help you avoid the draft if necessary." Hot paused, then continued. "You've a lot more to give up than I do. We just come from different circumstances, that's all."

"Are you saying my, or anybody's, inquiry into morality is a waste of time?" Corey asked. "Not at all; I know I'm being selfish, but I'm not predisposed to change the world. The ideals of the kind you seek can better the human condition, I'm just not of the same ilk. And furthermore, I don't mind being a follower. It's actually a lot easier road than the one you're going down. The difference you don't understand is that your morality makes you feel responsible for everyone else. Just think about our little surfing clan — you're the center of our clan, the one who makes things happen. Our apartment is the central meeting place not because of me, but because of you. Being a leader will always make your road far more difficult than mine."

"Are you saying I shouldn't be the way I am?" Corey said, more confused than before. "No, you are the way you are because you were born the way you always have been. Look back at your high school days. Haven't you always been the center? That's why this assignment is so damn intriguing for you. That's why, although you probably won't admit it, it was tougher for you to kick out Aaron than his leaving was on Dougie."

"Hot, sometimes I think you are smarter than you pretend, or maybe I'm dumber than I think."

"Neither. I'm less encumbered than you, but that has nothing to do with intelligence. Your nature makes you think that your self-worth is determined by what you do for others. That's beautiful, man, and that's why I'll always be one of your most loyal followers, even if I spend the rest of my life in Australia and never see you after this year. I'm the real Huck Finn, just doin' what feels right, but you're like Ahab; you just don't understand why people like me don't ask as many questions as people like you."

Corey chuckled, then confessed, "Both Karen and Joey say I overanalyze, only Joey calls it 'weirding out.'"

"You know why Joey sees inside you so clearly? Because

he's destined to be like you. Turk is an idol too, but in the end Joey is going to be another you, and that is beautiful."

"Joey comes from a less fortunate situation than yours. Why do you think he's gonna turn out like me?"

"No! He's just smarter than both of us," Hot said as he laughed. "Instead of trying to be philosophical with me, why don't we get a couple of beers from the frig, smoke a joint, and who knows, I might even be able to interpret *Moby Dick* for you. The nice thing about discussing heady things while drunk or stoned is they sound great at the time, but in the morning, you can't remember half of what you said the night before; less heavy shit weighing on your mind."

"Or it gives you an excuse to drink again the next day," Corey said as he went to retrieve a couple of beers while Hot rolled a joint. After the beers were nearly empty and only the roach remained, Corey said, "So what's your take on that?"

"On what?" Hot answered.

"On *Moby Dick*? You said you'd interpret it after we got stoned."

"Oh shit, you know I wasn't serious. I read that back in high school, and then I thought it was one it of the dumbest books I ever read. You've got this whacko sea captain making the crew chase this monster whale. You and I would have thrown the dipshit overboard; but no, he fools them into thinking there is some evil force behind the whale, so in the name of God they must pursue and destroy it. Kind of like the con job our government's doing to us with the Vietnam war, but I don't want to go there. I'd rather put on some music and bullshit with you. Let's just enjoy the moment, dude. Ten years from now, wherever we are, we will long for the times we are in now."

"Okay, but what about Ishmael? Why did he survive?" Corey asked.

"Fuck! Someone had to survive to relate the story. Besides," Hot said, drinking his remaining beer in one gulp, "that's for you to figure out. I'm not going to do your whole fucking paper for you. Besides, if I leave some things unresolved, using your logic, we'll have a good excuse to do this again. By the way, and changing the subject, did you know that *Butch Cassidy and the Sundance Kid* is playing at the Rialto? It's supposed to be one the best pictures of the year and it's light comedy. I think we all should go Tuesday night. It will clear your head of all this intellectual crap you're obsessed with right now."

"Where did that come from, and why did you bring that up now?"

"I told you, I don't like heavy conversations, and I want to see the movie."

"You're right," Corey said. "Let's just have another beer together while you're still in this fucking country. We'll get everyone together and go see the movie Tuesday night."

"There you go being the leader again, but that's cool," Hot said, and went to the refrigerator to retrieve a couple more beers.

CHAPTER FIFTEEN

MOVIE THEATERS IN THE GREATER SAN DIEGO AREA WERE on a circuit where films rotated every Wednesday. The Rialto in Pacific Beach, the city closest to Mission Beach with a movie theater, offered a Tuesday special — fifty cents admission on the last night before the changeover. The current film, *Butch Cassidy and the Sundance Kid,* was playing with a second feature, *The Reivers*, based on William Faulkner's last and Pulitzer Prize winning novel. The movie received critical acclaim, but not much of a popular following at the box office. It was the real reason Corey wanted to go to the movies, although he pretended he wanted to see Butch and Sundance like everyone else. Almost any popular movie playing at the Rialto became a Tuesday night ritual for the clan. Everyone wanted to go not only to see Butch and

Sundance, but also to meet Dougie's new roommate, Sean Diozio, known as Dizzy.

Turk was responsible for finding Dizzy. As expected, when Eric learned what happened in Mexico, he evicted Aaron. Even if he hadn't, the social pressure from the clan would have. Turk came across Dizzy, while surfing one day. He noticed this guy riding a board with a colorful sunset design pigmented on the surface of an obviously homemade surfboard.

"Who did the artwork for your board?" Turk asked after he introduced himself. "I did," Dizzy said proudly as he lifted his board for Turk to inspect.

"Absolutely a terrible job of shaping, but that's okay because the glassing is decent, but primo on the artwork." Turk then explained about his shaping, and to his surprise, Dizzy already knew Turk by reputation. He was excited to meet him, and even more excited when Turk offered him a job doing artwork on Turk's designs. Turk explained his shaping business was growing into a full-time job whether or not he wanted it to be, which of course he didn't, but it was lucrative enough for Dizzy to pick up extra cash by painting psychedelic pictures on the decks. Turk threw in a bonus by making a new board for Dizzy as part of the deal. With Dougie needing a new roommate, Turk made the introduction. Dizzy, as it turned out, had been kicked out of the dorm when he got caught smoking pot. He was currently living out of his car while searching for a new place to dwell. Dizzy was only a freshman and therefore younger than Dougie, but like Dougie, he was an art major. They hit it off immediately, so that night they all met at Dougie's to meet Dizzy before going to the movies.

Dizzy introduced himself by offering to share some of the grass he got from Turk. Dizzy, being a shrewd businessman himself, had negotiated that as part of his salary. Everyone but Jan, who still was a little uneasy about smoking grass, and Corey, who wanted to stay awake for the second feature, did not imbibe. Karen had a midterm the next day, so she passed on the evening. They found Dizzy to be a total contrast to Aaron. Dizzy had a very affable personality augmented by his laid-back, weed-enhanced California surfer attitude. He was a perfect fit for Dougie.

Sufficiently high, they went to the movies, where between the beginning and the end scene when Butch and Sundance die in the final fury of a gun battle, the clan consumed two jumbo boxes of popcorn, numerous candy bars, and several soft drinks a piece. They were coming off a sugar rush and a pot high that left everyone wanting to go home and sleep by the end of the first movie. Corey, who had come in Dougie's Volkswagen bus, announced he was going to stay for the second film and would walk home afterward since it was only about a mile walk back to the Surf Rider. Jan asked if he wouldn't mind if she stayed to keep him company.

At the end of the second feature, the theater was nearly empty, yet Jan and Corey remained in their seats, as did the few remaining viewers. After the last credits were shown and the lights turned on, Corey and Jan sat in silence, overcome with emotions aroused by the film. After several minutes Jan turned to Corey.

"Powerful," she said, her eyes moist. "I had no idea what to expect from that film, but you did, and that's why you wanted to stay wasn't it?" she asked.

"You know I'm an English major. I discovered Faulkner a year ago and had read *The Reivers*. Most movies don't follow the book that closely, but this one sure did, and I'm glad it did," Corey said.

"At first I thought it was a cute comical story, but at the end I realized how insightful the story line was," Jan said.

"That's Faulkner at his best — exploring universal moral dilemmas in a very humorous way. He's like the flavored cough syrup your mom would give you when you were a kid; it tastes good so you don't think of it as medicine. If I become a writer, I'd like to spin a yarn like him," Corey said.

"Spin a yarn? That sounds like something the old-timers would say in Olmsteadville," Jan said with a remorseful tone in her voice.

They began their walk back toward the Surf Rider. There was a definite fall chill in the cloudless winter air which made the moon and stars look larger than usual. The waves were easily seen in the moonlight. Nothing was said for a while. Corey was thinking about the movie and assumed Jan was too. Finally, she interrupted the silence. "I know the movie was set in early nineteen hundred, but the town in the movie could have been where I grew up."

"You miss it, don't ya? That's why you're so quiet ... you're thinking about back home," Corey said.

"Ya, but I know I can never go back for reasons I haven't told anyone." She hesitated. "I know we haven't known each other that long and that well, but — " Jan stopped walking and looked Corey in the eye. Ever since he had first met her, Corey had sensed that she was hiding something inside. By her expression, he knew she was ready to share whatever troubled her. A gust of cold late-autumn wind blew from the east, making them both shiver.

"Come on. Let's sit and talk for a while." They hopped the boardwalk wall and sat with their backs against it to give them some shelter from the chilly wind. "I can be a good listener," Corey said.

They sat in silence for a few minutes and watched the spume from the crashing waves sparkle a soft white light from the reflection of the bright moon. Jan, unlike Christy, had not shown herself to be a touchy-feely person, yet she surprised Corey by snuggling close against his shoulder. Her body felt very tense at first, but she slowly began to relax.

"My sister's name is Joyce ... we're fraternal twins," she began, her voice sounding as if she were an embarrassed child reluctantly confessing her sins to some parish priest. "Not only did we not look alike, but we were at opposite ends of the pole in every aspect of our lives. I was the good one and Joyce the bad one. Our parents were third generation Olmsteadville and pillars of the community. My father was a deacon in the church. Because Joyce was always defying our parents and constantly getting into trouble, Dad and Mom always said something to the effect of "Why can't you be more like Jan," then they would point out how wonderful I was by contrast to her. This distanced us as sisters even more. We became adversaries whose differences were accentuated by our parents constantly insinuating we were like good and evil twins. I tried to understand my sister. I wanted to be her friend like other siblings we knew, but I was put on a pedestal while poor Joyce was placed beneath me as if she were some kind of troubled freak.

"Toward the end of our junior year of high school, Joyce had to tell our parents that she was pregnant. Our father went into a rage; he called her a 'harlot, a Jezebel,' and ordered her to leave his home."

Jan began softly weeping. "I went to our room and tried to talk with her as she packed. She said to me, 'Let's face it, Dad's probably secretly happy I got pregnant. It gives him an excuse to kick his bad daughter out of his house. Now the three of you can live happily ever after and not be disgraced by this harlot.'

"I told her they just misunderstood her and I would go talk with them. That's when I realized how much she despised me. She looked at me with anger in her eyes and said, 'You know as well as I they've always loved you more. Now they don't have to pretend that they love us equally.

Don't try and placate me; at least let me leave with some dignity.'"

Jan paused and snuggled closer to Corey. He felt her anxiety. "That's when I did something really stupid," she continued. "A couple of days later, I went to a neighboring town. I looked older than my age so I went into a bar. There was this guy, just out of the army. He bought me a drink, then another, and before I knew what was happening, I was back at his apartment."

She began crying. Corey put his arm around her. "It's okay ... It's okay, you don't have to continue if you don't want to."

She collected herself, then said, "No, I need to tell someone. I got pregnant too. It wasn't out of love or for wanting a child. I just wanted to somehow bond with Joyce. That's the only way I can explain my actions." She began to cry softly and pulled away from Corey, but he held her fast and gently stroked her shoulder. She relaxed and even put her arms around him. With tears returning, she continued, "I guess I had some warped notion that it was the only way I could empathize with her and I understood her. How could I have been so stupid?"

"You might have been drunk or confused, but what you did was out of love, an honest love for your sister. I understand that and think it is a beautiful thing."

"No," she snapped. "I knew what I was doing was wrong. I didn't even think I might get pregnant. It wasn't until I learned I was pregnant that I realized what I had done. You don't bring a child into the world to spite your parents. I was so wrong." She began crying uncontrollably.

Corey held her closer and said nothing as he massaged her neck and shoulders, trying to comfort her the best he could.

After several moments, she was able to continue. "When I told my parents, there was no tirade this time. My father slumped into his chair and began to pray to God asking him why he was being tested like Job." She paused. Her eyes held a distant look as if she was still in the movie theater, only this time she was watching herself playing the role of an agonizing sinner.

"Christy," she continued, "was Joyce's best friend, and just as wild as her. She wanted to see the world, but mostly she wanted out of Olmsteadville. She got a letter from Joyce not saying exactly where she was, but it was postmarked San Francisco, California. However in the letter, she said she was going south to explore the San Diego area. We decided to try and find her, but first there was something I knew I had to do. I had to get an abortion. Christy knew of a doctor in New York City who was qualified and would perform it at a reasonable price."

"So when you got the prostitute license in Mexico —" Corey said, only to have Jan start crying again.

"I tried to correct one sin with another. I know abortion is wrong — I know I shouldn't have done it. I thought no one would find out, but you can't hide from God! It was he who gave me the prostitute license, not the Mexican police."

Corey sat in silence and watched the silhouettes of the

waves roll onto the shore as if they were cleansing the sand. He waited for the tears to stop and her labored breathing to ease. "Wow, girl! And I thought that movie was heavy." Corey thought for a moment, then offered, "If there is a God, I think he knows even better than I do that you are a good person."

Jan's body tensed again. "I am responsible, and I sinned in the eyes of God; isn't that obvious?" She sounded almost maniacal in her self-deprecation.

Corey patiently waited until she calmed herself once more. "I'm not the person to talk religion with. I think I've doubted the existence of God ever since I've intellectually thought about it, but if there is a God, or better yet if I could create the perfect deity, my God would want us to lead our lives as if he didn't exist. He would want us to accept full responsibility for our actions, no matter how wrong they might seem to others ... others who appear to delight in passing judgment on someone else's actions. The God I would create would forgive us our trespasses providing we suffered enough to learn from our mistakes and made ourselves into a better person than we were before. The way I see it, you've punished yourself enough. It's not what you did, and I know your intentions were not evil, but what are you going to do from this moment forward?"

Jan stopped crying and sighed. "I'm so confused. I'm so scared. I can't stop thinking about my sin."

"It would be so easy being the son of God and having your destiny predetermined," Corey said. "Wouldn't it be great to know that your actions were foreordained like the Bible says of Jesus? Then you wouldn't be responsible for a fucking thing you do. It's a helluva lot harder being a mortal than the son of God, isn't it, kiddo?" He put his arms around her and gave her a gentle hug. "What I heard you say was you loved your sister so much you were willing to give up the dream of the good life your parents wanted you to have in order to walk in your sister's shoes and to feel her pain and her frustrations. You wanted to see and feel from her point of view. That, to me is an awesome act of love. I know I've never done anything that bold."

"What about the child I destroyed?" she shouted.

"What about the God you were taught to believe in? He let his son die painfully on the cross... That was supposedly done out of love."

"What am I supposed to learn from what I did? I don't even know where my sister is. Did she have her baby? Will I ever see her again? Will she know or even care about the sacrifice I made?"

"I think the only mistake you made was thinking you could put yourself in your sister's shoes. People say that you should never judge anyone until you walk a mile in their shoes, and I've never understood that expression. I've come to a different conclusion. You can call it the Corey axiom," Corey said with a smile as he stroked her hair.

"And what's that?" Jan asked as she wiped the moisture off her cheeks.

"That the best we can do for anyone we love is not to try

to walk in their shoes, but rather walk alongside them for a while, help them up if they stumble, give them food and water when they hunger and thirst, but allow them to find their own path. Each of us must take the lead for ourselves in discovering that path."

"But it was still so wrong for me to get pregnant, and even worse to get an abortion," Jan answered.

"Do you want me to agree that you're an awful sinner? I will if that's what you want to hear from me."

Jan shook her head no.

"I think I know why that movie had such a powerful effect on you. At the end when the little boy returned to his hometown, he said, 'It looked just the same as when I left. After all that I had seen, after all that I had learned, it seemed wrong that my town was still the same.' Your parents lived the same way as their parents, but you've changed; you've experienced life from an entirely different perspective. When the little boy in the movie — who of course is now the old man narrating the story — made that comment, you felt an uplifting ... maybe one you couldn't put into words. The old man knew that when he was a boy his parents raised him with love and the best of intentions, but he realized that he lived in a different time. It was now his time and his town."

Jan said nothing for a while, then in clear, crisp voice said, "I'm sorry to have burdened you with my problems, but thank you."

"Sorry for what? Tonight I'm walking beside a friend who has stumbled and I'm helping her pick herself up and I'm willing to walk beside her for a while until she finds her own path. That makes me feel good too, definitely not burdened. I'm honored you trusted me enough to confide in me." Corey laughed. "Besides, you probably feel better confessing to me than you would have if you had confessed to a priest or minister. I won't demand any penance."

Jan arose, saying, "Thanks again. I think I'm ready to go home now."

They walked the rest of the way back in silence until they reached Jan's apartment, where she turned and looked in Corey's eyes.

"There's one more thing, one more favor." She sighed. "I don't know how to say this without you getting the wrong impression."

"Just say it. I'm your friend."

"When I had sex, despite my feelings of guilt, it still was delightful. My upbringing taught me to believe sex is sin disguised as pleasurable in order to trap us. I've been afraid to do it again, but it was so pleasurable. I'm not afraid anymore. I want you to come in, Corey. No strings attached, but I want you to come in."

Corey stepped forward and kissed her on the forehead. "You are a beautiful human being and you unloaded a lot of heavy baggage tonight. With the lifting of that weight, you are very vulnerable. You're feeling a freedom you've never thought possible and you're not sure how to handle it. I'm honored you want to celebrate that newly discovered liberty with me, but I can't. Not because I don't want to, but because just a few hundred yards from here lies the girl I want to marry. I tried to see things from your side tonight, now try to see them from mine. I can't."

She stepped forward and kissed him lightly on the lips. "I understand. It was wrong of me to ask."

"No! Like I said, I'm honored, but I must leave now," Corey said as he gently kissed her forehead, then hurried away.

The next morning, Corey awoke early. The waves were good, so he decided to surf some before going to class. There were several other surfers already in the water. One was Dougie who, when he spotted Corey, paddled over to him.

Dougie wore a silly grin on his face. "I have to tell you this, man. That Jan is sure changin' fast. I was awakened by a knock on my door shortly after midnight. It was Jan. She wanted to come in and talk. I didn't expect to get laid last night, but I did. Wow! Has she changed." He then giggled like an adolescent bragging about his sexual conquest in a high school locker room environment.

"Lucky you. As soon as Aaron is gone, you score." Corey paused, then added, "But I'd be careful with Jan if I were you."

"Is the mighty Corey a little jealous that she didn't go to your apartment?" Dougie said with a mocking laugh.

"Ya! I guess I am. Just the same, she's been pretty confused about running away from home. She hasn't embraced her situation like Christy. For her to suddenly change like that ... Well, man, I just don't know."

"Admit it, man. I've just got more sex appeal than you," Dougie said with a snicker.

"That's probably it, man. Listening to your luck is making me horny. Let's get to surfing while the waves are this good."

CHAPTER SIXTEEN

When Thanksgiving arrived, Corey was torn as to whether to go home and spend the day with his parents or stay in Mission Beach and host a meal for his New York friends who would not be going home for the short holiday. He wanted to see his parents, but he knew his hair length would probably lead to another argument with his father. The more he thought about it, he realized the reason he even considered going up to San Marino was because Hank had the operation on his legs and was feeling much better. Finally, he decided to go home Thursday — Thanksgiving Day — and Friday, and return and do a barbecue on Saturday for the East Coast clan. Karen agreed to come back and help.

When he reached his parents' home it was around four o'clock in the afternoon. He found his mother, Bloody Mary in hand, watching a quiz show on television. She looked up when Corey entered the room and said a quick, "Hello, honey. Get yourself something to drink and watch TV with me."

As Corey searched the refrigerator, he heard the show host ask, "What is the capitol of Missouri: St. Louis, Jefferson City, or Joplin?"

"Jefferson City," his mom answered.

The contestant said, "St. Louis." "Idiot," his mom called at the TV.

"I'm sorry," the host said. "The correct answer is Jefferson City."

"Of course," his mother exclaimed.

Corey returned and sat on the couch next to her.

Without looking at him she said, "I ought to go on one of these shows, but I think they intentionally go after stupid people."

"You're probably right, Mom. You're too smart for this," Corey said.

The host said it was time for a commercial, so his mother turned and looked at her son for the first time.

"You've got a great tan. Are you spending all your time at the beach, or do you go to class once in a while?" She smiled.

"I live at the beach, remember? And yes, I go to class and study hard so I won't flunk out and get drafted."

It was then she noticed his hair. "Oh my! You haven't gotten a haircut yet. Your father is not going to like that." But before she could say anything further, the show returned and small talk about tans and hair length gave way to naming the tallest mountain peak on the North American continent.

Corey excused himself and went to his room, where he began unpacking his overnight bag. Rolled up in a sock, he had a plastic baggie with a small amount of grass. When he made the decision to go home, he decided it was inevitable there would be a confrontation with his old man and he wanted to be stoned for it. Sometimes, when he was high, he felt as if his mind became a third person observing himself from some safe outpost. When he felt like that, he remained much calmer. He became an observer, not a participant.

He rolled the joint, put it in his pocket, and returned to the TV room. "When's Dad getting home?"

"In about an hour," she said, her eyes remaining glued to the screen. "I think I'll go say a quick hello to Hank and Millie, okay?"

"The Rhine River," his mom said, answering the quiz show question rather than Corey. The host confirmed she was right. Corey got up to leave but not before giving her a soft kiss on the cheek, which forced her to turn and acknowledge him.

"Sure ... a ... fine, ah, say hello for me," she said, but immediately turned back toward the TV to concentrate on the next question.

Corey never intended to go and see the Victors, and of course he never would allow himself to be high while visiting them. Instead he drove to Lacy Park in the center of town. The park was once a large lake that long ago had been drained and now was home for numerous trees, shrubs, and various exotic plants transplanted from all over the world. It was there he had always found a solitary space when he needed to be alone. In recent years, it was where, among the foliage, he could hide and smoke his weed. Normally Corey wouldn't smoke an entire joint by himself, but rather share it with a friend or two. He considered himself a social smoker, because he preferred smoking with friends so you could laugh at some of the ridiculous things you said to each other while high. He thought about smoking just half, but he smoked the whole thing and immediately felt a paranoia that made him too self-conscious to face his dad, so he decided to take a long, slow walk in the park instead.

His favorite place in the park was a large rose garden at the far west end. The caretaker, ever since Corey could remember, was an elderly Japanese man. If you asked the man his name, he would never say "My name is Ben," or just plain "Ben." He would answer "Call me Ben," like maybe he had another name but preferred to be called Ben, or maybe he felt his Japanese name was too hard for Americans to pronounce so he just picked an English one that sounded close to his native name. It was kind of like "Call me Ishmael," Corey thought, a result of his preoccupation with his assignment.

When Corey was younger, and relied on imagination more than logic, he and his friends fantasized that Ben had some wicked past, like he had been a spy during World War II and was never discovered, but for some reason couldn't return home. Whatever Ben's past, it no longer mattered to Corey since the gardener was always cordial and seemed to delight in the pleasure his rose garden provided so many visitors. Call Me Ben's rose garden was pristine, displaying roses of every color and species. Through the years he had grafted the different varieties, creating roses that you saw nowhere else but Lacy Park. Corey remembered hearing somewhere that only God creates and man copies, yet Ben had created a garden that had to be as beautiful and fragrant as the first garden.

As Corey wandered through the garden in his euphoric state, he was like a small kid in a candy shop, overwhelmed by having to choose between so many delicious-looking flavors. The colors of the petals seemed so intense that they radiated a fog-like aura over each plant. He was so immersed in their beauty he hardly noticed Ben working just a few feet away until the man said, "Oh, hi! They are even more beautiful in the spring." The man was smiling at Corey with an expression that said, "I know you are stoned, but if that allows you to enjoy my flowers even more, I don't mind."

He took a deep breath as if to drink the rose fragrance as if it were liquid nectar. "You are a miracle worker, Ben," Corey said, then added, "It is said in the Bible that Benjamin sat on the right hand of God. Is that where you got your inspiration?"

Ben's smiled widened. "I'm driven by seeing the delight people receive from walking in my garden. You've been coming here since you were a boy, which is an even bigger compliment. Thank you."

Corey said, "No, thank you." Then several more onlookers arrived and interrupted his sanctuary and private bond with Ben. Seeing the old gardener and the new arrivals made Corey aware that his paranoia was lifting. He made gregarious small talk about the roses with the new sightseers. He felt a perfect balance of natural high and stoned to face his father.

Frank Jameson's car was in the driveway. Corey walked in and with a big smile said, "Hello, Pops," in as friendly a voice as he could muster.

Mr. Jameson was in the kitchen fixing himself a martini.

"Hello, son," he answered, and in the same breath said, "I see you still insist on keeping your hair long." His father's tone was more like ordering his secretary to retype some business letter he felt unsatisfactory.

"Karen loves to run her fingers through it, and I spend more time with her than you." Corey mimicked his father's tone.

Frank Jameson looked at his watch. "We still have time to get you a haircut with the club's barber. He's open another forty-five minutes."

"Now why would I want to do that?" Corey said.

"Because we are having our Thanksgiving Day at the Country Club and there are a few members I want you to meet. They are very successful and would make excellent contacts in getting you that first job after you graduate. Besides, your mom won't have to cook."

"Do you know what river in Western Europe flows from Switzerland through Germany and the Netherlands and empties into the North Sea?"

Anger erupted on his father face. "I don't know, and why would you ask that?"

"The Rhine. I was pretty impressed that mom knew that," Corey said. "I didn't know that either. I guess like father like son, huh?"

"Get in the car," Frank Jameson said, raising his voice. "No!" answered Corey.

His father took a sip of his drink, then sat the glass down. "Let's go into my study. I want to have a serious and civil conversation with you."

Corey walked into the living room and sat on the couch.

"I said my study. We'll have more privacy there," Mr. Jameson said.

"You pick the topic, I'll pick the location," Corey answered. When he saw his father's anger swell, Corey wished he could take back what he had just said. Instead he quickly added, "I'm sorry. I'm out of line. We need to talk civilly, the way we used to."

Corey arose and followed his father into the study. Frank Jameson immediately seemed pleased. He wheeled his office chair around from behind his large, antique, cedar-wood desk and sat side by side with his son. He said nothing at first, but just gazed into his son's eyes. Corey wished he had used a little Visine before he confronted his dad. Mr. Jameson's glance lowered to Corey's legs. Corey was wearing shorts. His dad patted Corey's calf.

"Man, your legs are strong. You didn't inherit that from your chicken-legged father." He smiled, then continued. "Look, son, I don't mind a little rebellion. I had some difficult times with my father when I was your age. I think youthful rebellion is normal. I'd be more worried if you didn't start questioning things at your age ... Lord knows my generation has made its share of Mistakes." He paused.

Corey said nothing.

"I want to share something with you that I just heard a few weeks ago. I don't know if you remember meeting the Parkers. Bill Parker has a son just a few years older than you. Last summer his boy went down to Alabama to join in a civil rights march. He was stopped by the police, who searched him, and they found a small amount of marijuana in his possession.

Alabama laws are a lot tougher than California's. He ended up being sentenced to three to five years in an Alabama penitentiary.

"I wish you could have heard the anguish in Bill's voice as he described the pain and suffering he and his wife were going through not knowing how his son's health, both mental and physical, were holding up. You've heard tales of what happens to young men in prison. Bill's son is slight of build and not nearly as strong as you. Bill said the helplessness feeling, coupled with not knowing, was like being in prison themselves. His wife cries almost every day.

"Bill told me his boy is a good boy. He's definitely not a criminal. As he described him, I couldn't help but think that he is much like you; his ideals are noble ones, but his passion for his beliefs can cloud practical judgment. Three to five years in an Alabama prison. Do you hear what I'm saying?" He reached over and grabbed Corey's shoulder as if by touch he could squeeze his point into his son. "Despite of our arguments, you know I love you. I would never want you to wind up in Bill's son's place. Let's get that haircut, buddy. You can start growing it back as soon as you return to school."

Corey glanced around the room. His eyes came to rest on one of his father's model collection of old sailing ships displayed on an antique bookcase. They were about the only decorative object in the Jameson home that had not been chosen by an interior decorator. Corey remembered his father telling him the origin and use of the old ships. He had sensed that his dad loved those ships because they represented some kind of longing for adventure his dad had in his youth but had been denied by the war, or maybe by his own father choosing his son's path. Corey remembered as a boy going to bed after his father's stories and dreaming of sailing away into some tropical paradise.

"Remember when you told me about your love of the old sailing vessels? In those days, I wanted nothing more than to live up to your expectations. I'm older now, and I've got my own dreams, ones that are different from the ones you have for me. That doesn't mean that I don't respect what you've accomplished, and you know I will always love you and Mom, but it's time to go my own way. Can you understand that?"

Mr. Jameson said nothing for a few long seconds, then slowly said, "I want you to be your own man, but because I love my son, I can't sit idly by and watch you possibly make a mistake that could tragically affect that future."

"I appreciate that, but did you hear what you just told me?

You said that the kid's parents are suffering more than him. You always explain things from your point of view. Do you think his dad is suffering more than his kid? Look, I'll comb my hair back and even put on a coat and tie, I'll make polite conversation, which I do well because of the way that I've been raised — you've taught me well — but no haircut. That's a compromise I'm not willing to make now."

Frank Jameson almost jumped to his feet. "Fine, we'll go without you. I'm sure you can find something in the fridge, but hear me loud and clear. DON'T COME HOME AT CHRISTMAS WITHOUT A HAIRCUT." Then in his calm but best authoritarian voice, he said, "If your hair isn't cut by then, you pay your fifth year of college. I've met any obligation. You're on your own if that's the way you want it."

"Fair enough," Corey said, and nearly brushed his father's shoulder as he walked past him and went upstairs to his bedroom, where he immediately called the Victors' home.

"Hello," Hank answered.

Upon hearing Hank's voice, Corey suddenly forgot the conversation he had just had with his own father. Not only was Hank feeling well enough to answer the phone, but his voice sounded so it uplifted Corey's sagging spirits like the sails of an old Cutty Sark schooner being expanded by the wind as it set sail on another adventure.

"Good to hear your voice. It's the strongest it's sounded in some time."

"So, you're home for Thanksgiving. Hope you can come

see us. Maybe come by and have a little dessert. Millie baked a delicious pumpkin pie, and it's just the two of us."

"I can do better than that if you've got enough food for three," Corey answered.

"I take it you and your dad didn't have a real feel good conversation," Hank said, chuckling. "I go to bed early these days," he said, "so we plan to eat about three, if that's okay?"

"See you then. ... and thanks a lot."

CHAPTER SEVENTEEN

HANK ANSWERED THE DOOR. HE WAS NOT USING HIS CANE.

"Look at you," Corey said. "Want to go out and toss around the football?"

Hank laughed. From the kitchen, Millie called, "Amazing. He's even working out in the garden with me."

"Plastic arteries. Millie and I went to the movies recently to see that film everybody is talking about. There was a line in the movie about plastics being the wave of the future. What was the name of that movie?"

"*The Graduate*," Millie answered from the kitchen.

They went into the living room, where Millie brought in a plate of various hors d'oeuvres.

There was a pitcher of cold lemonade and three glasses. "What? No VO?" Corey said, looking at the pitcher.

"The doc says no more booze. He's a good surgeon, but a

lousy dietitian." Millie filled the three glasses then passed around the snacks.

"Well?" Hank said. "I guess your visit didn't turn out all that well?"

Corey sighed. "It's partly — no, mostly — my fault. I've gotten to the point where I take the opposite view from the old man just to piss him off."

"Why do you suppose you do that?" Hank asked.

"Because with my father there is only one acceptable point of view, which is his. I only have the right to my opinion if it agrees with his."

"Don't all young people think that?" Millie asked.

"Probably, but here's an example of what I'm talking about. This summer we went out to dinner. When the waiter asked me what kind of dressing I wanted on my salad, I answered balsamic. Dad looked at me with the most disgusted expression and said, 'Balsamic? Or maybe poppy seed? I bet you really don't like balsamic vinegar, but even the choice of salad dressing has to be a source of rebellion for your generation because your parents' generation prefers creamier dressing like blue cheese and thousand island.' Can you believe he actually said that?"

"Did that just pop out of his head from nowhere?" Hank said. "That sounds awfully random to me."

"Well, not exactly. We had been in another pretty heated argument about why we were in Vietnam."

"Oh! That explains it. I think I heard somewhere that most balsamic vinegar is manufactured in the Mideast where the profits go to North Vietnam to help fight the war." Hank winked at Corey and chuckled.

"Don't ever say that to my dad; he'll accuse me of being a traitor. Seriously though, can't my generation question some our parents' values without being labeled an immature radical?"

Hank smiled and said, "It's normal and healthy. There are always things that need changing. The problem is if when you throw out those old values, with what will you be replacing them?"

"Same old Hank; answer my question with a question. Don't get me wrong, I love that. It's just quite a contrast from my dad who only has answers."

Hank looked at Millie and said, "These snacks are delicious. They're from an old recipe of your grandmother's, aren't they?"

"I'm not sure. I've had them a long time. I don't how many times I've had to give someone the recipes. Some things are worth keeping," she said and winked at Corey.

"A good recipe is an easy thing to hold onto. All you have to do is taste it and you know that's good, but what about values?" Corey asked.

"Baseball has always been a love of yours. What kind of win is the most rewarding, the one in which you slaughter some weak team fifteen to nothing, or a hard-fought game against a good team which you win by one run ... hell! ... even lose by a run?"

"I know where you're going with this; things that are hard

to come by are more rewarding than stuff that comes easy," Corey answered, then reflected as he sat silent for a little while.

"You guys know who Bob Dylan is, I'm sure?" Corey said, breaking his own silent contemplation. "The singer and songwriter who has sort of become the poet laureate of my generation. My dad hates him ... calls him a communist sympathizer. One of his songs, 'Blowin in the Wind,' has become my generations' anthem. One of the verses asks the question 'How many times must the cannonball fire, before they are ever banned?' Does being against war make you a communist? Does it mean you are a coward?"

"How does Mr. Dylan answer that question?" Hank asked.

"He says,

'The answer, my friend, is blowin' in the wind.'"

"And what do you suppose he means by that?"

"I guess it means that there are questions that mankind can't answer. The reason has to come from some outside force which is greater than ourselves."

"Should we accept that as an answer. or should we keep questioning even though we know that most answers are blowing in the wind?"

Corey let go a hearty laugh aimed at himself. "I love you because you always play me in to close a ball game. I know my father loves me and wants the best for me ... and I love both my parents. I just don't want to be like them because I can see, despite their material wealth, they're not happy, and so why would they want me to be like them?"

Hank smiled, then said, "When I had my blowout with my father and left the reservation, before leaving I paid a visit to an elder tribesman who was my mentor. He told me something that I didn't understand at the time but remembered, and its meaning became clearer with age. He said, 'Always have a strong curiosity but be cautious in your beliefs. Be bold when expressing your inquisitiveness, but humble in giving your opinions.'"

Corey nodded. "What yesterday's fight was about was his bugging me over my hair. He wants me to get it cut so I will appear more presentable at his beloved country club with all its conservative, hawkish members. He's always wanting to drag me over there to meet some pompous ass who, because he has money, Dad thinks is successful and can somehow help me get started in a future he has planned for me. I'll bet three quarters of the club membership comes from inherited money, not earned like my dad, which is why I respect him. It pisses me off seeing him act so servile to them when he has probably accomplished more on his own than they have on theirs. What I see in much of that old money membership is their main concern in life is how to protect what they were given. They could care less about social problems or anyone else for that matter. I've yet to meet anyone over there who you can engage in a conversation about any deeper meaning in life other than the new Mercedes they bought, or the trip they are going to take to Europe."

"Mercedes is a good car, but to be honest, I also like balsamic vinegar."

Corey laughed. "You know what I mean. I won't mention any names, but there is this one club member who I'm sure is very wealthy, but I don't think I've ever talked to him when he wasn't drunk. I don't remember how we got onto the subject of marijuana — probably because I'm young and they assume I need a lecture on drugs — but anyway this guy says to me, 'You want to know the difference between a pot smoker and an alcoholic?' I didn't, but just like my father who also frequently asks rhetorical questions, he told me anyway. He said, 'If an alcoholic is hard up for a drink but has no money, he might steal from you, but as soon as he's sober, he'll realize what he has done and will pay you back. A pot head, on the other hand, will also steal from you, but he'll just sneak away without ever admitting he stole and, of course, never pay you back.'"

"Millie, if that turkey isn't finished cooking, we ought to move into the kitchen. Corey's letting off enough steam to cook it the rest of the way," Hank said, chuckling to himself.

"We could probably have him over every time he needs to vent. We'd save enough money on gas for *you* to join the country club," Millie answered.

"All right, I'm sorry, but I had to get this off my chest. I appreciate you guys listening and having me over."

"Just out of curiosity, how did you answer that guy on the marijuana thing?" Hank asked.

"I didn't say anything, because my father and everyone

else at the table agreed with him and acted like he had just come down from Sinai with some profound truth. They couldn't even recognize it for what it was — pompous, drunken ramble."

Hank laughed, then said, "I never joined the country club, although I've dined there with friends who are members. I couldn't help but notice that all the help was Mexican and all the members white. I wondered where us Indians stood on their racial tolerance ladder."

"You know what amazes me the most? Those conservative snobs provide more entitlements and more subsidies for their children than the broadest of welfare reform ever proposed by McGovern. In San Marino, it is automatic to get a new car for your sixteenth birthday."

"Now you are the one who's overstating things," Hank interrupted. "I know some families that only provide used cars so their kids will learn the value of the dollar."

Millie said, "I'm going to stay out of this discussion. I'm more worried neither of you are going to like the lemon-poppy seed dressing, although the lemons came from our tree, not the Mideast."

After more laughter, Cory continued to give more examples of San Marino welfare programs until Hank interrupted him and said, "I think I know what bothers you most about the country club. You are young, and the world, despite its injustices, is still filled with wonder. Your dreams are unfulfilled, and your passion for pursuing them is at its optimum. At the club, you see a lot of listless old men whose passion burned out sometime ago; only ashes of cynicism remain. Now what you see in those old men is repetitive, predictable lives whereby diversions like card games and golf seem paramount. You see garrulous old men who think that young men should want to listen to their exaggerated stories about their life's accomplishments. What scares you the most is you knew your father once had the same aspirations you have now. It's not your hair, not your opposition to the war; it is your youthful zest for life he and many of them lost somewhere along the line. Next time you go over with your dad, instead of thinking about how uncomfortable you are, see if you can determine how many truly satisfied people sit among them."

Millie, who had quietly listened to the conversation, softly spoke up. "Maybe your father, like many of those club members, want their children to follow in their footsteps so as to deceive themselves into thinking that if their children choose the same path, then that gives validity to the choices they chose for themselves. If you want to be a bigger man than them, show pity, not scorn."

Hank looked at his wife as affectionately as Corey had ever seen. He coyly smiled, then said to Corey, "Now you see why I married her ... She's smarter than I am."

"Both of my parents once talked with me like you guys do. Now they only talk at me," Corey replied.

"That was before the war," Hank stated more than asked.

"Yes, before the war. Before that goddamned war," Corey answered.

"That's the one bump in the road that you can't find an

answer for," Hank said, then added, "I think you need to ask yourself a few real tough questions before blaming your dad or anyone else. You need to ask yourself: am I opposed to all war on a spiritual or ethical level, or is it just this war that you're opposed to for political differences? Or maybe, and what would be the most difficult to admit, you need to ask am I just plain scared? I know I was, and thankful because as an Indian, I was allowed to avoid the draft during World War II."

"I'm not a pacifist," Corey answered. "And yes, I'm afraid of dying or being maimed — only a fool or a liar would say he wasn't — but this war is so wrong. We are supporting the wrong side and we are doing so for business reasons, not ethical ones. When I believe in something, I'm a crusader, a fighter, a patriot. Because of that I can't see myself leaving the country, nor am I willing to go to prison for draft evasion. I've got another year to think about what I'm going to do. That even makes it worse ... another year to torture myself mentally over this dilemma."

"I didn't mean for you to answer me. However, it seems to me before the war, life was pretty easy for you. You were playing in a lot of fifteen-to-one games. Are you sure a close game is what you really prefer? Well! Maybe the country club life isn't so bad after all." "Well what?" Corey said, caught off guard by Hank's response.

"I was just thinking that maybe something good has come out of this war for you on a personal level. I hear you asking questions far deeper than those asked at card games over at the country club." Hank winked at Corey.

"Right now the only thing I know for sure is that I know a lot less than I thought I did," Corey confessed.

"We're sort of back to where we began — opposing the values of old and how to replace them. Admitting what you don't know is a great start. It might be a good time to tell you why I left my family and how I arrived at where I am today. A word of caution though; remember what I'm about to tell you is only what worked for me and does not necessarily apply to you. That being said, I can tell you I left the reservation because I did not see any dignity in reservation life. It didn't matter to me if the white man committed injustices in robbing the native people of their land. They outnumbered us and were technologically way more advanced. That's the way things worked. Cro-Magnon conquered the Neanderthal much like the white man conquered my people. To me it was assimilate or die out. My values did not come all at once. I did not read any philosophy or the ideas of profound writers. I simply delved into a new culture that forced me to make many decisions at a very young age. I was only eighteen when I left the reservation.

"Sometimes my choices were the right ones, sometimes not. I often found my old values were often in conflict with those of the new society I was entering. The actual conflict was between what I felt at a gut level and the laws of both my old and new worlds that were supposed to govern my behavior.

At first that uncertainty scared me until I learned to embrace it. The more difficult the decision, the more questions I had to ask, and each answer led to yet another and more difficult question. That's when I realized I was learning, and as strange as it seems, feeling more comfortable with being uncomfortable. At first I was searching for some absolute revelation that would guide my life. I thought I could climb Mount Sinai and bring back some missing commandment that would better not only me, but all of mankind. Now I simply enjoy change and all the new and wonderful questions that being alive allows. I never cease learning or want to. That's what works for me, but maybe not you. Perhaps you'll find something even better."

Corey smiled at the old man. "Like I said earlier, my father used to talk to me like you are doing now, but not in a long time."

"Things change. He might again," Hank said, then added, "Both of you might."

Corey returned to San Diego that night. Alone in his apartment, he picked up his copy of *Moby Dick* and began skimming where he had yellow marked certain phrases and passages. He found the one he had been thinking about for almost the entire drive back to the Surf Rider.

It was the chapter where Starbuck realizes Ahab is mad and needed to be stopped. He came to the captain's quarters with a pistol hidden in his jacket. Ahab's back was to his first mate; Ahab never turned to face the first mate, yet it was as if he sensed why Starbuck was there.

> *"Vengeance on a dumb brute," cried Starbuck, "that simply smote thee from blindest instinct! Madness! To be enraged with a dumb thing seems blasphemous."*
>
> *"Hark ye yet again — the little lower layer. All visible objects, man, are but as pasteboard masks, but in each event — in the living act, the undoubted deed — there, some unknown but still reasoning thing puts forth the moldings of its features from behind the unreasoning mask. How can the prisoner reach outside except by thrusting through the wall? To me, the white whale is the wall, shoved near to me. Sometimes I think there's naught beyond. But tis enough. He task me; he heaps me. I see in him outrageous strength; with an incredible malice sinewing it. That inscrutable thing is chiefly what I hate."*

Corey opened his notebook and quickly added to the journal he was keeping for Professor Vanderhoof's assignment. He wrote:

Starbuck's use of the biblical term smote, his reference to blasphemy, showed his deep religious conviction. A conviction so strong that before he could kill Ahab, he had to be sure he was carrying out God's will. But Ahab's answer stopped him, for Ahab was not seeking the whale, but the force behind the whale. That thing that moved all living things, which to Starbuck was God. He and Ahab sought the same thing, just in different ways.

In parenthesis, he wrote, *How could two people value the same thing from such different points of view. How could Starbuck not see insanity has nothing to do with God. Who was really mad — Starbuck or Ahab, or maybe both? Hot is probably right. Starbuck was a dumb shit.*

CHAPTER EIGHTEEN

The New Yorkers came to Corey's Thanksgiving Day barbecue along with Joey and Karen, who came back early as promised. During the meal, Dougie suggested that since they would be out of school a full week before they would be going home for the Christmas holidays, they take a surfing trip to Matachen Bay that Hot and Corey talked about and described during their recent trip to Hector's. As they sat around the fire that evening, they asked Corey to tell them more about the place.

"Hot and I first went to Matachen Bay the summer after our freshman year in college. At that time, the sleepy little ocean village was virtually unknown as a tourist town except for the wealthy Mexican nationals. It was unknown as a surfing spot. Gradually word got out, but as recent as one year ago, probably because it is about fifteen hundred miles below the border, south of Mazatlan but on the mainland, it still hadn't attracted many surfers. The first time we went there, we met a local young dude about our age named Lalo. Lalo was a turtle diver who worked six days a week. The town of San Blas is right on the bay. It is a poor town, and the capturing and slaughtering of sea turtles is necessary for food, but local artists and craftsmen let no part of the turtle go to waste. Shells and bones were made into various ornaments and jewelry which were exported to Guadalajara and other larger cities that had a greater influx of tourists. The primitiveness of the place was as interesting to us as the outstanding surfing.

"At the time we made our first visit, surfers were such an oddity, Lalo, along with several of his buddies, came to the bay to investigate. Hot and I loaned them our boards and taught them to surf. In return, Lalo invited us to join him and some other divers for a few beers at Enrique's, the town's most popular bar. It was there they boasted about the town's baseball team, for whom Lalo played. The San Blas team played other towns every Sunday afternoon following church.

When Hot mentioned I played baseball for San Diego State, Lalo's eyes sparkled and he immediately invited me to play with the San Blas team that Sunday."

"The other team made no objection to an American playing until I got lucky and hit a tie-breaking home run late in the game. Then, for the first time the manager of the other team objected, saying I was not a resident of San Blas and, of course, not even a citizen of Mexico. After a long argument, the umpire, who happened to be the priest from the San Blas church, ruled that since there was no objection at the start of the game, it was legal for me to play, but in the future, only residents would be eligible. The ruling was fine with us since we had not come to San Blas for the baseball, but for the waves.

"After the game, Hot and I were invited to Enrique's bar for a victory celebration. With several beers under everyone's belt and our testosterone levels elevated by the game, everyone began challenging each other to arm wrestling matches. Hot and I watched until Lalo challenged me to a contest, with one footnote. The match would be governed by Mexican rules, which meant you took a shot of tequila, then a swig of beer, followed by five chin-ups on a wooden beam that ran the length of the bar ceiling. You had to do it five times before the match began. If I lost, Hot and I would buy a round of beers for Lalo and his friends, and of course if Lalo lost, he would buy a round for me and Hot. After the second shot of tequila, I noticed that Lalo's shot glass looked different than mine. My glass had alcohol legs running down the interior. Lalo's vessel looked smooth, like it is when it is only filled with water."

"What did you do?" Joey asked.

"Nothing. I realized that the bartender was filling Lalo's glass with water so I would be drunk on my ass by the time the match began. I had trouble putting my elbow on the table."

"You didn't say nothing even though you knew they were cheating?" Joey protested.

"Of course not," Corey said. "I lost and paid for the drinks. The few dollars lost that day was nothing compared to the friends we gained."

Karen suggested if they decided to return at Christmas, Corey should contact the San Diego Padres baseball team. She had read that they were changing their uniform design for the upcoming season and might give some of the old uniforms away. She suggested that, since San Diego, being close to the border, and the Padres having a big following south of the border as well as a large Hispanic population in the greater San Diego area, that the gesture could be used for publicity purposes. She had been to Matachen Bay on previous trips and had noticed how shoddy the poor San Blas team uniforms were. Most players wore T-shirts with hand-painted numbers on the back.

The Surf Rider clan agreed the trip was a great idea, so the next week Spook and Corey went to the Padres. Their publicity department loved the idea and gave them twenty old uniforms in return for an agreement that the clan would take pictures of the team in their "new" Padre uniforms, and Spook would write up an article on the team. Everything fell into place. Joey's mom, seeing an opportunity to spend time with her new boyfriend free of Joey, gladly signed a permission slip and produced a copy of Joey's birth certificate so

Joey could go along. They left in a small convoy for San Blas a week before Christmas.

They reached Matachan Bay in the early afternoon and drove to the bay before getting their rooms and going to town. It was a large natural bay at the southern end of town. There were three points located at the far northern end of the bay. When there was a large swell, ocean waves wrapped around the first point, passing dangerously close to the jagged rocks near the shoreline of all three points. When the waves were large enough to clear all three points, well-shaped walls of water entered the bay where you could ride one wave almost a half mile. After catching two or three waves, your legs felt like rubber, so just a few rides a day with long rest periods between waves was all a surfer needed.

When they arrived at the beach, they were shocked to see at least fifteen campsites, all belonging to Americans, but mostly hippie surfers, not die-hard surfers. Hot and Corey exchanged glances; their secluded spot was no longer a secret. A freshwater river ran from the jungle into the bay. In the past, Corey and Hot would bathe in the stream to clean the saltwater from their bodies. They now saw several of the Americans nude bathing in the river. The campers openly smoked pot.

Near where the river entered the sea were about eight thatched Quonset huts owned by a widow, who rented them to poorer tourists who could not afford to stay in the one extravagant hotel in town, which was at the extreme south end of the bay. Lalo had introduced the boys to her on a previous visit to San Blas. He told them it was okay to camp out, but if they paid a modest rental, it would put them in higher regards with the towns' people. She only charged an equivalent of two dollars per person per night. There was a central bathroom and shower for all the huts, which each comfortably slept four people.

None of the huts were rented, so she was delighted to see the boys had returned and had brought so many friends. They rented three rooms and gave her a hundred dollars for four nights. Spook, who spoke Spanish fluently, learned from the old women that she, and most of the town's people, were upset with the surfer tourists. Not only did they frequently parade nude and were open about drug use and sex, but they spent very little money in town, which meant no tourist income for the poor village.

Once settled in their modest accommodations, they went into town and to Enrique's, where they hoped to find Lalo and other members of the baseball team relaxing after a day's work.

Before they entered the bar, they were surrounded by children offering to wash their car windows, but also trying to sell jumping beans and small boxes of Chicklets chewing gum. "Chicklet," Hot said as he got out of the car, not referring to gum but rather to a small boy whom they had met during earlier visits to the village. Because he appeared to be the ringleader of the diminutive hucksters, they nicknamed him Chicklet. The boy was the same age as Joey, but much smaller and younger looking. Despite his size and youthful appearance, he was definitely in charge.

The boy ran over to Hot and held out a soiled box filled with small packages of Chicklet gum — two pieces in each mini cardboard box. The faded printing on the gum containers housed stale, hard gum. Corey had not seen boxes like those in America since he was about eight or nine years old.

Hot took a handful of gum, then said "window wash." Chicklet snapped his fingers and two boys and a girl, all taller than Chicklet, emerged from the group and began washing the windows of the clan's dust-covered windshields with dirty rags that just redistributed the dirt rather than cleaned the windows.

"How much?" Hot asked as he held out his hands so the boy could count the number of pieces of gum.

Chicklet quickly counted the gum and pointed to the cars. "One dollar, twenty-five cents American," Chicklet answered. Hot paid him in coins so he could divide it among his workers. They went inside where Hot dumped the gum in a wastebasket. At the bar, Lalo sat with his back to the entrance and did not see his friends when they first entered.

"Amigos," Lalo shouted as he jumped up, hugging Corey as he lifted him off his feet and spun him around. Lalo spoke a little English, as did his friends. Between their English and Spooks's Spanish, they explained the uniforms they had in the car. The bar emptied and its occupants excitedly went out and surrounded Turk's Volkswagen bus.

They began passing out the uniforms, sorting sizes as best they could, but the scene looked like a shark feeding frenzy as each one tried to grab his favorite number. They acted as happy as children opening presents beneath a Christmas tree. Everyone hurried back into the bar and into the men's room to try on their uniforms, Karen all the while snapping pictures at a furious pace. The bartender gave the clan the first round of beers on the house, along with a bottle of orange soda for Joey. During the celebration, Karen tapped Joey on the shoulder.

"Joey," Karen said, "follow me." She led Joey outside to the village square.

In almost every small town or village in Mexico there was a park or town square that faced the most ornate building in the village, the Catholic church. San Blas was no exception. The church was more than just a place of worship, and similar to almost every small town in Mexico, the church was located looking over the town square, where it also served as the primary information source for local news as well as town meetings. Even in the twentieth century, many of the people in poor and remote areas were partially illiterate. The plaza itself also served many purposes. Since the town was void of arcades, night clubs, and movie theaters, the square also became the entertainment center.

In San Blas, in the southwest corner of the promenade was a small bandstand where Friday through Sunday evenings local musicians played mostly flamingo and mariachi music. On the northeast corner were two volleyball courts where the teenage boys played competitively, not so much for victory over their opponents, but more to show off their athletic skills for the young female onlookers. On the southeast side were park benches and small tables where older town folk gathered either to gossip or play chess.

Karen led Joey to the northwest corner where the children gathered to play foosball. Joey immediately became intrigued by the game. A young Mexican boy saw Joey's fascination and motioned to him asking if he wanted to play. Joey nodded yes. He lost the first two sets, the second set five to four, then he won the next three, the last with a five-to-one score.

Soon the young American boy had a small audience around him. The young onlookers were amazed at how quickly Joey jumped from handle to handle, both to protect his goal, but also to attack his opponent. Karen too was admiring Joey's play and how remarkably quick he seemed to master a game he had never played, when she heard someone walk up behind her.

"Just look at that church," Jan said. "Yes, it is beautiful," Karen answered.

"What I meant was in every town we passed, the churches are pretentious while the rest of the country is locked in poverty. Doesn't that bother you?"

"Do you think that if they tore down the church, sold all the artifacts, and gave the proceeds to the townsfolk there would be less poverty in Mexico?"

"Probably not, but it just seems wrong that these poor

people should give so much of their meager income to the church."

"I've always thought of the church as a collective source of pride. In every country there seems to be something — a statue, a garden, whatever—but it serves that purpose. Besides, look around this square. Do you see any desperate or angry-looking faces. Ever since I first came this far below the border, I've marveled at how happy the people seem, and how young or old, wealthy or poor, they commingle so much at ease with one another. You rarely see anything like this in the States, do you?" Karen replied.

"It just seems that there is a lot of exploitation by the haves against the have-nots in Mexico," Jan said.

"We're on vacation, relax. Why don't you watch Joey play with the local kids?" Karen said. "Look how happy Joey and the local kids are. Don't spoil the fun by telling them how poor they are," Karen added, chiding Jan for her seriousness.

Karen turned to see how Joey was faring when she spotted Chicklet among the gathering crowd of youthful lookers-on that had gathered. Chicklet had been playing at another table when they first arrived and was obviously the foosball champion of San Blas. He said something in Spanish to the boy who had been playing against Joey. The boy stopped and moved away from the table. Chicklet took his spot.

Chicklet won the match in four sets, but all of them were close games. Joey wanted to play him again, but the Surf Rider clan had left the bar and congregated at the foosball games. "You've got all week to play," Corey said. "We're going back to catch the evening surf. By the end of the week you'll be beating Chicklet. Comprende, Chicklet?" Chicklet responded with a challenging glance toward Joey, who smiled back confidently.

"One more match," Joey said.

"Not now, champ. Let's go, kiddo. We came here to surf."

CHAPTER NINETEEN

When they got back to the bay, Corey and Hot told the rest of the clan that Lalo suggested they maybe talk to the influx of campers about spending a little money in town, and maybe be more discreet about the pot smoking and nude bathing.

"Haven't you camped out just to enjoy the solitude of camping?" Jan immediately defended the college campers.

"Sure, I love doing that. Nothing beats going to some secluded lake, skinny dipping, smoking a little weed, and just kicking back. The key word is 'secluded,' but they're camping next to a poor fishing village where the town's people are steeped in old Catholic religious convictions," Corey answered.

"I agree with Jan," Dougie said. "They are far enough away from town's people. They're not hurting anybody."

"Look around. There are a number of small huts similar to the ones we're staying in, only families with children live in many of those shacks," Hot said.

"Then the way I see it is that these folks are like the ones I fled from in my old hometown; they are too concerned with everyone's morals but their own," Jan continued to protest. "Did you notice how ornate the town's church is? Why doesn't the church do something about the people who live in these dilapidated hovels rather than worry about some college kids blowing off a little steam during Christmas break? What's more obscene: a few young people occasionally skinny dipping while on vacation in a remote place, or people living year-round in poverty?"

"Whatever," Corey said. "From my perspective we've found our own private paradise and we can keep it that way by simply respecting the local villagers' cultural beliefs. If you want, when we get back home you all come over to our apartment, smoke a little pot, sip on wine, then have a nice morality discussion."

Jan shook her head, threw up her hands in disgust, and walked away with Dougie quickly following her as she headed toward the beach.

Although the bay was crowded, there was a nice swell rolling in, providing ample waves for anyone wanting to surf, which was only a small percentage of the American campers. The clan members were much more serious about surfing, so they stayed in the warm tropical water until dusk, still amazed that it was just a week before Christmas.

Back in San Diego, the air and the water temp would both be about fifty degrees. With the summer-like temperatures, and away from the bombardment of war news that continually dominated the media, the clan felt as relaxed as they probably had during their respective high school summer vacation years. Corey was sure that the others felt the same sensation as he. Somehow, he had traveled back in time and he wished he could remain there — at least longer than a week.

Hot paddled to Corey. "I know we told Lalo we would talk to these guys, but I was thinking it would be a helluva lot nicer to sit around a campfire, smoke a little pot, sip on a beer or two, and bullshit about surfing or whatever comes to mind."

"I'd prefer to do that too, but I've got this weird feeling that we ought to try to approach the subject. Didn't you get the feeling that Lalo was making more than a casual request, like maybe if this crowd continues doing what they are doing something bad is going to happen? Besides, we can be cool about it," Corey said. "Even share a joint and mellow out with them to show them we have a common ground when it comes to having a good time."

"Are you having some kind of premonition?"

"I can't explain it. I just think we need to say something. Maybe these guys are so caught up in having a good time of their own that they are not aware of the towns' attitude."

"We can give it a go, but I think we ought to find a way to leave Jan and Dougie out of coming with us, because you know they will become part of the problem and not the solution," Hot cautioned.

Corey talked them into staying and helping Karen and Joey fix dinner. He and Hot filled the others in on what Lalo had suggested, and they agreed to infiltrate the beach campers with them and, in a friendly way, educate them regarding the locals' attitude.

"How's the surf been wherever you all are from?" Corey asked as they reached a blazing bonfire where most of the campers congregated.

"Good, but nothing like these waves," someone answered.

"Where is home for everyone, anyway?" Hot asked, trying to sound as if he cared.

It turned out they were mostly from northern California, where the winter surf was even colder than it was in San Diego. To the clan's surprise, most of them were not students, not even die-hard surfers, but rather hippies who surfed some and who thought by living a nomadic lifestyle, it would make it hard for their local draft boards to locate them. By sunset, the fire had attracted a crowd of about fifty people, which was almost the entire population of campers.

The clan smoked a little weed, then made it a point to confirm they shared the same anti-war and establishment views as the visiting campers before easing the conversation into local attitudes. Hot casually remarked how shocked he was that although Mexico was a close neighbor to America, how different the villagers' values were in in the small towns of Mexico from the attitudes in America, mostly brought about by the war.

Turk said with smile, “Yeah! In the States, change is coming fast, but down here, it's so slow by contrast.”

“It's about time they come into the twentieth century,” someone in the crowd replied.

“Their culture is so steeped in religious virtues I don't know if change can come that fast down here", Corey said, then added, “It might be best to adhere to the old saying, ‘When in Rome do as the Romans do.’”

Hot then suggested that buying a few trinkets or food from the town's merchants might be all that was necessary to make them welcome guests rather than looked upon as immoral intruders, “which they think you are whether you realize it or not.”

“Then they've got a problem,” someone else said. Nothing any of Corey's group would say, direct or subtle, could make any impact. Their attitude was bluntly expressed by a bikini-clad young lady. “We're here to have a good time and we're not hurting anyone. They should mind their own fucking business.”

Later, when they returned to their lodging, Corey would remark he had a notion that back in the States these same hippies probably argued that there is nobility in poverty, yet down here they looked upon the poor as ignorant peasants.

The Mission Beach clan left knowing they failed to get their point across, causing Corey to feel the brunt of the disappointment. Hot must have sensed it. He tapped Corey on the shoulder. "I don't exactly know what you are thinking, but I feel we tried and can honestly report to Lalo we gave it our best shot. Right now, I'm pleasantly stoned and exhausted enough to want to enjoy nothing more than a nice dinner, maybe take a short nap, then head into town. Besides, your intuition could be wrong."

Corey answered, "You're right, but just to be safe I think we ought to keep our distance with these guys and make sure the rest of our clan does too."

After dinner, they decided to go into town for the nightlife and to see how the baseball team fared in their new uniforms. They thought maybe Lalo might have an idea or two concerning a different approach to reasoning with the hippies, and if so, they could try again in the morning. If nothing else, the surf was great, and that was their main reason for the trip. Jan, Dougie, Dizzy, and Weirdness wanted to stay on the beach and hang with the campers for the evening, but Corey demanded they all go into town. As soon as they arrived, Joey headed straight for the foosball tables, where he and Chicklet began playing. Chicklet won most of the games at first, but each one became more fiercely contested until finally they were playing even. Karen saw how heavily each boy perspired in the balmy, tropical climate, so she brought over a couple of soft drinks, which both boys quickly gulped down. Joey nodded thanks, but Chicklet looked confused. No American tourist had ever done anything like that for him. Then when he saw Joey nod, Chicklet tipped the bottle toward Karen and gave her a warm smile. Both boys went at it with restored vigor. By then a large crowd began gathering. Karen and Christy, who also had been watching them play, went into the bar to get the others.

"You guys have got to see this," they said. The Surf Rider clan and most of the baseball team followed them out.

The San Blas team was in good spirits. They had won handily, beating a team that had beat them in their two previous meetings. They attributed their better play to the uniforms, which they claimed still held the energy from the major league players who had worn them previously and gave them a source of power and team pride they had never experienced before. The clan bought the first round of beers to toast the victory, then the team insisted that beers the rest of the evening were on them. They bought another round and followed the girls outside.

Chicklet glanced around at the onlookers. He was used to drawing a small crowd, but nothing ever this large. He pulled out a quarter, probably one Hot had given the day before, and laid it onto the side of the game platform.

Joey had no money, so Turk took a quarter from his pocket and laid it next to Chicklet's. The match had meaning. It took nearly forty-five minutes, but Joey, in the end, gave a quarter back to Turk and put the other in his pocket.

Chicklet slammed another quarter down, but before Joey could match him, the police chief, who was the third baseman on the team, stepped up to the table, holding up his hands and announcing in Spanish at first, then turning to Corey's group to translate to English, spurring excited conversation from the crowd.

"Tomorrow evening we are going to have a party at Enrique's in honor of our American friends and their generous gifts of these uniforms." The chief paused and turned to model the jersey he still wore instead of his police uniform. "Before the party," he continued, "we will have a match game between Chicklet and your boy. I sanction gambling on this game," he said, smiling at the crowd. "Afterward, the party will be held at Enrique's bar. We will celebrate our new uniforms and Niko's (Chicklet's birth name) victory over our friendly American challenger."

The crowd let out a joyous roar. Many came over to Chicklet and either ruffled his already uncombed hair or patted him on the back, saying words of encouragement. Lalo began collecting bets, which the police chief collected for safekeeping. The clan put up twenty-five dollars on Joey. Numerous side bets were made, hands were shaken, and further pleasantries exchanged. The clan finished their beers and offered their final congratulations on the victory before returning to the bay.

When they got back to Matachen Bay, Corey asked Joey to take a walk with him on the beach. As they passed the campers, there was the wood-smoke aroma from the campfires mingling with the pungent scent of marijuana hanging over the encampment. A bare-breasted girl, whose glazed eyes were further enhanced by the dim glow of the campfire, danced slowly as a couple of guys strummed on their guitars. One guy got up and kissed the girl on her naked breast.

"Wow!" Joey said, his eyes widening. Corey pushed him on after letting him watch for few more seconds.

"I have a feeling you'll get plenty of that in a few years, but not just yet," Corey said as they continued their walk.

"How come everyone is so hung up over these guys anyway? All of you smoke pot, and I'm pretty sure my mom's not the only one screwing," Joey asked when they were out of earshot of the campers.

"It has nothing to do with smoking weed. We've even had tokes with Lalo and his friends," Corey said. "Only we did it discreetly. That's just the way things are done in a small town like this where church and old values are still a way of life."

Joey said nothing as they continued their walk a little further. "Let's sit on the beach for a while," Corey said, then continued. "You know that old man I've told you about, Hank? He's been my mentor for about ten years, maybe longer. He used to take me on camping trips into the High Sierras. At night, we would sit around the campfire and talk about any number of things. The conversations were never meant to be profound. In fact, he encouraged me to do most of the talking. Our talks never started out to be anything heavy, but before you knew it they became kind of deep anyway, at least for a ten-year-old kid. I remember one conversation in particular; we were discussing an old grouch who lived on our street. All us kids steered clear of his house. God forbid a ball got away from us and rolled up on his lawn.

Next thing you know, Hank brought up the subject of boundaries.

"'You all knew his house was out of bounds. You knew that without anyone having to tell you. You knew your space ended where another person's began,' Hank said sort out of the blue."

"Are you saying it's kind of like that now?" Joey said.

"Yeah, kind of like that now. Most of these tourist kids don't understand how they can be pissing off the locals. It was just like me and my neighborhood friends not knowing why the old man was such an asshole, but we both hated and feared him. That evening, in the most unassuming way, Hank mentioned that the man and his wife had lost their only son to polio.

'Right or wrong,' Hank said, 'I suppose they see other peoples' kids as a sad reminder of their own loss.'

"A couple of weeks after we were back home, I was walking my dog when the old man came out to get his morning paper. I picked it up and handed it to him. 'I just learned about your son,' I said. 'I bet he was a really neat kid. He would have fit in real well with the kids on this block.' The old man looked at me real peculiar. It wasn't a look of anger or grief. I guess he just looked confused and didn't know what to say, but a few days later we were playing touch football in the street when our football got loose and rolled up on his lawn. We all hesitated, trying to decide who would make a daredevil run to get the ball when that old man came out. He didn't say anything at first. He walked over to the ball and looked at it as if he never had seen a football before. He held it for a few seconds then to our surprise, he tossed it back, actually threw a pretty good spiral. 'Have a good game,' he said, and went back inside."

"But if you can't see the boundaries, then how do you know what to do?" Joey said. "You do what you always have done, little man. Do what feels right, what makes sense."

Joey looked a little puzzled and was about to say something else when they heard footsteps come up behind them.

"Nice night," Karen said as she sat down, nudging herself against Corey. They noticed she had her camera. "What are you two talking about?"

"The situation going on here. I'm trying to explain to Joey that in our eyes these kids are doing nothing wrong. But the people down here see things from a different point of view. I'm trying to tell him it's not a question of right or wrong, but rather just the way things are. It's a lot like surfing; first you size up the wave, then go with the flow."

"Oh! Is that what you were trying tell me?" Joey said, his impish boyish smile escaping. "Why didn't you just say so to begin with?"

"Because I like teaching you lessons so as you grow up you'll be as neat an adult as you are a kid," Corey said and playfully punched Joey in the shoulder.

"I didn't mean to interrupt your man talk, but I came here because I've got a new idea for my photography. It probably has nothing to do what you guys are talking about, but maybe in way it does."

"There's no way to interrupt our conversation, because it is one of those random talks you have at a time like this," Corey answered.

"Well then, the reason I'm here is because yesterday I took a picture of the bay at about this same location, only at sunset. This morning I shot the scene right at sunrise. The color of the water was starkly different. At sunset, the sun melted into the water like butter dripping over the edge of a stack of warm pancakes. In the morning, it reflected a much more silvery light that made you squint your eyes as you looked at it. I want to shoot the same picture under the moonlight. I want to show how the same thing can have such contrasts when viewed under different circumstances and times. It kind of shows how your perspective can, through time, change the way you see the same thing. Look at the moonlight over the water now. It kind of looks like a golden stream running through black water. At night, it's like someone poured a truckload of floating golden glitter that sparkles on the rippling water's surface."

"Way cool!" Joey said.

"It sure is. By the way, Joey, I got some real neat shots of you playing foosball. I hope to get even better ones when you win tomorrow."

Joey shifted uneasily. "I wish everyone hadn't made such a big deal out of it. I'm just playing for fun, you know!"

"Bullshit! I was there and I saw how intense both you and Chicklet went at it," Corey said. "You both are natural competitors."

"But it was still just for fun," Joey protested.

"Maybe for you, but it meant something far greater for Chicklet. You understand me, don't you?"

"Yeah, I think I do," Joey said softly.

"I think it's going to be a great match, but just keep playing for fun, okay?"

Corey put his arm around Karen. "You know, as the moon shifts location there could be a lot of interesting effects. Why don't we stay up for a while and see what kind of pictures the moon allows you to capture?"

"I was thinking the same thing, but I think Joey ought to get his rest for the big day tomorrow."

"Yeah right, I can take a hint. Pretty late for the town people to be up, and too dark to see what you guys are doing even if they are still awake," he said as he jumped to his feet and headed back toward the huts. "Remember to have fun," he shouted back at them as he left.

They waited until they were sure Joey was long gone, then Karen said, "He's amazing. Sometimes I think he really is already an adult."

"Yep! He's had to grow up faster than he should, but there's still a lot of little boy in there. It wouldn't surprise me if he doesn't sneak back to spy on us."

"I don't think he will. It doesn't matter anyway since I really am just here to take pictures. I just won't be taking them all night," she said and poked Corey in his rib cage.

"I'm glad you're here. There is something we've talked about before and I have to bring it up again."

Karen sighed. "It's about marriage, isn't it?"

"I love you, and that night on the beach at Hector's — you can't tell me you don't feel the same love for me."

"You know I do, but, well, people go into marriage thinking that their love is so powerful that they will compromise their likes and dislikes and meet each other halfway. Didn't your parents do that? They were high school sweethearts whose love could conquer all obstacles. I think you told me that. You've said a number of times how your mom ended up making greater sacrifices than your father and that's why she became an alcoholic. I think their relationship is more the norm in most marriages, at least from what I've seen, and in our society, it's the woman who's expected to make the greater sacrifices."

"What makes you think that I'm not willing to allow you to put your profession ahead of mine?" Corey answered. "Your parents seem to be happy."

"That's because my mom is willing to sacrifice more — That's what women of her generation have been taught to do."

"Hey, times are changing! What makes you think I wouldn't be willing to sacrifice more for you. Do you realize how much I enjoy watching you work, then talking like we are now?"

"I know you do, and that's one of the many reasons I love you, but at the same time I recognize you will want to have children; I know how happy that will make you. I can see that by the way you interact with Joey. I love Joey too, just as I would love our children if we had them, but children would make me further compromise my true passion. You always tell me how important it is for people to follow their passion."

"Don't you think that maybe marriage and children might broaden your work rather than take away? I heard you say to Joey just now how you got some great shots of him playing foosball against Chicklet. Aren't you here to see how the same thing can change so radically when viewed from another angle? Besides, we don't have to have children," Corey said, giving her a hug. "I would rather give up children than you. We could be like Hank and Millie and be surrogate parents for other peoples' kids."

"Oh boy! This is so hard. Could you make my life primary in our relationship? Think about it; you've always been the center of things, heck, you're even an only child. For right now, let's just live for the moment. As for now, I see us staying together for long while, then who knows what might happen. I might change — or both of us will," she said, then began laughing.

"What's so funny? I'm dead serious," Corey said, getting a little angry.

"I know you are, but you said this night spurred random thinking. I just thought about that poster you and Hot have hanging in your apartment — the one that parodies the Gibran quote. Corey, what does your poster say?"

"Well babe,

'I did not come into this world

to meet up to your expectations.
Nor did you come into this world
to meet up with mine.
I am I, and you are you.
And if by chance our paths were to cross,
Let's just fuck our brains out'

Ouch! I told Hot we should take that down," Corey said.

"You didn't, so let's just enjoy the night," Karen said, putting her arms around him. "This could be a better night than the one at Hector's. Let's just enjoy it for what it is. After all, isn't that why we came down here in the first place — to forget about tomorrow?" She snuggled closer to him, taking his hand gently in hers, but still holding her camera in her other hand while they observed the way the moonlight reflected upon the water.

CHAPTER TWENTY

THE NEXT DAY THEY MADE JOEY STOP SURFING EARLY SO HE would be well rested for the match. Dougie, Dizzy, and Jan wanted to remain with the campers at Matachen Bay, but the rest of the group insisted they should go to town to show support for Joey. The town crowd would overwhelmingly be in support of Chicklet; besides, it would be an insult if they didn't attend the party thrown in their honor.

When they arrived, the band had set up near the foosball tables. They were playing bullfight music. Some of the shops that usually were open at night were closed so that their owners could watch the match.

When Chicklet approached the table, a loud cheer deafened any other conversation. Joey went to his corner. The clan cheered as loud as their few voices could muster. The two boys stared at each other like two boxers before a championship bout. The police chief went to the center of the table. He made the boys come together and shake hands, then they returned to their respective sides. The chief dropped the ball and the game was on.

Right from the beginning Corey saw something different about Joey. There was a calmness, an effortless motion in every limb of his body. Corey had always been amazed at how great athletes made their game look so easy. "The zenith of athletic performance was the appearance of effortlessness," he had heard some great athlete say.

The game seemed to slow down for Joey. It was like he was the only movement in a scene of suspended animation, while Chicklet rushed. His body moved in spasmodic muscle jerks. Quickly Joey was up three nothing.

A man in the crowd who Corey recognized as the owner of a small ice cream and candy shop stepped forward and said something to Chicklet. Chicklet nodded, stepped back, and took a deep breath, then nodded for the game to continue.

The next point was bitterly contested, but Chicklet lost. Joey needed only one more point to win the first set and skunk the reigning champ.

Chicklet finally scored, but it was a short-lived satisfaction as Joey easily won the next point. A collective groan rose from the disappointed crowd. Someone stepped forward and massaged Chicklet's shoulders, then the next game began.

In the blink of an eye, Joey was up two nothing. Before the next ball was set in motion, Joey requested a sip of soda and a towel to dry his hands. He looked around the crowd and saw panic and disappointment in their faces. He then looked Chicklet in the eye. All the cockiness in his manner was gone. What he saw was not fear but humiliation. Joey looked over to Corey and smiled in a way that confused Corey. The next ball dropped.

Chicklet managed to tie the score at two, then they exchanged scores until they tied at four. Since this was agreed to be a three-set match instead of five, if Joey won the next point, all would be over for Chicklet, the pride of San Blas foosball.

The final point took about ten minutes, but Chicklet won the point. He turned and smiled at the crowd, who cheered as if he were the Pope come to give mass at their church. It was now one game each and the final set was ready to begin.

No point came quickly, but Joey went up three nothing. The clan started talking about how they would spend their winnings. The citizens of San Blas were eerily quiet. Once again Joey looked at Corey, and now Corey understood. He nodded to the boy.

Once again Chicklet tied the score and lifted his hands in triumph. The crowd was back in the game and raised their collective voice as Chicklet hoisted his hands. But even with a tied score, there was still fear in the smaller boy's eyes, while Joey remained calm. They tied at four, then the last point took at least twenty minutes. Both boys' brows dripped with sweat while their mouths became dry.

Chicklet won and was immediately lifted onto Lalo's shoulders. Lalo paraded the boy among the crowd. He bent over and slapped or shook hands with nearly everyone in the crowd. At last Lalo took him to Joey, where he put him down. Chicklet extended his hand. Joey put his hand in his pocket and pulled out two quarters, which he placed in the boy's palm, then he gave the boy a hug and shook his hand.

The police chief announced that it was time to party at Enrique's.

"I'll be there in a few minutes," Corey said to the police chief, then he and Karen went to Joey.

"I think the ice cream shop will be opening in a few minutes. They make the best strawberry ice cream I've ever tasted. Karen and I would like to buy you a cone. I'm sure you worked up quite an appetite."

As Corey thought, the ice cream shop lights came on. Several people entered. Chicklet remained in the crowd, glowing with ecstasy as congratulations were being continuously bestowed.

Once inside the shop, Corey ordered three strawberry cones. "Make one a double for the boy."

The man finished making the cones. He handed Joey his and in broken English said, "The boy's is free."

"I'll gladly pay," Corey said. The man shook his head no.

"The boy you call 'Chicklet' is my only son, Niko. We lost his mother when Niko was six. It's been hard. Tonight he's a town hero and very happy. The boy's cone is free."

Corey paid for his and Karen's, then the three of them walked over to Enrique's. Inside Hot came over to Joey.

"I thought you had him. It was a helluva fight. He had the

home field advantage though." Joey smiled and said to Hot, "When in Rome —"

The band had moved inside and an evening of drinking and dancing began. The police chief came over to Corey.

"I'm going to have to attend to some police business; you all stay here until I get back. I want to buy you all one drink before the evening is over."

Joey was the first person up in the morning. He had fallen asleep in the back of Turk's van and was the only one to get a good night's sleep. The rest of the clan partied until almost two in the morning and had more than enough to drink.

Joey was careful not to wake anyone, but he wanted to get surfing early. He returned immediately and woke everyone.

"The beach is completely empty," he said excitedly. "There's not a single surfer or hippie in sight."

Everyone woke. Sure enough, the beach was empty. A few abandoned campfires were the only thing that remained. Carmen, the owner of the huts, came out and spoke in Spanish to Spook.

"During the night the Federales came and arrested everyone on the beach because of drugs," she explained.

Immediately, Jan protested to the others. "Those kids weren't hurting anybody. It's just another way to steal money from tourists; just like what happened to us in Ensenada."

"It's kind of cool that we got the bay to ourselves. This is the way it was when Corey and I first came here," Hot said.

"What about those kids, and just before Christmas?" Dougie remarked.

"They'll spend a few days in jail, maybe through Christmas. We did try to warn them.

Eventually they'll discover 'mordita,' just like it worked for you girls in Ensenada," Turk added. "It's exploitation anyway you look at it," Jan said.

"I don't know," Corey said. "To me this is kind of like what's going on in Vietnam. We go into a foreign country and invoke our morals and beliefs without regard for the traditions of the people who lived there all their lives, and we end up in a mess."

"I hate to say it, but those kids don't care about the Mexicans who live here. They didn't care that their behavior was an insult to local beliefs. Look at us, we partied all night because we just showed respect for their ways," Karen added.

"Why should they care what those kids did as long as they weren't forcing the locals to join in?" Jan continued to argue.

"It just is," Corey said. "Guess we know why Lalo and the police chief, Reuben, wanted us to party and stay late.

"Let's take advantage of the surf," Hot said. "There's nothing we can do about it anyway."

Karen took Corey aside. "You don't need to surf right away, do you? The beach will be empty all day."

"What do you have in mind?"

Karen smiled. "The other night was almost as good as the one at Hector's. Last night went late, so let's just stay in bed awhile longer."

CHAPTER TWENTY-ONE

THEY GOT BACK ON DECEMBER 23, AND EVERYONE HEADED somewhere for Christmas. Christy and Jan either could not or did not want to return to Olmsteadville, so Christy went home with Hot while Jan accompanied Dougie back to Montauk for the holidays, saying that was as close as she wanted to get to Olmsteadville. Turk decided he would visit his older brother in the San Fernando Valley. They had never been close, but Turk said he needed to at least make an attempt to reunite some kind of friendly relationship with his brother.

Corey was sure his father would welcome him home, at least for Christmas. He had bought some gifts in San Blas and wanted to give them to his parents as a peace offering, and, if nothing else, his parents had always stressed that the holidays were a time families should put aside their differences and spend quality time together. Just to be on the safe side, when he reached San Clemente, he pulled off and stopped by his parent's beach house. He called home to say he was coming and what time he thought he would arrive. His father answered the phone.

"Dad, we just got back from a surfing trip to Mexico. I got some things for you and mom. I should be there around four."

There was a pause before his father answered. "I hate to have to ask this since your mother and I are looking forward to having you home, but did you get your hair cut?"

"No, I haven't. But come on, it's Christmas. There is even a truce in Vietnam. Let's put aside our differences for a few days."

"I told you the rules. It's my home, and it is very simple — either you comply, or stay down there."

"Merry Christmas anyway. Can you put Mom on? I would like to wish her happy holidays also," Corey said and waited.

Finally, his mom came to the phone. Her voice sounded weak. "Honey," she said, "hair seems like such a silly thing to mess up our Christmas together. Would you get it cut for me? You can start growing it back for the rest of the year."

"Mom, when I was a little kid we would go back to Iowa and visit your parents. Grandpa would take me fishing or something else just as neat. But the times I remember best were just sitting around and listening to you and Grandma talk about when you were a little girl. You seemed so happy. I know you never wanted to leave your hometown. But you did because you loved Dad and were willing to follow whatever path he wanted ... and you followed. Mom, are you happy now?"

There was a long silence before she said, "That's a very cruel question."

"I didn't mean it to be. I love you and Dad very much and always will, but, Mom, I've got to find my own road and begin my own journey. You must know why I feel that way. It's why you thought my question cruel. Do you want me to allow Dad to dictate my future like he did yours? I'm sorry ... don't answer that. I know you love me and want what is best for me. Maybe, through time, you can help me make him see why I feel the way I do. Maybe I'll discover that I'm wrong and will be apologizing to the both of you, but for now, well, I just want you to know I love you very much and wish you a Merry Christmas."

There was another period of silence before his mom answered. "I love you too. I wish you weren't as stubborn as your father and would just get your hair cut. You are more like him than you would ever admit, but I understand. Hope to see you soon. I love you too," she repeated.

Corey headed back to Mission Beach, trying to figure out why he felt so low when just a few days ago he experienced such a high. He stopped at the store to pick up a few groceries and thought about calling Karen. He was sure that she would either invite him to her parents' home in Fallbrook or would return to San Diego to be with him. He knew the relationship she had with her parents was not strained like his own and she looked forward to being with them during the holidays. He didn't want to spoil her Christmas because he was feeling lonely and wanted company. He headed back to Mission Beach without calling her.

Back at his apartment, he pulled out his Vanderhoof assignment. He had been thinking about his paper all the way back from San Blas. The events in the small village made him want to write; not just to write the paper for the professor, but for himself. Somehow he felt the dilemmas of Ahab and Huck were about everyday human choices which was Professor Vanderhoof's motive for the assignment in the first place. Yet when he tried to write, he could only think of more questions than answers, at least not easily recognizable answers. He began thinking about Ahab, and what a lonely man he must have been, as lonely as Corey felt presently. Corey knew his own solitude would pass, but what would it do to a man to feel as lonely as Corey felt at that moment ... but feel like that all the time? The thought scared him. He didn't want to know the answer. Ahab had no friends in which to confide. His hatred for the whale sustained his only emotional outlet. How awful would it be to have hate as your only emotional outlet?

Corey put down his pen and thought until the word compassion entered his mind. Huck had compassion, even for scoundrels like the Duke and King. It was as if the boy instinctively knew that meaning in life is not something revealed by isolation, but through relationships with others ... Almost as if our purpose in life can only be revealed through our interactions with others. Where was compassion in Ahab? He thumbed through the yellow highlighting he had done in Melville's novel. He found not one single instance of compassion in Ahab. Without compassion for his fellow men, Ahab had no regard for their lives and made them pawns to carry out his insane vengeance against the whale.

Suddenly he saw the comparison between Melville and Twain. The God they saw, the God their contemporaries revered, seemed to have no compassion for the congregations that worshiped him. Pestilence, war, natural disaster — all killed and maimed randomly. God seemed to have no moral sense, no compassion himself, and yet expected his flock to worship him for his mercy? How the hell could they be such easy believers? They should be shouting, "God damn you, God," as Twain once uttered to a minister friend.

Before Corey had another thought, there was a knock on the front door which startled him. He could not imagine who it was, but instantly his mood shifted at the sound of another person. He gladly put down his pen and went to the door. It was Joey.

"What are you doing here?" Joey asked, as surprised at seeing Corey as Corey was at seeing the boy.

"What are you doing out on this cold Christmas Eve night?" Corey asked.

"I saw the light and thought maybe you guys left it on. I was going to let myself in, (they had given Joey a key in case of emergencies), but I thought I better knock first," Joey said.

Corey told him of his confrontation with his father, then asked Joey why he wasn't home with his mom on Christmas Eve. "She wanted me out of the house because she's got a new boyfriend. You know what she meant? They don't want me around so they can fuck. Mom thinks I don't know what she does with all her boyfriends. I was heading to Eric's when I noticed the light," he explained.

"Give her the benefit of the doubt. Maybe she doesn't want you around because, in her own way, she feels guilty having you around while she's having sex. But since I'm here, I'd rather you stay here than go to Eric's. In fact, if neither Hot nor I were here, I'd want you to feel welcomed here; that's why we gave you the key in the first place. Since Hot is not here, you don't have to sleep on the couch either. You can use Hot's bed, unless of course you like looking at all those fertility gods at Eric's?"

"Yeah, right! To be honest, I was going to spend the night here figuring you guys wouldn't mind. I'm sorry about what happened between you and your pa, but I'm glad you're here. I really don't like being alone, especially on Christmas Eve."

Corey put away his notebook, then went to the closet where he pulled out a brown paper bag. "I didn't have time to wrap this cuz I was planning to wrap it at home and give it to you when I got back. Merry Christmas," he said, and gave the boy the bag.

Inside was a new baseball glove. Joey's eyes lit up as he pulled out the glove. The smell of new leather permeated the room. "Wow!" he said, but his eyes showed even greater delight than his voice. "I wasn't expecting anything from you. I don't have anything to give you."

"You just did, kiddo, you just did. Now give me the mitt for a second. I want to teach you something about how to care for a new glove."

Corey put the glove on his hand, popped his fist into the pocket a few times.

"You play shortstop; that's why this glove is small. Middle infielders only catch the ball on tag plays and put outs. The rest of the time they are just blocking the ball, so they can get rid of it quickly. If you oil it or soak in water, you break down the leather fiber. Soften it too much and it starts looking like a taco. This is the proper way you break in a new glove. Take a ball and put it just above the heel, then fold the little finger under the thumb and tie a string around it. If you check that bag, you should find a jar in there."

Joey pulled out a plastic jar. 'Mink Oil,' it said on the label.

"Mink oil is the only thing you put on your glove and just a little bit at a time. You don't want your glove to dry out and crack either. Mink oil will keep the leather its natural self.

Unfortunately, it smells like a bedroom after sex, which I shouldn't have said since you won't appreciate that comment for a few years."

The boy laughed, opened the jar, and smelled the contents. "Shit! Does sex smell like that?" "Like I said, you are a few years away yet from appreciating that. You ready for some dinner? I bought some sliced turkey and Swiss cheese. Bought a ham to cook tomorrow." Corey went into the kitchen to fix dinner. The boy followed.

"You still love baseball, don't you?" Joey asked.

"What makes you think that?" Corey replied.

"Nobody would talk about caring for a glove like you just did unless they loved the game. It was your voice too. It sounded the same way as when you talk about Karen."

Corey laughed. "Baseball was my first real love until I met Karen, but don't tell her what you just said or else she'll think I compare her to a baseball glove."

"So why did you quit playing?"

"That's a hard question to answer." Corey paused, then sighed. "Remember last year when I took you and couple of your friends over to the park and threw you guys some balls for batting practice?"

"Yeah."

"You started laughing at me and I asked you why. You said because I always grin while I pitch," Corey said.

"And you said because you were having fun," Joey said.

"I was, but there was another reason. When I looked at your face, I was looking in the mirror — I was seeing myself when I was your age. You wanted to hit. You weren't watching where the ball went. You just wanted the next pitch. Your expression was just like I'd seen on the best hitters I'd ever played with. I'd like to think I had that look at one time."

"So, doesn't everybody?"

"Nope, your friends didn't. They were out there because that's what kids do at that age. They surprised themselves when they hit a ball hard and had to stop and watch it." Joey still wore a puzzled expression, so Corey continued.

"I once played the game because I loved it, but I lost that sometime in high school when it became about results and getting a scholarship. When I got the scholarship, I became a poster boy for the school's athletic program and bragging rights for my father at the country club. I began playing for other people's agendas. I was playing because it was expected of me. What I did on the field was who I became."

Corey put a plate with a turkey sandwich and some potato salad in front of the boy. "Milk or water?"

"Milk," Joey answered. "But you still love the game, so I don't understand why you quit."

"My freshman year I had a great year because I was still playing more out of my passion for the game than headlines. My sophomore year started out just as solid. The whole team was playing well. We were in second place — an unusually high ranking for a school not known for winning records in baseball. We had a weekend series against the first-place team and we were only one game behind in the standings.

On Friday, the first game of the series, we were in a two-to-two tie. They had a runner on second with two outs. I was in center field, and all I could think was hit the ball to me and I'm going to throw that guy's ass out at the plate. Sure enough, the hitter hit one up the middle. I got a great jump, charged, fielded the ball cleanly, and made a quick strong throw to the plate. From the corner of my eyes, I saw the runner just rounding third. Ha! I thought. I've got him, except for one thing. My throw was too strong. I watched it sail right over my catcher's head, and the go ahead run scored. I couldn't wait to get into the dugout. I was third up and I knew I would make up for that error."

My coach didn't say a word. The lead-off hitter walked, and the next guy bunted him over. I walked up to the plate knowing I would drive him in. I had no thought of failure, only my inevitable success. Just before I stepped in the batter's box, my coach yelled 'time.' He called me away and put in a pinch hitter. The guy he put in wasn't ready. He struck out. I sat out the last inning and watched us lose. I had never experienced such a low in anything I'd ever done in sports as I did then.

There was silence in the locker room. Several of my teammates came over to console me, which struck me as odd. I made the right play. I aggressively, with no thought of failure, made that throw. I made an error, then that son-of-a-bitch coach took away my opportunity to right it.

And he did so by embarrassing me, by letting me go all the way up to the plate before calling for the pinch hitter. I've played for all kinds of coaches, and none of them ever got into my head like that.

I didn't think it could get much worse until what happened next. Just as guys were undressing to shower, coach came into the center of the room and told everyone to take a seat. He spoke real calm and quiet at first.

He said, 'When I was in high school, we made it to the city championship game. We were up by one and had two outs on the other team in the last inning, but they had the tying and winning run on second and third.'

His expression was as if he were alone in his living room looking at a home movie of the game. He was not in the present with us but alone in a bad memory. At first I thought instead of being mad, he was going to tell some inspiring story to get us up for the two remaining games, but instead he tells us, 'The hitter hit a routine grounder to short. He makes the routine play and we are city champions.' Then his voice changed and anger rose. 'But you know what he did? He threw the ball away.'

He looked around the room at everyone but me. Then he shouted, 'He threw the ball away! All that work, all that glory we had fought so hard to attain and he threw the fuckin' ball away.'

By then his face was red, his eyes bulged, and the veins in his neck swelled the way a balloon does when being filled with water from a garden hose. He walked over to me and screamed, 'He threw the fuckin' ball away.'

Spit spewed from his mouth as he shouted and hit me in the face. Then he shouted again, sounding madder still. I don't know why, but I took off my uniform. Naked, I walked toward the shower.

'I'm not finished,' he shouted.

I didn't stop. I walked right into the shower, turned it on, and began washing myself. Fully dressed, he followed me in. Water splashed off my body and began getting him wet.

'He threw the ball away,' he shouted several more times, his nose almost touching mine he was so close. Finally, he threw up his hands in disgust and walked to the coach's locker room. My teammates were stunned. They waited for me to finish showering before anyone else began.

I gathered my uniform, folded it neatly, and went to the coach's locker room. I knocked and he came to the door. I handed him the uniform and said, 'Looks like you always lose the big ones.' Well, that was that. I told my dad and almost everyone else who was following my career that I quit because of an arm injury. Said the sore arm was what probably caused my bad throw. I told them it wasn't fair to the team to try and play hurt. I lied to save face, but you just heard the truth."

"I still think you want to play," Joey said with a wry smile.

"Maybe, but I'm honest with myself now. I'm good enough to play college, but probably not beyond, but that's not important. What's important is I lost my passion for playing. It's easy to blame it on the coach for what he did, but I don't. I recognize he did what he did because he thought it was the right thing. Hell, he was probably the player that threw the ball away and his coach chewed his ass just like he chewed mine. That's sort of the way things seem to work; we teach the way we were taught. I hope I've learned enough so if I ever coach, I would never do that to a young player."

Corey paused again, then continued, "As much as I liked

baseball then, I like surfing now because it gives me the same high as baseball once did."

"Honestly," Joey said, "I think I like baseball more."

"Well good, as long as it is fun, keep playing. I've come to think that whatever anyone does they do it because the activity itself is the high, not the result. It's like when you're trying to catch a wave. You paddle like hell and don't think about nothing else but catching that wave. Then it happens — the wave catches you. You feel yourself falling into its magical force. Whether or not you get a four-second tube ride or wipe out, that thrill, that adrenaline rush is always the same, and it is what keeps you wanting to come back for one more ride."

Joey said nothing for a while, nor did Corey. Finally, Joey said, "Sometimes a double strawberry ice cream cone is all the reward you need, right?"

"Yeah," Corey said. "Exactly. Now let's pop some popcorn for dessert and plan what we are going to do tomorrow, roomie. I'll let you make the decision. Do we go to church or surf New Break?"

"Church?" Joey said, frowning his brow. "I've hardly ever been to church in my life. Not to worship anyways."

"Yeah, it's surfing then."

"Corey, can I ask you a serious question?" "Depends. About what?"

"I know you were kidding when you said church, but all my friends go to church. They invite me from time to time and I've gone to church or church functions with them, usually around Christmas or Easter, but I feel weird cause I don't know how to do religious things. If there is a God, shouldn't I be going to church?"

"I didn't mean to have a religious talk with you, although I guess this is about as religious a holiday as we have. To answer your first question ... I don't know, but if God is real, I don't think he's anything like what I was led to believe when I went to church when I was younger. I've pretty much concluded that when you're doing something you love, like playing baseball or surfing, you're more likely to find God in those activities rather than in a building. Good chance with tomorrow being Christmas morn, we're likely to have New Break all to ourselves, and that would be heaven to me."

Joey looked a little bewildered, so Corey said, "You know that old man Hank I always talk about? One time we were camping in the Sierras, sitting under some shady pines near a stream. We were just enjoying the serenity and the lulling sound from the stream when Hank says, 'You know our entire galaxy is simply made of gases. Somehow our tiny planet was given two atoms of hydrogen mixed with one atom of oxygen, then simmered with the right amount of heat from the sun to turn the gases to water, thus causing this planet to come to life. People complain about things, talk about bad breaks, injustices, or just plain bitch. Seems like everyone thinks they're entitled to something more than what they were given. Just sit by this stream and look at the water; it's the rarest commodity in our known universe. What more do you need than these two gifts? The sun is our father and water is the milk from our mother's breast.'"

"He said that?" Joey asked.

"Yes, although not exactly in those words, but that's the gist of it, and why I think surfing tomorrow is just as good as church. Now let's turn in so we can get up early."

"Good night," Joey said, then added, "Thanks. This turned out to be a pretty neat Christmas after all."

CHAPTER TWENTY-TWO

Outside of a light fog and haze from a chilly northern breeze, New Break looked inviting with six to eight-foot waves. The rising sun penetrated the clear water so the waves seemed almost artificially translucent. The ocean floor at New Break was rock bottom so even big surf rarely kicked up sand clouds, which was why the water always appeared clearer at New Break than most other surfing spots along the California coast.

The cliffs were jagged, shaped by erosion over a long period of time. The only visible sand was maybe a fifty-yard sunken beach between the rocks and the cliffs. The land above the cliffs was owned by Cal Western University, which had not developed the land, so it had looked like it was now for several hundred years.

The boys slowly climbed down the cliffs, then eyed the

waves from the sandy beach. As expected, they were the only ones there on a Saturday morning, with near perfectly shaped waves, an occurrence that could only happen on Christmas morning. The only other life was a pelican gliding low across the face of the water, fishing as he did every morning. The bird knew no significance to this morning as he did any other.

"You get the feeling that we are standing on the first morning of creation, don't you?"

"Awesome," Joey answered.

The water was cold, so even in a full body wet suit they would only be able to withstand the cold for an hour or so, but being the only surfers, and plenty of waves, they would catch any wave they desired.

Had Hot been with them, he would have broken the morning silence on numerous waves, shouting his cries of jubilation for friends who got great rides. But to Corey and Joey that morning was their church, and they silently preyed upon the waves like the pelican quietly preyed upon the fish, only their silence was out of reverence, not stealth.

Maybe because they caught so many waves, or maybe because they rarely fell into the cold water, they surfed longer than they planned. It was an hour and a half before they returned to shore, and just as they did, they heard voices among the tumbling rock as two more surfers climbed down the cliffs.

They recognized the first surfer to hit the sand – Aaron. The guy behind him was a short stocky guy who looked to be in his early thirties. Corey knew him too. He was a local rogue everyone called Mad Dog. It was rumored that Mad Dog had done prison time for mayhem he dispensed on a person in a bar room brawl. He got his nickname because of the way he growled and went crazy in any fight.

Aaron spotted Corey and Joey, then turned and whispered something in Mad Dog's ear.

Mad Dog gave them a sinister smile.

"Keep quiet and stay behind me," Corey whispered.

Aaron and Mad Dog walked directly toward the two of them. Mad Dog got close to Corey's face. Mad Dog was about three inches shorter than Corey. He had a scar above his right eye and on his left cheek.

"I understand that kid with you dodged an initiation because of you," he said to Corey.

Corey, as a boy, had boxed "golden gloves". He had learned to read faces, and he knew immediately that a fight was inevitable. Whenever Corey fought, instead of tensing, he relaxed. He felt a calmness that slowed everything down and gave him an edge over his opponent.

"The waves are great. Aaron, why don't you and your friend surf all to yourself. Joey and I were just leaving," Corey said, but did not take his eye off Mad Dog.

"Oh, we will, but first why don't you and the boy take off your trunks and give them to us along with your wet suits?" Mad Dog said, then he tried a quick sucker punch.

Corey expected the blow and stepped aside. Before Mad Dog could regain his balance, Corey landed three quick, left-handed jabs into Mad Dog's nose. On the third one, there was a dull crack and blood spurted from his nose.

Mad Dog growled and began swinging wildly. Corey delivered a powerful right upper cut that landed firmly on Mad Dog's chin. His head snapped back and before he landed on the sand, his eyes rolled back so nothing but white showed in his eye orbits. He was out before he hit the ground.

Suddenly, Corey felt a blow hit him on the side of his head. He had trouble staying conscious and fell to his hands and knees where Aaron kicked him in the ribs and was about to kick him again when Corey heard a crack, then a loud groan, as Aaron fell to the sand. He put his hand over his forehead, blood oozed from between his fingers.

Corey looked up and saw Joey, rock in hand, standing over Aaron.

"I'm going to kill you, you little bastard," Aaron said, grabbing the boy's heel and lifting it up, so Joey fell onto his back. Aaron pulled back his fist, but never threw a punch. Corey recovered and caught Aaron's arm. He hit Aaron with three powerful rights. Aaron sprawled on the sand completely unconscious.

Joey walked to the still body, rock still in hand. Corey stopped the boy.

"The fight's over. We won. Now let's get out of here. When Mad Dog wakes up, that crazy bastard won't know he lost and will want to fight some more," Corey said and pushed Joey toward his board.

. . .

After they got to Corey's apartment, Corey put an ice bag on the side of his head, started the ham, then called Karen. When he told her about not being able to go home for Christmas, she immediately told him that he should have called her. "You could have come here," she said.

"I know, that's why I didn't call until today. You are close with your family and should spend Christmas with them, but if you want to come back to school a little early, I won't mind that," Corey said.

Then he told her about meeting Aaron and Mad Dog and about the fight. "On Christmas Day?"

"Letting that happen, I feel like a fool." "Was there any way to avoid it?"

"Yeah, if Joey and I would have walked naked back to my car."

"It was inevitable. Hope you kicked their butts good. Tell Joey I owe him a kiss for smokin' Aaron."

CHAPTER TWENTY-THREE

COREY WAS PLEASANTLY SURPRISED THAT HIS FATHER'S banishment worked to Corey's advantage. With so many of the Mission Beach residents being college students who were visiting family during the holidays, the beach seemed deserted. Without the excessive sounds of human voices and their noise machines, the repetitive sound of the ocean and the constant northern wind provided an atmospheric mantra conducive for contemplation. He began each morning surfing with Joey at any one of San Diego's good winter breaks, then went back to his apartment to work on the Vanderhoof assignment.

The problem that had been blocking him from progressing in his term paper was removing his own moral dilemma concerning the Vietnam War from those of the characters in the novels by the two authors. Just before leaving for San Blas, he went into Professor Vanderhoof's office to talk to him about his quandary.

"Having a difficult time, are you," the professor said, not asked. "Well, good. Hard will make your ultimate resolution more enlightening."

"Enlightening it is, but where the trouble lies is in finding satisfactory answers," Corey replied. "Sometimes I think the assignment is a lifetime sentence, not a semester task."

"Thank you," the professor said. "That makes me feel like a teacher, not a court stenographer."

Then he asked, "Have you ever read William Faulkner's acceptance speech for winning the Nobel Prize for literature?"

Corey's expression answered for him: no.

"He said the essence of all good writing shows

> *'the human heart in conflict with itself ... because only that is worth writing about.'*

If Melville and Twain are worthy writers — well, you answer the rest."

Corey left the professor's office feeling the assignment got more difficult, not easier. The San Blas excursion made him forget about his paper altogether until he sat on the unusually quiet Mission Beach strand, where the ocean's peaceful hymn coupled with the revelations from the recent trip put him into a meditative state of mind.

"The human heart is in conflict with itself. What does

that mean?" Corey thought. "The heart doesn't think. It's an engine that works to provide blood and nutrients to the body because the brain orders it to function that way." Then he began to think about watching cartoons when he was little kid. Often some animated character was depicted as having to make a choice. On one shoulder was a caricature of the devil urging him to do the wrong thing, while an angel sat on the other side pleading for him to make the right choice. The devil always based his case on the material gain rendered for choosing his side, while the angel appealed to him to do what his heart told him was right.

The Greeks talked about "logos" and "mythos." "Logos" required you to contemplate the laws and customs of the society in which you lived in order to be a good citizen. "Mythos" on the other hand dealt with legend and intuition. Laws dictate the actions required of its citizens, but then "there is a place where laws end and people begin," as Faulkner so eloquently stated in the *Reivers*. "Human spirit, people, are connected by the struggles we share with all living creatures."

Huck was on a journey to whose end was some city, but he had no idea as to where that was. By everything Huck had been taught, not only was what he was doing against the law, but it was also immoral by accepted religious beliefs. Not only was what he was doing subject to criminal punishment, but also to eternal damnation. Yet on the raft he discovered exactly who he was, a friend to Jim, the slave, who Huck realized shared all the love, the humor, the passions ... the human spirit that Huck felt. That bond was stronger than those of both man-made law and God. That conclusion came from leaving civilization and just trusting what felt like the right thing to do.

"Wow! Talk about the human heart in conflict with itself," Corey thought. but then he wondered, "What about Ahab?" He remembered the two cartoon characters and realized Vanderhoof had said to compare and contrast the novels. Corey's focus had been on doing a comparison. Both Ahab and Huck were confined on a vessel headed toward an unsure location, and both were surrounded by water, which made for obvious comparisons, but that's where it ended. Ahab was oblivious to his crew. They were merely pawns in his personal chess game.

Ahab demanded to know why the creator made the whale, which Ahab perceived as an evil force of destruction that he was destined to destroy, yet all the while it was Ahab who chased the whale and not the other way around. Ahab never showed a hint of empathy for his men, while Huck felt uplifted by connecting his emotions with Jim, which in turn made him realize his interconnectedness with all of mankind.

"When you understand the importance of where you are, then your destination is inconsequential," Corey wrote. *"Ahab needed certainty of purpose to define good and evil so he could be like God and make moral judgment. Huck, when he let go of the moral sense, found something satisfying by the journey itself, where Ahab could not."*

Corey glanced at the twenty typed pages he had before him. He had compared and contrasted many aspects of the novels. There was the symbolism of the journeys on water; there were supernatural beliefs; there were the concepts of the "moral sense" and "easy believers." He expanded on the moral dilemmas of Huck and Starbuck. He introduced the idea that Huck, who put friendship before the laws of man, found peace of mind, but Ahab had no friends and no sympathy for his fellow voyagers, which ultimately led to the death and destruction of himself and crew.

Now that the paper was done, it somehow seemed not long enough, yet too long. It still seemed unfinished. He attached a note to the professor.

Dear Professor Vanderhoof:

This is not intended to be an addition to my paper, nor an attempt to get bonus points; it is merely an observation I wish to share.

I have come to realize that this assignment is not a one-semester task, nor did you intend it to be. But rather it will be the beginning of a lifetime deliberation. Interesting, isn't it, that the word liberate is contained within the word deliberation? I have agonized many hours and poured over these two authors. Not just the two novels in question, but many of their other works and private letters. At times the jock in me came out and I called you a "motherfucker." In the end, I felt liberated not because I finished the assignment, but because I felt the awakening of a new beginning. Maybe there is no such thing as an end, simply just new beginnings. I wonder if that is why the bible starts with, "In the beginning ..."

Thank you,

Corey Jameson

CHAPTER TWENTY-FOUR

THE SECOND SEMESTER OF THEIR SENIOR YEAR HAD BEGUN. All the fears, the anxieties felt at the beginning of the year, were accentuated by it being just four and a half months away from having to face either the draft, leaving the country, or going to jail. Graduation was secondary.

Then if things were not alarming enough, the whole thing was exacerbated by the announcement that there would be a career day set aside during the first week of the second semester. No one objected to booths being erected to expand upon future opportunities. Except for one — Dow Chemical was to have a booth.

On the cover of a recent issue of *Life* magazine was shown a young Vietnamese girl fleeing from a burning village, a village set fire by a napalm bomb. The little girl, about six or seven, was naked and crying from both fear and pain caused by blistering burns from napalm. The cover of the magazine had become a popular poster for the anti-war movement. Dow Chemical, the manufacturer and chief supplier of napalm, had become the symbol of the evil created by the military industrial complex. Although agricultural products, medicines for healthcare, and building materials for new and better homes were the bulk of the company's production and research was forgotten, profits from war material like napalm — which resulted in the maiming and killing of children like the little girl on the magazine cover — was the focal point of the anti-war group oppositions to Dow Chemical.

Corey knew of all the good things Dow Chemical did, and to condemn them for manufacturing napalm seemed ridiculous except for one thing. He and the clan, during one of their many evening talk sessions, kept coming back to one significant point about the Vietnam War in comparison to other US wars of the twentieth century. Patriotism was not being invoked but rather forced. Opposition to the war needed a rallying banner, and the manufacturer of napalm, Dow, provided that instrument.

Both in World Wars I and II, the United States had been attacked. Protecting one's own homeland invoked a surge of patriotism. Most of the leaders in America had fought in World War II and had vivid memories of the attack on Pearl Harbor. But the generation closest to Corey's age were the Korean War veterans, and they were the first generation asked to fight a war in the name of the international policing concept.

Congress declared war in earlier wars but not in Korea. It was a police action sold as a preventative step to avoid the US from being directly attacked. The soldiers coming back from Korea were confused. They had fought for containment, not victory. Corey and Hot both said they never once played a game in which they tried to make it a tie game. They said if they ever had a coach who asked them not to win, they'd find another sport or ask the coach to resign. In sport, they were putting their honor on the line, but in war it was your life at stake. All the Korean War vets they knew were disillusioned by that war.

One of America's most popular generals and war heroes, Douglas MacArthur, resigned over being unable to win the war. Yet the same containment policy was once again being employed in Vietnam. It was a police action, but rather than getting its police from people who choose that line of work, they used the draft concept, which began at age eighteen when draftees were too young to vote.

Corey's father and his friends had reminded their sons that looked at defending their country as earning the right to vote. When Corey pointed out that the average draft age in World War II was twenty-six, while in Vietnam it was nineteen, he was dismissed as missing the point. Corey agreed *someone* was missing the point.

One of the reasons so many young white kids not only picked up the anti-war placards, but joined forces with civil rights groups, woman's liberation, ecology advocates, and other minority voices, was because as non-voting draft-eligible citizens, they represented such a small percent of the population. Aligning themselves with minorities who had voting rights, but not equality, gave them a more powerful voice. Most of Corey's peers had read John Kennedy's *Profiles of Courage* and knew what international law had been invoked at the Nuremburg trials. In essence, it was said that there was a higher law than man-made law. Further, you could not dodge your responsibility of that higher law by pleading that you were following orders from superiors or your government. Hot called it a no brainer — the US was using a mandatory draft for a police action that the majority of Corey's generation found to be an immoral war, and because of the Nuremburg trials, they had every right to oppose it. To demonstrate against Dow and to march in Mississippi were the same thing — a chance for a minority coalition to make their voices heard by the ruling majority.

A couple of days before career day, a number of new faces appeared on campus. They were young, maybe early twenties, perhaps recent graduates, but they were not students. They engaged the students in small groups and talked mostly about the "military industrial complex," but also other minority issues. They handed out leaflets with quotes from hippie leaders like Abbie Hoffman and Mario Savio. Corey picked a couple of them up and took them back to the Surf Rider for the rest of the clan to read.

> *Become an internationalist and learn to respect all life. Make war on machines. And in particular*

the sterile machines of corporate death and robots that guard them.
- *Abbie Hoffman*

And:

There is a time when the operation of the machine becomes so odious, makes you so sick at heart, that you can't take part, you can't even passively take part, and you've got to put your bodies upon the gears and upon the levers, upon all the apparatus, and you've got to make it stop. And you've got to indicate to the people who run it, to the people who own it, that unless you're free, the machine will be prevented from working at all.
- *Mario Savio*

In Corey's mind, it was unfortunate that Dow was the target, but there had to be a target. Somehow, his generation needed to make his parents' generation realize that the conditions of their time were no longer applicable to his generation. Also, ever since their return from San Blas, Corey was going through a change in his own emotions.

When the clan was protected from the raid on the beach at Matachan Bay; when the party was thrown in their honor at Enrique's; when he saw the enthusiasm for both Chicklet and Joey at the foosball showdown, Corey began feeling a strong spiritual connectedness to all of mankind. Simply by respecting the rights of other people, even if you disagreed with some of their beliefs, peaceful opposition was more powerful than antagonism. Then when he wrote his paper and thought about universal verities, he became more convinced that you had to embrace friendships and expand humanitarian causes.

He and Hot invited the clan and a few other friends to their apartment the night before the demonstration. Spook and Dawn brought a poster they had made and intended to display at the rally. The poster had pictures of bodies piled up outside a German concentration camp. The bodies were emaciated, naked, and contorted in gruesome display. Then there was a picture of a huge mushroom cloud explosion in the Nevada desert. Next there were several pictures of the mass destruction of Hiroshima and Nagasaki after their bombing during World War II. At the bottom, in bold, blood-red, dripping letters it read, "When Will It Stop?"

Eric had come to the meeting and announced that he was going to be at the demonstration in a working capacity. He was to be a photographer for a small local underground newspaper called *Voice of the People*.

The only one not in attendance was Turk. He told them that his sympathies were with the protesters, but at the same time he felt empathy for the soldiers in Vietnam. "They don't want to be there anymore than you guys don't want to go. They're just unlucky because the system is so fucked up."

The more they talked about taking part in the demonstration, the more excited they got. Corey's feeling that he was taking part in something larger than himself made the notion of spiritual connectedness and universal conscious grow stronger.

Dougie expressed their feelings best of all when he said, "This is going to be more fun than the San Blas trip."

The festive mood that Dougie hoped for was well in progress when the clan arrived the next day. The grass square in the center of campus was filled with students and outside sympathizers. The career booths were assembled along the perimeter of the square, with the Dow display at the south corner. The majority of the crowd was packed in front of that display. A young man playing the guitar was leading the congregation, who were singing "We Shall Overcome."

The Dow booth was manned by two young men who looked to be recent college graduates themselves. Although they wore coat and tie, their hair, neatly combed, was still longer than the stereotypical businessman's. "A good move on Dow's part," thought Corey.

A young man Corey had never seen on campus before stood in front of the Dow booth. He appeared to be a spokesman for the demonstration. By contrast, his hair was much longer and slightly unfurled. He wore faded bell-bottom jeans with holes in one knee. His shirt was collared with long sleeves and decorated by small orange and pink wildflower patterns. In his hand, he held a blow-up picture of the *Life* magazine cover of the burned child.

"What do you feel when you see this picture?" he shouted

at the two Dow men. The crowd applauded the question, then grew quiet as the Dow men answered.

"Pity," said one.

"Sadness," said the other.

"Do either one of you feel responsibility?"

The crowd cheered wildly at the question. Neither of the Dow men tried to talk until the roar of the crowd quieted down. Corey noticed about a dozen campus police arrived and moved toward the booth. Before the Dow men could answer the second question, the protester began a new line of questioning.

"If you manufactured steel and I came to you wanting to buy steel to make leg braces for crippled people, would you sell it to me?"

The Dow men hesitated and looked at each other. They assumed every question from the young man was a trick question, bait for a trap.

Finally, one of the young men answered, "If I manufactured steel and you were a legitimate company, yes."

"Then what if I came to you wanting to buy steel to make bullets?" All noise stopped as the crowd waited for the answer.

"If you were a reputable manufacturer of ammunition, working for a firm making bullets for the United States government, who would be using the bullets to protect our shores from aggressors, of course I would."

The protester walked over closer to the Dow booth, but

looked around the crowd for several seconds before turning to face the young men.

"Then you are saying that the bullets would be used to keep the peace, huh, sheriff?" he asked, trying to sound like John Wayne.

The crowd laughed; some applauded, others just jeered. The protester spotted Spook's poster. He pointed to Spook.

"You, please, come here."

Spook walked up to the young man, who pointed to the picture of the atom bomb exploding in the Nevada desert.

"This was supposed to be a weapon that would keep the peace." He then pointed to the pictures of the aftermath of the bombing of the Japanese cities. "This instrument of peace killed two hundred and twenty-five thousand people, the majority of whom were private citizens."

There was a collective gasp from the crowd.

"About half of those people died immediately. The other half slowly died a painful death from the burns. It took several days for them to be laid to rest. Yes, two hundred and twenty-five thousand souls were laid to rest in peace."

The crowd cheered again. Behind the crowd Corey noticed a police captain began speaking into his radio. There was no way to hear what he was saying or to know who he was talking with.

Once again the crowd quieted and the young protester, whose voice sounded even more confident, said, "Once again I ask, do you feel any responsibility?"

The two Dow young men looked very uneasy. One of

them loosened his tie; the other took off his jacket. "I was one year old then. I feel no responsibility," the one who loosened his tie said. There was anger in his voice.

"How clever," the protester said. He pointed to the poster of the little girl on the cover of *Life*. "How about this instrument of peace?"

Someone tapped Corey on the shoulder. He turned and standing next to him were Mad Dog and Aaron. Mad Dog extended his hand in friendship.

"We're on your side, bro. I deserved that ass kicking, but this fucked-up war has got to be stopped. I'm with you."

Corey meekly shook his and Aaron's hands, but the minute he saw them, the affinity he felt with the crowd seemed to diminish. He wasn't sure what to do or think next when a commotion broke out in the crowd. About a dozen of the college football players pushed their way through the protesters and moved toward the Dow booth. Corey recognized the leader of the football players. It was Curtis Henson, the starting center on the team.

"I have a great deal of respect for all the good Dow Chemical has provided throughout the world. I would like to talk with these representatives about employment after I graduate," he said loudly and just as confidently as the protester.

Spook, who was nearest to Curtis, held his placard higher. Curtis snatched it from his hand.

When Spook tried to take it back, he was easily pushed to the ground.

Instinctively, Corey moved toward his friend. "We'll kick ass together," Mad Dog said, moving to Corey's side.

Before Corey took another step, another large, well-built student stepped up face to face to Curtis. The other young man Corey recognized immediately, as did the entire crowd. It was Dennis Collins, the team's quarterback, and rumored to be a top NFL prospect, but recently he had suffered some bad press — not for his game performance, but rather for his public criticism of the Vietnam War.

In an interview with a local sportswriter, when asked if the military draft might come in conflict with the pro draft, Dennis replied, "They played good football in Canada and the last I heard, Canada was not waging any immoral war."

Dennis was not there to take a snap from his center. The two young men looked directly into each other's eyes like two gunfighters in a western movie.

Corey stopped. He was stunned. As an athlete, he had more than once found himself defending the actions of a teammate that he did not personally agree with, but for the sake of the team camaraderie, tacitly defended. Seeing the face-off of the two teammates, knowing that Mad Dog and Aaron were at his side, nearly changed his fervent allegiance to the protest to ambivalence.

Before anything could happen, a voice came over a portable bullhorn from behind the crowd. It was the school's dean.

"It is the decision of this school's administration that career day, although well intentioned, has led to a disruption of the school's primary purpose — classroom education. Therefore, career day has been canceled and all classes shall resume as normal."

The crowd gave a loud cheer and Hot yelled his victorious "HHHOOOOTTT!"

Spook went up to Curtis and said, "You keep the poster as a souvenir of the day. You two shake hands and get back to the business of developing another undefeated football team."

Karen gave Corey a hug. He seized the opportunity to hasten her away from Mad Dog and Aaron and disappear into the crowd, which rather than dispersing, began singing "If I Had a Hammer," led by the folk singer.

CHAPTER TWENTY-FIVE

THE CLAN RETURNED ABOUT THREE THAT AFTERNOON. Everyone was in high spirits. Spook was getting high fives from everyone. Eric said he got a great picture of Curtis wrestling the placard from Spook's hand. He said he would get the picture enlarged and framed for Spook. He also boasted that it was the kind of picture that might get national circulation, even wind up on the cover of the *American Free Press*.

"Wait a minute," Hot said. "Getting career day shut down at San Diego State isn't exactly like burning your draft card in front of the nation's capitol."

"No, it isn't, but maybe a large number of small victories, like this one today, is better than an occasional large one in a major city, particularly if that victory is in a conservative military town like San Diego," Eric replied.

The clan decided to take up a collection to get food for a barbecue and some cases of beer to celebrate the day. Eric pulled a couple of twenties from his wallet and laid them on the table.

Spook and Dawn volunteered to do the shopping. They had been gone less than ten minutes when the front door flung open.

Joey stood at the doorway. His body shook and he was crying uncontrollably. "Turk's dead," he managed to say through his sobs.

For a moment, only the constant violent crashing of the waves could be heard. The room became as still as if they were silently posing for a picture. Karen was the first to move. She went to Joey, who during the year had grown almost to the same height as she, but now he appeared more childlike as he bowed his head and began to cry again.

"Don't try to talk," she said. "Just tell us what happened when you are ready."

Eric asked to use their phone. He was well-connected with both of San Diego's newspapers. He quietly spoke with someone on the other end of the line. Everyone waited, trying to hear the conversation.

"Thanks," Eric said into the phone, and then looked up at the group.

"Apparently, the Tijuana police had set up a sting operation to catch a Mexican marijuana dealer. Turk just happened to be there buying his usual couple of ounces. He panicked and ran when he saw the police. Someone ordered him to stop. When he didn't, a warning shot was fired above his head, only by a freak chance, the bullet struck a building and ricocheted into the back of Turk's head, killing him instantly."

Hot went over to the TV and turned the knob to find a news channel. The man on the TV was finishing up the latest Vietnam War news.

"When we get back from commercial, we'll be looking at local news and the demonstration at San Diego State this morning. Also, a local man was killed in a drug raid in Tijuana."

Joey lifted his head from Karen's shoulder. "Bullshit!" he screamed. "Turk was no drug dealer. Why do they call him a drug dealer? He was a veteran."

"He was that and more," Hot said. "He was a craftsman, a surfboard designer who happened to buy a little weed to share with his friends, but mostly he was another fatality of this fuckin' war. I'll bet that whatever the final combat death toll is at the end of the war, within three years there will be double the number of deaths by veterans who wind up dead through suicide, drug overdose, or die in some stupid way like Turk, all because they can't piece their lives back together. They won't be listed as war fatalities; they'll call it something else, just like they're doing with Turk's death."

Karen forced Joey to stand up. "Walk outside with me a minute." She led the boy to the boardwalk, where they hopped the wall and sat in the sand facing the ocean.

"I knew Turk better than most people realize. I was one of the first of our little circle to befriend him when he got back from Vietnam. What most people don't know is he had a rather tough childhood, maybe rougher than Aaron's. He knew how hard it was to grow up without much parental guidance, especially not having a strong father figure. He wanted to make sure you got every opportunity to make something of yourself, which is why he took so much interest in you. It's okay to cry as long as you need to in order to wash the pain away." She patted the boy on his head and stroked his hair. "There's something I must do right away. Stay out here until you are ready to go back inside. I'll be back in a few minutes and we will talk some more if you want."

Spook and Dawn returned with the food and drink just as the newscaster was reporting Turk's death. No one felt like eating or drinking. Corey was on the phone with someone, but no one paid attention to him until they heard him say, "Well then, fuck you," and he slammed the receiver down. He looked at his friends in the room.

"That was Turk's brother. He, his mom, and stepfather are going to Mexico to get Turk's remains. They don't want any of us at the funeral services. They blame the crowd he hung with — US, for Turk not getting his life together. What a bunch of bullshit. We were the only family that he cared about, and we cared about him more than his family. We're going to have to honor him in our way — in a way he would have wanted."

"Turk hated his parents," Dougie said. "He told me some horror stories about how they treated him growing up."

"It doesn't matter," Eric said. "You wouldn't want to be

with them anyway. We'll have our own memorial service for Turk this weekend. What were you thinking, Corey?"

"New Break was his favorite surfing spot and we were his best friends. I think we should contact his many other friends and have a memorial there, then all surf a wave in his honor. Joey can help get the word to the others," Corey said as Joey came back in the room. Corey went to the boy and put his arm around him. "I'm so sorry for you, little man. You're spending the night here."

The boy tried to hold back his tears, but a few escaped and slowly rolled down his cheek.

Corey gently wiped them away. "Where's Karen?" Corey whispered.

"She said she had something to do and would be right back," Joey answered.

"You know what else I think we should do — what Turk would probably have liked?" Hot said. "We should let anyone who wants tell a story about some fun time they had with him. It has to be a happy remembrance; that's the only requirement." They agreed and began offering other ideas for a memorial service when Karen came back. She had the picture of Turk and his friends at the Saigon bar.

"You know they are going to seal off Turk's house and search it. I wanted to get a few things I know Turk would want removed. I think he always knew how vulnerable he was, which is why he gave me a key to his place. A while back, like he had some kind of a premonition, he told me if anything ever happened to him, to as quickly as possible remove certain items from his house which he designated to go to particular friends. He wanted you to have this," she said to Joey, handing him the picture of Turk and his army buddies at the Saigon bar.

Joey stared at the picture for several seconds before pressing it to his chest. His eyes grew visibly moist, but he held back the tears this time, and even managed a shadow of a smile. "Thank you," he said.

"He was as fond of you as those friends in the picture," Karen said.

When Saturday morning arrived, Corey awoke to a warm stream of sunshine filtering in through the cracks between the curtains. He opened the window. A mild onshore breeze pushed the clean smell of the ocean into the room. The sun and air seeped into the room and warmed the cool evening air inside his bedroom like a heavy blanket warms your body on a cool winter's night. The day looked more like a spring morning rather than a late winter's day.

The clan and several other friends of Turk's formed a car caravan heading toward Point Loma and New Break. Hot, Karen, Christy, and Joey rode with Corey. They carried their boards on top of Corey's station wagon. No one said anything until they reached the Sunset Cliffs region.

"Look at the swells. It's an early southern swell moving up from Mexico," Hot said. "New Break is going to be piping."

You had to park on the street and walk about a half mile

to New Break. A dirt road ran through a eucalyptus grove you passed through on the way. The warm sun heated the leaves, freeing its mint-like aroma and natural decongestant medicinal qualities. It seemed to make the air both sweet and therapeutic.

Nearly a hundred people showed. The surfers wedged their boards nose down into the sand to form a circle enclosure. Everyone stood in the middle. Eric, who was to lead the ceremony, stood in the center.

"We are all gathered here, not to mourn our friend Turk's death, but to celebrate his life. I would like anyone who has a fond remembrance of Turk and wishes to share it to please come forth and do so now."

The first person to come forward was Dawn. She wore a necklace that Turk had fashioned for her. She took it and held it up for the crowd. She began to tell the story about what the shape symbolized, and why Turk made it for her, but she began to cry and could not continue.

"Come on now," Hot said, walking to the center. "He was about the overcoming of tragedy, about the fun of life," he said, giving her a hug.

Then he related a story about how many of the clan first met Turk. It was when a red tide had hit Mission Beach. As ugly as the water looked during the day, it turned eerily beautiful at night as the crashing waves cracked open the skeletal plankton remains, releasing the trapped phosphorus inside. The waves lit up an iridescent mixture of blue and green. When you ran your foot or hand through the wet sand, blue-green sparks flew like the sparklers you played with as a kid during a Fourth of July celebration. Turk called for everyone to find any container they could use to fill with wet sand.

"Like the Pied Piper, he led us back to his house. He turned off all the lights, then turned on a black light and put on a Jimi Hendrix album. We painted our faces, arms, and legs with the wet sand and began to dance. Our bodies glowed like ghost-like apparitions. Eventually we stripped naked and painted our whole bodies. It was AWESOME." Everyone laughed, and soon others came forward sharing their personal remembrances of their mutual friend.

Corey looked toward the ocean. The waves were as perfect as New Break gets, matching the perfect spring-like weather. There was not a cloud in the rich azure sky, which appeared almost liquid blue. The breeze, being from the south, was warm and blew slightly offshore.

Eric's voice sounded drone-like as the wind and surf blended together in a harmonious duet. Under any other circumstances, Corey would have become mesmerized by the glorious day. But it was not perfect, for it lacked the presence of one particular friend — Turk.

Then he heard Eric say, "Does anyone else want to relate a story about Turk?" There was silence. "Then before we surf, I would like to —"

"I have something to say," Joey said. He walked up to Eric.

"Turk loved music. He had a favorite song. Karen helped me find the lyrics and music to this. Do you think you can sing this?" Eric looked over the piece of paper, then tuned his guitar. "I'm not familiar with the singer, but these lyrics are beautiful." Eric paused, then announced, "This is a song by Tim Buckley," Eric said, taking a piece of paper on which Joey had written the lyrics. "It's called 'Once I Was.'"

He began playing and then singing in his finest voice:

Once I was a soldier
And I fought on foreign sands for you Once I was a hunter
And I brought home fresh meat for you Once I was a lover
And I searched behind your eyes for you And soon there'll be another
To tell you I was just a lie

And sometimes I wonder Just for a while
Will you ever remember me?

As he sang, Corey once again looked at the perfect day and the perfect waves. Flying low coming from the south he saw a brown pelican gliding effortlessly in the warm breeze. Corey grabbed his board and paddled toward the break. Although Corey was unaware, Eric stopped singing as every eye shifted toward Corey.

He did not surf the waves in his usual graceful manner. He attacked them. He used the fin of his board like the blade of a knife, slashing and carving into the clear, clean faces of the waves. He was not trying to impress any onlookers or win any contest. He surfed to destroy their perfectness. The sea had no right to offer such perfect waves this day. He was like the madman he had read about who smuggled a knife into Amsterdam's Rijksmuseum and began slashing the Rembrandt paintings.

Corey attacked the waves until the waves, like Ahab's whale, had had enough and finally retaliated. He took a bad wipeout, scraping his shoulder on the rocky bottom. He swam ashore to retrieve his board, his shoulder bleeding. As he stood on the beach, a thin stream of blood trickled down his arm from his shoulder. Someone said, "You okay? You're bleeding." Corey watched his own blood as it slowly fell onto the sand, disappearing as the sand sucked it beneath its surface. "All new seeds are nurtured by the blood from those that came before. How well we learned today," Corey said, speaking to everyone but looking at Joey.

The singing had stopped as everyone had watched Corey's surfing, then were hushed by his words. Joey quickly retrieved Corey's board.

"That was a beautiful tribute, man," someone said. "Nobody else needs to surf. That was totally awesome."

"Better than any words could express," Dougie said.

Corey took his board from the boy and walked up to Eric. "I would like to hear the rest of the song. You are sounding better than I've heard you sing before."

Once again Eric played and sang:

And though you have forgotten All of our rubbish dreams
I find myself searching through the ashes of our ruins
Or the days when we smiled And the hours that ran wild With the magic of our eyes And the silence of our words
And sometimes I wonder Just for a while
Will you remember me?

As they walked back to their cars, Corey walked up to Joey. "I think you should spend the night on our couch again. Is that all right by you?"

Joey nodded. "I already asked Hot if I could." Corey said nothing more, nor did Joey.

Late that night, Corey was awakened by what sounded like a frightened puppy's lonely whine. He went into the front room, where he found Joey softly crying as he lay on the couch. Corey turned on a light and the boy sat up. "I'm sorry," Joey whispered as tears rolled down his cheeks.

Corey said, "Take your time," and patiently waited for the boy to compose himself. When Joey had, Corey asked, "Do you know why I surfed the way I did this afternoon?"

"To honor Turk."

"No, that's what everyone thought, but I did it out of anger. All I was thinking was if there is a God, how could he create such a beautiful day when Turk's death was so wrong ...

so unjust? How could he take away Turk's life when Turk was finally getting the pieces back together? If there is a God and he wants our respect, then he damn well should be willing to take our criticism." Corey's eyes watered, which he quickly wiped away before continuing. "Yet a funny feeling overcame me when I saw my blood dripping onto the sand and sinking into the ground. Do you remember what I said? Because Turk's life only has meaning if you believe that every seed of life, in order to germinate, must be soaked in the blood and rotting flesh of the lives that came before." Corey stopped and retrieved a pen and paper and handed them to Joey.

"I want you to write down everything that Turk meant to you and every important thing he taught you."

Joey began to write. He took a great deal of time, as if he were taking a test he must pass.

Corey sat quietly, occasionally reminding the boy he could take as long as he wanted. When Joey finished, Corey quickly glanced over the list until he saw Joey's final remark. Joey had written, "— and most important, Turk told me to not just see things for what they appear to be in the present, but all the wonderful things they can become." As he read the last statement, Corey could almost hear Turk saying the words the way Turk would have spoken them — not sounding as if he were trying to be profound, but just letting the thought escape.

"Very good. Now we need to do one more thing." Corey took some matches that were on a table next to the couch. There also was an abalone shell. He struck a match and lit Joey's notes, placing them in the ab shell to burn. When the paper was reduced to ashes, Corey rubbed his fingers in the ash, then smeared them on the boy's cheeks. The moisture from Joey's tears turned them to a black paste. "The words on the paper weren't destroyed because they were nothing more than images of what is inside of you and always will be," Corey said, then the two sat in silence for a while.

Words were as unnecessary as the writing on the paper. Joey sifted his fingers through the ashes for almost a minute, turning them to gray powder. "I'm okay now if you want to go back to bed," he said.

"I will in a while, but if it's all right with you, I think I'd like to sit and listen to the ocean.

The waves are not pounding against the shore. Tonight they are much quieter — more like a hymn — don't you think?"

CHAPTER TWENTY-SIX

About two weeks later, Corey was reading on the beach. He was trying to forget the phone call from the night before. It came from Millie. She told him that Hank had another mild stroke. He was already out of the hospital, but the doctor said it was inevitable, that he needed a bypass surgery on his carotid artery. Again, Hank had said no.

Corey asked if Hank was willing to talk with him, and Millie got him to the phone. To Corey's surprise, his voice sounded strong. Corey could not detect a slur.

"Go ahead," Hank said.

"Go ahead with what?" Corey asked.

"Aren't you supposed to talk me into another surgery?"

"Do you want me to?"

"No!" Hank answered. "Can I ask why?"

"You can ask, but I don't have to answer."

"Then fuck you," Corey joked.

Hank laughed. "I deserve that, I just wasn't expecting that."

Then the old man gave Corey his reason. He told Corey that since he and Millie were never able to have children, they traveled a lot. Throughout the years, many of their friends traveled with them. "Most of them still do, but health hasn't let us do much in the last couple for years, yet I know Millie would love to."

He then explained that being ten years older than Millie, he fully expected to die before her. He had made good money in his life, enough to allow Millie to live comfortably and travel with friends. He had planned on that.

He explained that although his insurance paid for much of the first operation, it still took a chunk from their savings. The second would take another chunk.

"The truth is I'm old and dying. Millie is younger and in good health. She is going to outlive me whether or not I get the surgery. The more I leave her, the better."

"She's made it pretty clear that she's happy having you around and wants it that way as long as possible," Corey reminded him.

"Everyone I've known that had to care for a dying loved one who lingered for some time, it wore on them, exhausted funds, and the quality of the dying person's lifestyle wasn't worth a shit. She'll be better off if I go quick. She'll still have quality time left."

"What if you have a major stroke that makes you linger,

whether or not you want to? She won't make the decision to pull the plug," Corey said.

"I've thought of that. Maybe it was a good thing after all that I was born on the reservation.

Not all the old ways were wrong."

"I think I know what you are thinking. I respect you too much to try to tell you that I think you're wrong."

The old man said nothing for a moment, then said, "When the time comes, can I count on you?"

"When the time comes, can I cont on you? Hank said then added, "You okay with that?"

"I'm fine with that," Corey said. "But I'll still be pestering you for advice until that time comes. You okay with that?"

Hank laughed again and said, "Fine," then they said good-bye. Corey was sure he knew what Hank wanted him to do; he just couldn't figure out how and was still pondering that when Joey walked up to him.

"Are you studying?"

"No, thinking, and it hurts. Good time to stop. What's up?"

"You know my baseball season starts in three weeks. Since you aren't playing anymore, do you think maybe this weekend you could throw me and some of my friends a little batting practice?"

"Love to. In fact I was going to suggest it if you hadn't brought it up. Is there a good place to hit around here?"

"I called my coach. He's a good guy. He said he could meet us at the diamond Saturday morning, open up the equipment room, and get the pitching screen. He'd bring some balls."

"Why doesn't he throw?"

"He does, but he's an old fart and doesn't throw that hard. He doesn't last too long either."

Saturday morning Corey picked up Joey. Three friends met them at the PONY league diamond. Joey's coach, a retired army officer named Fred Thompson, was already there and had the screen set up in front of the mound with a milk case filled with balls off to the side.

"Fred Thompson," he said, extending his hand to Corey. He had a strong handshake. He looked younger than Corey expected from the "old fart description of Joey's. Fred's body was lean. His crew-cut hair, being short, looked blond in the sun, but up close, Corey could see it was gray.

"Corey Jameson," Corey answered.

"I know who you are. I follow State baseball very closely. I love the game. I thought you were going to be a pretty good player. I was sorry to see you quit after two years," Fred said.

"It wasn't an easy decision. I still love the game too," Corey explained.

"No need to tell me your reasons. The school hasn't won league for as long as I can remember. Hell, they have trouble playing five hundred ball despite getting well above-average talent. I don't know why they keep that coach around. You're not the first player he's run off."

"I'm not sure I was that good, but you're right, he is a terrible coach."

"Well! We can talk later. I'm just here to watch. Why don't you get the boys going? I know they're anxious."

Corey threw a full hour of batting practice, only stopping to collect the balls periodically.

As the boys got used to his pitching, he threw a little harder, challenging them. After hitting, he fungoed a few grounders and fly balls until they had enough.

"Okay! Let's pick everything up, put away the screen, and rake the mound and home plate," Fred yelled when they finished. "Corey, let the boys do that. Come here. I'd like to talk with you a minute."

Corey sat next to the coach, who said, "I'll get right to the point. I need a young coach with your energy and knowledge of the game. You interested in working with me coaching this team?"

Corey did not answer right away. He said to Coach Thompson, "I'd like to know something about your coaching philosophy first."

"Fair enough. I have only two rules. We don't talk about winning or losing; we only talk about trying to play each game better than you played in the last one. Next, there is no such thing as a mistake, only learning opportunities."

"I wish I had played for a few more coaches with that concept. I think I would like coaching with you," Corey said.

Coach Thompson pulled a business card from his wallet and gave it to Corey. "Here's my number on the card. Now give me yours. I'm ready to write."

"Looking forward to this," Corey said as he got up.

"One more question," the coach said. "You want to know why I made up my mind to ask you to coach?"

"Because you're getting too old to throw batting practice that long?"

"That too, but mostly because you were smiling the whole time you worked with the kids."

Corey looked surprised. "I was? Joey told you to say that, didn't he?"

"You always do. I've told you that before and I'm not the only one who notices," Joey said, having come over after finishing the field maintenance.

"The tryouts for new players are next Saturday morning. Can you be there to help me grade the players?"

"See you then," Corey said, then he and Joey went back to the Surf Rider.

On the drive back, Joey said that he was really glad that Coach Thompson and Corey liked each other. He said, "I thought that might happen, and I'm stoked it did."

Corey laughed. "You knew that was going to happen all along, didn't you?" "Sure," the boy said sheepishly. "My new glove has a great pocket in it."

The next weekend Corey went to the tryouts. He and Coach Thompson were pretty much in agreement with their evaluations of the players. It wasn't just their physical skills, but the body language, the makeup that, as a player, Corey had come to realize was just as important as the physical skills. Coach Thompson saw those things too.

After the tryouts, Coach Thompson bought Corey lunch

and they went over the players, ranking them for their baseball draft. Again, Corey was impressed with Fred's insights.

"I'm really going to enjoy coaching with you," Fred told Corey when they finished.

"Likewise, likewise," Corey answered.

Later that evening when Fred called, Corey assumed it was to ask further questions about his opinion on a player or two. He was not expecting the real reason the coach was calling.

"We've got what I hope is a minor problem," Fred began. "The president of the league called me and asked about you. I told him about your baseball background and how impressed I was with the way you worked with the kids. He said he was not questioning your baseball knowledge or ability, but as he explained, a lot of the parents and coaches are either military or military dependents. He said your hippie appearance rubbed him and a few others the wrong way. He wants you to get a haircut. I hope that's not a problem?"

"How do you feel about that?" Corey asked. "You're retired military."

"I argued like hell on your behalf. You know more baseball than me and all these other coaches combined. You'd be the best thing that could happen for the kids and the league."

"So my hair length, and not baseball, is the issue?" Corey stated, rather shocked.

"That's what I argued, but the league president's position was that youth sports are just a vehicle for teaching life skills.

Our country is at war, and the peace movement on the home front is damaging the morale of the troops."

Corey was caught off guard. He didn't know how to respond. His silence was broken by Fred saying, "Are you still there?"

"Yes, I don't know how to respond. I guess they're making Vietnam an issue instead of baseball. So how do you feel about that?"

"I'm with you. They are two unrelated issues and how you and I stand on the Vietnam War has nothing to do with baseball, but the people in power don't see it that way. Will you get your hair cut? You can still oppose the war with short hair."

Corey paused again, then said, "I appreciate you defending me, but since they made the war the issue, I would like to know where you stand."

It was Coach Thompson's turn to hesitate before speaking. He spoke slowly and guarded at first, then let his emotions come through.

"I was one of the first military advisers to go to Vietnam back in sixty-three. I was there when we sent over the first wave of troops. Then, our troops had great morale, because they believed in their purpose — to stop the spread of communism. 'Better dead than red' was the rally cry. I saw that enthusiasm turn to bewilderment, not because of protests on the home front, but because it was Korea all over again. Young men were putting their lives on the line fighting a war we can't and won't be allowed to win."

I was eligible for early retirement and did. I'm not opposed to the military — it has been my life's obligation — but I'm as opposed to the Vietnam War as you."

"I really do appreciate your honesty," Corey said. "I need to think it over. I'm really coaching for Joey and I would like to talk with him first."

"I don't know, Corey. I don't think we should get the kids involved."

"I think that *is* the whole issue is it for the kids or not? I'll get back to you by tomorrow."

"I really want to coach your team," Corey told Joey later that evening. "I like Coach Thompson a lot. He's a good man and I want you to know he's on my side. If you say the word, I'll fake being part of the establishment. I'll cut my hair."

Corey saw the disappointment in the boy's eyes. He felt miserable putting Joey in that position while the boy was still mourning Turk's death, but sometimes life makes you grow up faster than you should, he rationalized.

"Turk was my friend," Joey said. "Another kid on my team had an older brother who was killed in Vietnam over the summer. I think their lives are bigger than baseball."

Corey shook the boy's hand. "That was a tough decision, I know, but you made a very adult choice," he added, seeing the disappointment still in Joey's eyes.

"I still can throw you batting practice anytime you want.

And there is no law saying I have to get a haircut to watch you play."

"Okay," Joey said, trying to hide his disappointment.

"Thanks, man," Corey said, and ruffled the boy's hair in affection.

CHAPTER TWENTY-SEVEN

Corey explained to Karen what had happened with the coaching.

"Some good did come out of the whole experience," he said, then explained how he discussed it with Joey and Joey's decision.

"For a kid who has had no father around, and you know what kind of a role model his mom is, he still manages to think like an adult. I'm proud to be one of his mentors," Corey concluded.

Karen listened patiently to Corey's story. When he finished, she said, "You have impressed me from the moment I met you. You always seem to make good decisions, but this wasn't one of them."

Corey was caught off guard. "I told Hot and Spook about what happened and they completely agreed. Hot called the leagues governing board "a bunch of motherfuckers" and said I was too good for their kind.

"Spook, being much more politically inclined and analytical, felt that the PONY league governing board was just a microcosm of our federal government. 'Suppress the opposition so you don't have to address the real issue.'

"Joey was disappointed, but he understood and said I was doing the right thing."

"What did you expect him to say? He's still trying to cope with Turk's death and he idolizes you. Remember he is a kid, not an adult. What were you thinking about when you were his age?" Karen said. "You always talk about your mentor, Hank. Do you think he would have handled it that way. You always talk about trying to see things from another person's point of view. Well, try to see it from Joey's. Think back to when you were thirteen." There was disappointment in her voice, and she knew she hurt Corey's feelings, so she added, "It sucks what they did, and I'd have told them to go 'f' themselves if I had been in your place, but Joey shouldn't be involved."

Corey still meekly defended his position. "How could I have not involved him? The reason I was coaching was to help him out."

"Really? Now I think you're lying to yourself. I think you miss baseball and wanted to get back into it."

Corey felt real uneasy. He tried to think of some powerful counterpoint that would change her opinion and make her come over to his side. He could think of a number of logical arguments for what he had done, but he realized even when he talked with Joey, something didn't feel right. He sighed. "Guess I'd better go talk to Joey, huh?"

Karen said nothing else. She kissed him and smiled.

Later that day, Corey sat on the boardwalk wall in front of the Surf Rider trying to think of what he should say to Joey. The never-ending drone of the waves lapping the shore resonated in his mind. The afternoon sun seemed to reflect on the water like light passing through crystal. As beautiful as it was, he thought about what realistically went on beneath the surface — the daily struggle for survival between predator and prey, or even more correctly, between higher and lower forms of predators. Then he thought of his paper last semester. Above the surface Ahab hunted the whale relentlessly, although the whale was not the aggressor until Ahab gave it no choice in the end. His thought was interrupted when he heard a familiar voice.

"Hello," Joey said, coming up behind him.

"Hey, Joey," Corey said. "You're just the man I was thinking about."

"You were? I was coming to see you. I talked with a few of the other kids on the team. I told them what happened and they thought what the league did sucked. We are thinking about boycotting opening day."

"Well, that kind of leads into why I wanted to talk with you," Corey said. "Playing baseball was the most important thing in the world to me when I was your age. The night before the game, all I could think about was the next day's game. I dreamed about Willie May's type catches and Mantle-like homers. I looked forward to the end of the game as much as the game itself. You know what I mean — the kidding of friends on the other team, and of course having to decide whether to have a fudgesicle or a lime popsicle for an after-game treat. Then too were the girls my age who had come to watch the game. I wasn't sure whether to tease them or what. I was noticing their developing breasts and how that made me feel kind of weird inside. Everything I thought about the game, or all the things that were associated with the ballpark, were all one. The world stood still and I could move through the day knowing it was created just for me and my friends."

"You're talking kind of strange, you know, but you do that every once in a while," Joey said.

Corey smiled. "It's because when I think about all the crap that is going on in the world, I would give every dollar I've ever had to have one more day like those I had at age thirteen.

Instead, what I did was make you take a step into a world of shitty adult problems. It was wrong for me to do that. You should just be having kid fun, not struggling with world shit. I apologize to you for that."

"I'm the one who wanted you to coach. I got you into this to begin with," Joey protested. "Maybe, to begin with I wanted to coach more than you know. I did it for me; that's how much I miss the game. That's not entirely true either. I miss the purity, the fun for fun's sake. It was a magic time and I wanted the magic back. You tell your friends what I want you, and all of them to do, is to go out there and play your asses off. Nothing would make me prouder."

"Does that mean you are going to cut your hair and coach?"

"No, I'm not going to coach your team. But I'll throw you and your friends batting practice anytime they want. We'll just have to be secretive about it. Plus, they can't stop me from watching your games unless they want to find out I'm a badass warrior disguised as a hippie."

Joey was silent for a minute, then said, "When you were my age was there a war going on?" Corey shook his head no. "Why do you ask?"

"Because there is a kid on my team who had an older brother, just a couple of years younger than you. He was a real nice guy too. He was killed in Vietnam over the summer. His brother is taking it real hard. These are different times," Joey said.

"Maybe. There will always be ugly and mean in the world, but hopefully there will always be something like baseball and surfing to escape the mean, even just for a little while. And like my friend Hank said, because there is sun and water, there is life, and that's all you need," Corey said, then added, "Look at the waves right now. They're not very big, and they're poor shape, but I bet if we go surfing right now, we'll have a blast. What do you say? Go surfing with me."

When they went to get their boards, they found Spook, Weirdness, Dougie, and Dizzy with Hot watching television.

"Why are you guys getting your boards? The surf is crap," Hot said.

"I know," Corey answered. "We are going to have a bad wave riding contest. Whoever can catch the smallest wave and still get a good ride wins."

"And the winner gets the loser to buy him a box of fudgesicles," Joey added.

CHAPTER TWENTY-EIGHT

Hot and Corey often talked among themselves about how the real learning experience of college took place not in the classroom, but in bullshit sessions sitting around somebody's apartment — usually theirs. Hot said that the philosophy department should offer a class called Bullshit 101 and should be required as part of the general education class curriculum. Then if you chose philosophy as your major, you would take Advanced Bullshit. Corey thought this was what Hank meant when he said you would learn a lot more if classes were held sitting around a campfire rather than in the conventional classroom.

It was not that they thought that most professors delivered boring lectures. In fact, the subject matter of many lectures was the stimulus for many a late-night bullshit session. What bothered them was in the classroom setting, the professor was strictly a teacher. It was assumed his rhetoric was almost biblical in proportion. It did not have to be proven, and definitely would not be questioned, for it came from the same divine enlightenment of prophets and saints.

Whenever Hot and Corey — and any of the rest of the clan for that matter — talked about a favorite teacher, past or present, it was always an instructor who acted more like a bright student contributing ideas. They shared their thoughts as a peer, and were just as interested in the student's response as they were in their own beliefs. In that environment, the clock was the enemy, for no matter how provocative the idea, the learning was cut off like the executioner clicking the switch of the electric chair. But around the campfire, or the informal setting around a friend's apartment, the clock was forgotten and the participants could stretch the night as long as they needed.

Spring in San Diego is the poorest time for surf. The northern storms have stopped, and the southern storms have yet to begin. The wind blows less without the pressure systems so the ocean fog lingers, often past noon, only to return before dusk. Gray is the predominant color of the sky. The number of good surfing days are few and far between. With the nearness of graduation approaching, coupled with the external conditions, apartment house congregations became more frequent, but all the bold talk against the war mellowed out as the reality of having to make an actual immediate decision concerning their own futures became imminent.

Those evening parlor conversations were less theoretical and philosophical and more practical. Corey, through switching majors, had put off the decision another year and could remain more in the lofty moralist position. Even immune to the pending reality of the draft, Corey found his once-staunch beliefs were losing their potency. Ever since the demonstration against Dow, he was confused because Mad Dog and Aaron had stood at his side as allies, not adversaries. He had always taken his respective stand on any issue because he believed in the cause, but he sensed those former foes where at his side for no noble reason, but rather they simply enjoyed fighting. He mentioned it to Karen on their way home from the rally.

"That happens in war," she said. "You find yourself needing the strangest of confederates."

Eric was too old to be drafted, but he still opposed the war on the highest-principled plateau. He felt it his duty to play the role of spiritual adviser and so wanted to make sure his tenants, whom he regarded more as friends, would maintain their anti-war views, because they would be doing the morally right thing even if they had to become martyrs. Since he viewed himself in that role, he began attending their informal talks more frequently.

Their most in-depth discussion took place because of what normally would have been a joyous announcement, but in reality, the first definitive decision concerning the war and the draft changed the entire mood among the clan.

Hot gathered everyone together to announce that he and Christy were going to get married. Just as everyone seemed delighted by the news, the joy turned a bit sour when someone asked if they had picked a date and a place. Hot told them that they were leaving for Canada right after graduation and would be married up there.

"You plan to run rather than make a stand?" Eric asked.

Before he could answer Corey asked, "Can you really leave this country? You may never be able to return."

"To answer both of you at once," Hot said, addressing Corey first, "I never told you this before, but the first year of college, when your parents came down and took us to a fancy restaurant, I didn't know what half the things on the menu were. Your family was discussing cordon bleu and chateaubriand while I searched the menu for fried chicken or a steak. When your dad insisted that we have escargots as an appetizer, I about died when they brought out snails.

"You see, my family was blue collar all the way. We lived month to month with both parents working. My parents struggled for me to go to state college. I had the grades to go to almost any private institution I wanted, but not the money."

He turned to Eric. "You like your protest songs. I was what John Fogarty sang about when he sang 'I was no fortunate son.' I'm not about to let the sacrifices my parents made get destroyed in some stupid government police action in some obscure country. Morality of war has nothing to do with it. I want to live my life so that my children can go into a nice restaurant and order cioppino or bouillabaisse and not be shocked when they see seashells and squid tentacles floating in their soup."

"Why can't you do that "here?" Dougie asked. Taxes are a lot higher in Canada than here."

"Call it my pioneer spirit. There are a lot of small towns and open wilderness in Canada.

You've got to struggle more against the weather than government ideology. Teachers get paid better up there too. I see myself teaching history in some nice bedroom community, maybe not a San Marino, but not in a tract home village where every fifth house looks alike."

"Is that what you want too?" Dawn asked Christy.

"I left home because I grew up learning to live my life in accordance to my parent's plan. They had a lot of rules intended to ensure happiness, but I don't think my parents were truly happy. Honestly, I'm not sure they really loved each other, so they weren't capable of showing me how to love. I've been happier with Hot than I've ever been before. I guess I have a very simple dream — a nice little house where I can grow vegetables and herbs and lie next to my husband at night, not in separate beds like my parents."

"The morality of war, the demonstration, the peace symbol on the bumper of your car," Eric said.

"I believe in them, but I'm not going to be a martyr as long as there is somewhere else to go," Hot said.

From there the discussion heated up. There was nothing new said, no point that had not been promulgated before, only the fervor of their arguments.

Spook and Dawn condemned all war, which had been their position ever since Corey met them. They repeated all their justifications for their opposition. As Spook became more heated in his denial of all wars, Corey interjected, "Looking back upon history, war seems inevitable."

"As to history showing war to be inevitable," Spook argued, "it was nothing more than a self-fulfilling prophecy. Because it has always been, we should just silently accept that it always will be," he argued. "There have been many beliefs — historical, theological, and scientific — that have been discredited and are now as extinct as dinosaurs," he added. "We can make the inevitable theory another such myth."

Eric was mostly in agreement with Spook and Dawn. He felt that most wars were fought by the greedy or power-hungry leaders who manipulated the masses into fighting their battles. If, through protests or education, the masses could reject the manipulation of their leaders, sort of like "suppose they threw a war and nobody came," then there would be a cessation of war.

Dougie simply found violence abominable. He reacted even to the make-believe violence of movies and television with repulsion. Corey thought that even if you tried to break down Dougie's gut-felt reaction to violence, as boot camp did, ultimately he still could not be made into a soldier, at least not one Corey would want at his side in combat.

Corey stayed out of the discussion. In the past, he would have gladly given his opinion, but he no longer knew what he believed. Melville's disdain for the "easy believer" came almost immediately to mind. "The masses will always be manipulated," he thought. Then the image of Aaron and Mad Dog standing at his side entered his mind. They were as strongly drawn to violence as Dougie was repelled by it. And what of himself? When he saw the placard pulled from Spook's hands and Spook was pushed down, Corey moved to defend his friend, his actions as uncontrollable as a knee-jerk response to the doctor's rubber mallet. He could rationalize he was called to arms for noble reasons, he could fantasize himself a noble warrior like those of the ancient Greeks, but in the end, he was no longer sure what he believed or why.

To Corey, Hot made the most sense of all. "Live and let live; don't make it any more complicated than that."

"What would you like?" Corey asked late in the evening, "Beer, wine or weed? Let's just toast to the happiness of Hot and Christy and quit arguing about war and Vietnam, which we've been doing for four years and where's that gone?"

Instead of reacting to Corey's comment as an interruption, the clan seemed to welcome the suggestion. Soon people were toasting Hot and Christy with the refreshment of their choice, and the gloomy mood turned festive.

Jan, had not only eventually tried pot, but like Weirdness, had developed a preference for it. She no longer believed she would strip and run naked into the sea. She asked for weed and shared a joint with Dougie and Dizzy. As the night grew late and they continued to imbibe, Spook talked Dougie and Jan into stripping and going skinny-dipping in the ocean.

Once again, nothing was resolved, only further contemplated. The day ended with mirth, but only because they altered their perception of reality. A thought lingered in the back of Corey's mind: things would never be the same for him and his friends.

CHAPTER TWENTY-NINE

Because the night went late, Corey slept in the next morning. He decided to skip school and work on a mid-term paper. About nine, he walked out to the boardwalk, hoping there would be some surf and he could catch a few waves. He didn't expect to find any surf because from Karen's apartment, just like his own, he could hear the ocean and judge the size of the waves by their sound as they pounded the shore. That night all he heard was the soft lapping of gentle surf as it brushed shoreline sands. He went to the wall anyway, where he saw something even more unexpected. There was a lone figure sitting on the beach, swaying from side to side. He recognized Joey immediately and hurried to where the boy sat.

"Hey, man, why aren't you in school?"

Joey turned and looked at Corey. His eyes were glassy and the pupils so shrunken they looked like penlights.

"Are you stoned?"

The boy nodded yes.

"Some cop comes by and asks why you're not in school, he'll see you're wasted and you can get in more trouble than just being truant. Hope you don't have any weed on you."

The boy reached in his coat pocket and pulled out a rolled joint.

"Shit, buddy. You get caught with that and you'll probably get kicked off the baseball team.

Those military clowns think that's a lot worse than long hair. Come on, let's get you out of sight."

Joey got up rather wobbly. "It won't matter. I'm not going to be able to finish the season anyway."

"What? Hurry up. Let's get you inside before a patrol car comes by."

Once inside Corey's apartment, Joey pulled out the joint and asked Corey for a lighter. "Give me that," Corey said, and snatched it from the boy's hand. "Now what's going on?"

"As soon as school's out, Mom's moving us to Arizona. Her new boyfriend wants to marry her and move there because he's got some high-paying job." Joey responded.

"Wow, I can understand why you're upset, but you'll have a father, and Arizona is a great baseball state. A lot of clubs have spring training over there. The surfing will be a bummer, but you'll find other things."

"He doesn't want me around. He wants Mom to try and

find my real dad. If not, he plans to put me in some kind of boarding school to get me out of their way."

Corey sat down next to the boy. "You're sure?"

"Oh, yeah. I'm just going to run away."

Corey put his arm around the boy. "This really had to catch you off guard; it does me."

The boy looked at the joint on the coffee table. "I just want to get real fucked up 'til I pass out."

"No!" Corey said. "You're going to go in and take as hot a shower as you can stand. Sweat out as much of what you've smoked as possible. I'll make some coffee and you'll just have to drink it whether or not you like it."

Joey just sat there.

"Go on. If I have to, I'll strip your ass and throw you in there."

Joey slowly got up and looked defiantly at Corey.

"Shut the window and close the bathroom door. Turn it into a sauna."

The boy reluctantly obeyed. Once Corey heard him get in the shower, he called Karen in hopes that she was still home. She was moving as slow as he was after their late night. She answered.

"You're still there, good ... Guess what? We're all playing hooky today; you, me, and Joey," he said.

"Joey! What the — Why? Is he okay?"

He then relayed what the boy had told him.

"Oh no! As if the kid hasn't had to deal with enough crap in his life. Do you have any echinacea tea? That's good for neutralizing the effects of pot. If not, I'll bring some over right away."

Joey was just getting out of the shower when Karen arrived. He walked zombie-like into the room with just a towel wrapped loosely around his waist.

"Careful. Don't let the towel fall, but nice bod," she said, trying to make light of the situation. "Go get some clothes on while I make some tea for you."

Joey pretended he was going to drop the towel as he smiled at Karen, then went into Corey's room to change.

"Good, you can't be that bummed out. You still can smile," Karen said.

Corey already had the water heating. Karen added a little milk and sugar to the tea and handed it to the boy when he came back to the front room. After he took a few sips, she said, "There's something I've been thinking about for a while, ever since Turk died. I don't know if it's possible, but it might work. You drink a couple of cups of this. You'll probably get sleepy and that's good. You need to sleep it off and get your head clear." She turned to Corey. "What time is low tide today?"

"About four this afternoon."

"Perfect. Once Joey is feeling better, I want you guys to go over to the Cliffs and dive for abalone. Bring them back to my place. We'll have dinner and by then I should know if my plan is going to work. You guys okay with that?"

"Can you give us a hint what this is all about?" Corey asked.

"Nope, but pick up a nice bottle of wine on your way back. I hope we'll be toasting something special at dinner."

She kissed Joey on the forehead and left.

Corey let Joey sleep for about two hours and woke him around two thirty. They headed for Sunset Cliffs in Point Loma. The road was the same one they took for New Break. At low tide, the rocky cliffs at the point were a diver's paradise. The rock bottom kept the water clear, while the rocky crevices were perfect homes where the abalone could attach themselves. There were thick kelp beds a couple of hundred yards from the cliffs which cut the swells, so the surf, even when big, just rolled slowly over the rocks.

The boy said nothing as they neared the cliffs until they were almost there. "Are you going to lecture me about what I did this morning?"

"Do I need to?" Corey asked. "No, I just was mad. Still am."

"I could say something like the worst time to turn to drugs or booze is when you're escaping from something, but if I did that, well, I've been where you are now ... I'd be a hypocrite. Nevertheless, it's still something neither one of us should do."

"I know! I know! Let's not talk about it anymore, okay?" Joey said. Anger still lingered in his tone.

"Okay, but just so you know, rumor has it that the sun will still rise tomorrow," Corey said, then playfully jabbed the boy's arm.

A remnant of a smile formed on Joey's face.

"What's that? Do I see a smile? That would be the first

one since early this morning, and it' not even three thirty yet."

"I'm a little better I guess. Sorry I kind of wrecked your day."

"No, you didn't. I understand how you feel, and you're the kind of a friend I'd help anytime under any circumstance. You ought to know that by now."

"Thanks, but I'm sorry just the same." Joey paused, then asked, "What do you think Karen is up to?"

"I have no idea, but I've learned that when she gets some mysterious idea in her mind, try not to figure it out. Just let her reveal it whenever she's ready," Corey said as he turned into a scenic outcrop where divers frequently parked while diving at the cliffs.

"Tide's going out. We ought to find abs in no more than ten to fifteen feet of water. Put your wet suit on; the water is still pretty chilly."

It didn't take them long to get several abs. They were back at the car in less than a half hour.

Just as they were about to take off their wet suits, someone yelled, "Hello."

The houses along Sunset Cliffs were all mansions. A man, who apparently lived in one of the homes and had seen the boys bring in their catch, walked down his driveway and approached them. He was wearing Bermuda shorts, a flannel shirt, and tennis shoes. All his clothing looked expensive but hung loosely over his slender, non-athletic looking body. He appeared to be about the same age as Eric, but unlike Eric, the uncovered skin was not tan, but a cream-colored white.

His hairless legs looked dry and speckled with liver spots. His thinning hair was almost entirely gray, yet his fingernails reflected a sparkle from having been freshly manicured. The wind pressed his clothes close to his body, revealing quads that were as thin and as underdeveloped as his puny calves. It was clear he lived at the ocean for the view, not for the recreation.

"Afternoon," Corey said back.

"I saw you bring up some abs. I was wondering if you wouldn't mind going out and getting a couple more, or I'll buy these three from you. My wife and I love fresh abalone."

"I'll have to go back out. These are for our dinner. I'll make a deal with you though. Instead of buying these abs" — Corey looked toward the man's house — "I imagine you have a nice wine cellar. How about while I'm getting the abs you grab a nice bottle of red wine. A Bordeaux would be nice if you have one?"

The man winked at Corey. "A man of taste," he said, then glanced at Joey.

"It's for me and my girlfriend, not the kid."

"I was pretty sure you aren't twenty-one," the man said to Joey, then laughed nervously to underscore he was only joking.

"Actually, I'm twenty-one," Joey said. "I come from a family that matures late."

The man forced an embarrassed laugh, then hurried back to his house for the wine. Corey and Joey went back to the sea. The boys got several abs and returned just as the man came back with the wine — two bottles.

"I'll give you both bottles if you cut out the meat and trim them for preparation."

Corey did what the man asked and prepared the three largest abs. They shook hands and thanked each other, then he and Joey left for Karen's.

"That guy seemed to be a little weird, huh?" Joey said. "I think his skin is whiter than Spook's, and he seemed real uncomfortable talking to us."

"When you go to college, don't become an English major or you'll find when you meet new people, they'll remind you of some fictional character and you'll start thinking of them as that character rather than who they are. I think we just had an encounter with J. Alfred Prufrock," Corey said.

"Who's that?" Joey asked.

"Just a character created by a famous poet named T.S. Eliot. The poem was about man who realized as he grew older, he existed to watch other people who tasted the pleasures of life while he was being careful not to

'disturb the universe.'"

"College intellectual talk," Joey said.

"Yeah. It means you've got to seize life by the balls, not hide in some dark place sipping coffee or smoking pot when you feel troubled."

"I knew it. You're going to turn it into a lecture after all," Joey said.

"No, I was just thinking out loud. You'll never be J. Alfred

Prufrock, and you'll know that the mermaids will always sing for you."

"Now you're really weirding out," Joey said.

"Yeah, I know, but you'll understand someday and, like that scar on your knee, hopefully it will bring another smile to your face."

They said nothing else until they reached Karen's, where they prepared the abs and waited for her return. About twenty minutes later, she arrived and seemed particularly excited to see them. Her eyes sparkled as she grinned like Joey said Corey did when he threw batting practice to the boys.

"As bad a day as you may have thought it was going to be when Corey found you on the beach this morning, I think it's going to turn out to be pretty darn good. Hopefully you'll learn how fast bad news can turn around. You just never know how quickly fortunes change," she said to Joey.

She inspected the abs, then noticed the wine. "See you had good hunting, but that wine looks expensive. Good! I think we have something special to celebrate; however, in the future, you and I might have to be a little more frugal," she said to Corey.

"Well, give us the news. I can't take anymore suspense," Corey said. "Not until dinner. Now you guys clean up while I start cooking."

She put on some early Beatles music, the "I want to hold your hand" happy stuff, not the more intellectual current Beatles music. She sang along with the record as she worked.

When they finally sat down to dinner, both boys in unison said, "Well?"

"As soon as you pour the wine. Make sure you give Joey a little so he can join in our toast."

Corey opened one of the bottles of wine and poured it into three glass. "So what big surprise are we toasting?"

"Joey, I'll start with you. I went to see your mother today. Before I tell you what we talked about, I want you to understand that she does love you, as much as she is capable of love anyway. Life has been real hard on her. I think you know that." Joey nodded yes. "She was raised without much love herself. Then, at sixteen, she had to raise a child before she had a chance to grow up ... had to figure out stuff on her own. I actually feel sorrow for her, but that doesn't matter now. We talked about you and you not wanting to move to Arizona. She understood and said she wished you had some relatives you could stay with and remain here."

"I told her" — Karen paused, her smile widening as she turned toward Corey — "I told her that Corey and I were going to get married this summer and would be back here at school for at least one more year. I said Joey could stay with us. It would buy time to figure out a better solution for everyone. She agreed and is getting some documents together to make us your legal guardians. Of course, it would make for a better case if Corey and I actually were married."

Joey looked as surprised as he had when Corey gave him the new glove, only something more. It was pure joy ... the kind that comes only a few times in one's lifetime. His body quivered as he fought back tears.

Corey looked at Karen as if what she had said hadn't fully sunk in. "And did she buy that story," he asked.

"Why not? Unless you've changed your mind about marriage? I didn't answer you down in Mexico because I wasn't ready. Today forced me to put everything into perspective. The answer is YES! I love you and want to marry you."

Corey stood up and almost knocked over the table as he hurried over to give her a kiss. "Girl, that's one crazy way of saying yes, but I'm used to your fickleness. It's one of many reasons I love you so much."

Her way of saying yes caught him so off guard he couldn't think of anything else to say, so he kept repeating how happy she made him. After several minutes and a sip of wine he started thinking more along practical lines. "You know my father is cutting off my income in June. I only have one additional year on my deferment. Joey is going to be an additional cost. And —"

Karen interrupted with a kiss. "We'll make it work. Here's the part that relates to Joey and why I think the whole crazy thing will work. My objection to marriage before was because I didn't want to have children for fear they would interfere with my career, yet everything that has happened this year has inspired me to do what I think is my best work to date. By having Joey live with us for what would only be, what — five, six years at the most — it would give me a chance to experience family life without taking time away from my career to meet the demands of raising a baby. Joey's old enough to take care of himself. He pretty much has for some time now. Joey's mom told me she could send us a little money from time to time and I think she will, but it doesn't matter if she does or not." She turned her eyes back toward Joey. "Here is the other surprise I've been hiding until I thought the time was right."

Both Joey and Corey gave each other a puzzled look while Karen went to her bedroom and returned with a box. She sat it on the table in front of Joey.

"I think Turk sensed that his life might not ever be put together. About a year ago, he gave me the key to his house. He told me that if anything ever happened to him, that he had something I was supposed to give to Joey. You can open the box."

Joey carefully opened the lid. "Oh my God," he shouted and lifted out a wad of money in each hand. "There must be several thousand dollars in there."

"A little under fourteen thousand actually. With every sale of jewelry, surfboards, or grass he made over the last four years, he put something aside for you. He wanted you to have the chance to go to college he never had. That's why I left the room the day we learned of his death. I've been keeping it for you in a safety deposit box at my bank. I figured that if I gave it to you right away, your mom would take it. On Monday, I think we should open a savings account for you without telling your mom. This is for college or some real emergency, okay?"

Joey's eyes glistened from the moisture that welled up

from within. “Of course,” he answered, his voice cracking, which made all three of them laugh.

“Well, what do you guys say?” she concluded.

“You know my answer,” Corey said. “You just made this the happiest day of my life.” He looked at Joey. “What do you say, little man? Before you answer, I want you to know if you get scared at night, you’ll have to tough it out. You can’t come get in bed with us, son.”

“Screw you.” Joey hesitated. “What should I call you now, Mom and Dad or is it still Karen and Corey?” Joey asked.

“It depends on whether you ditch school anymore or do something stupid like that. Then we will be your mom and dad,” Karen answered.

“But if we ask you to ditch school to go on a surfing trip, then it’s Karen and Corey,” Corey said, lifting his glass. “Let’s drink a toast to our new family.”

Joey waited for Karen and Corey to drink before he took a sip himself. “Ah! This stuff is terrible. How can you drink this?” Joey said with a sour face.

Corey emptied Joey’s glass into his own. “You might not be ready for wine yet, but you are ready for this move, aren’t you?”

Joey looked at Karen. “You’re right. This turned out to be a great day after all.” He paused and looked at Corey. “Right up there with last Christmas Eve. You guys are the best friends I've ever had.”

Corey laughed. “Quite a compliment considering all the experience you've gained in thirteen years.”

CHAPTER THIRTY

After what seemed like a full month of gray, Corey awoke one late May morning to bright sunshine and almost balmy tropical air. The surf was still small, but the gray gave way to bright blue. The weather seemed to lift his spirits. The anxiety he felt over his senior year coming to an end, although not completely resolved, at least was temporarily satisfied. Both he and his friends had come to decisions concerning their immediate futures, which appeared to be the right ones. Even if time proved them wrong, the mere fact that they took action brought about a peace of mind he hadn't felt in a long time. When he was in high school, his parents' wealth had provided a complacency that enabled him to believe that he could control his future and gave him a false sense of security. He now believed that everyone was subject to random occurrences that were beyond their control, but he had gained a self-confidence in his ability to adapt to most situations. It wasn't that he had eliminated his fear of having to inevitably make a decision concerning the war, but fear was now looked upon as a friend who taught himself self-reliance. The awareness of having this ability seemed to free him from uncertainties which had been hanging like an albatross around his neck. Like the ancient mariner, Corey's spirits were lifted by the wisdom gained through the agonizing that had been increasing since his senior year of high school.

Cory looked out the window and peered at the ocean. Numerous species of young sea birds either searched the sand for crabs or glided over the water, hoping to snare some unexpected fish near the surface. The natural cycle of life was right in front of him and as he viewed it, he felt his peace of mind grow.

"If the surf was better, I'd think there was surely a God," Hot said as he entered from his bedroom. "This is San Blas weather ... Sure makes it hard to study."

They contemplated going surfing anyway, but with finals so near, both thought they couldn't afford to miss class. The sultry air and the sunny clear skies remained throughout the entire day. By the time they got out of school and back to the Surf Rider, it was late afternoon. The surf had come up a little and almost every surfer in Mission Beach was in the water despite the nearness of final exams.

"Ever see such mediocre waves attract so many surfers?" Hot said as he and Corey sat on their boards praying that suddenly a larger swell would arrive. No miracle occurred, so after a short while, Hot suggested they get a game of volleyball going. "The Sun God is keeping us away from the Book God," he said. "After all the sunless days of the past several weeks, we've got to honor him now."

By dinner, without realizing it, they had played for nearly two and half hours. Because of the tropical-like heat, even after showering, their skin remained moist and sticky. Studying was uncomfortable in the uncharacteristically humid San Diego climate. Corey seemed to lose focus and had to reread almost everything he studied that night. As a result, he read until past midnight before giving up altogether. Yet once in bed — maybe because he was still thinking about his studies, or because the humid weather shocked his system so he couldn't sleep — he tossed and turned while frequently glancing at the clock. One thirty — two twenty — three a.m. Then without ever feeling he had dozed off, he found himself awake in a vivid dream.

He was in a desert somewhere. As a boy, he had accompanied his mother who, because she feared flying, drove herself and young Corey back to visit family in the Midwest. In his dream, he was in a landscape where the sands were brick red and jagged rock formations, eroded by time, revealed strata of myriad shades of red, brown, and pink in its sedimentary layers. He was in the unique topography of a New Mexico landscape etched in his memory during those boyhood trips.

In his dream, he was very thirsty and did not have any water container in his pack. He was toting a day pack, so he knew he wasn't far from wherever he had started his hike, although he did not know where he was or how he got there. He had no water, yet he felt no anxiety, for he sensed there was purpose for his being at that particular spot, at that moment in time.

He spied a cave and what looked like a stream of water trickling from the mouth of the cave. He approached the cave entrance and found the stream was no mirage, despite the intense heat in the desert. The clear water was ice cold, like the stream water in the High Sierras. As he knelt to drink the refreshing water, he thought he heard laughter, female laughter. He looked up and saw a young girl peeking out from behind a boulder just inside the mouth of the cave.

"Hello," he shouted.

The girl, who looked like she was an Indian because of her long black hair braided into two pigtails, and her moccasins, which were the same tan color as her dress, which appeared to be made from some kind of animal skin. When he called to her, she giggled and ran into the cave. He followed, running in the stream where the cool water soothed his hot bare feet. "Why am I hiking barefoot?" he thought, but heard the girl giggle again so he focused on his pursuit.

He wished that he had a flashlight or torch of some kind, but as he went deeper into the cave, he noticed the quartz walls reflected light coming from somewhere even deeper in the cave. Then too, the young girl kept playfully laughing while peeking back at him from up ahead, enticing him to continue his chase.

Corey stopped suddenly as he realized that the cold water

was gradually growing hotter as he went deeper into the inner chamber of the cave. He thought it odd that the water outside, in direct sunlight, was ice cold, yet in the cooler shade of the cave, the water was getting warmer. The girl, seeing he had stopped, tossed a pebble that splashed near him. He looked up and saw her waving for him to follow. She was not in the stream but stood on a small path next to it. The light on the walls no longer looked like a reflection but rather were coming from some kind of light source buried within the opaque quartz itself.

"How far do I have to chase you?" Corey yelled.

The girl smiled, then hurried down the path. He lost sight of her for a while, but her footsteps echoed within the walls so he maintained his pursuit. Finally, he came to a large subterranean pool. At the far side, the girl sat on a large rock with her back to him. He tested the water, thinking it would be quicker to swim to her, but the water felt like hot bath water, so he maneuvered around the rocks toward the girl. The closer he got, her body seemed to change before his eyes. The thick, shiny, black hair seemed to be thinner and streaked with gray. The closer he got, the more her hair turned gray. Soon streaks of white appeared and eventually completely changed to the yellow/white of old age. Her smooth and youthful taut tan skin became wrinkled and appeared to be draped from her hunched frame.

Finally, he reached her and tapped her shoulder. She turned, and for the first time in his dream, he felt fear. The figure was no longer a playful young girl. Instead, an old man looked him in the eye. The smile of the young girl became a sneer on the old man's lips. His eyes looked serpentine, hollow, and treacherous. Suddenly the old man hissed like a snake. Corey saw the old man's tongue was split at the end and darted from his mouth like two points protruding from one shaft.

Corey jumped back and began to run toward the entrance of the cave. He did not look back, but he could hear footsteps following him. The feet moved too fast, much too fast for an old man. He felt panic as he ran and wasn't even sure he was moving in the right direction except that he paralleled the stream.

Then he saw the light at the mouth of the cavern. He jumped in the stream, which was cool again and seemed to invigorate him, so he could run faster. Having reached the mouth of the cave, he leaped toward the sands outside. He lost his footing and tumbled down the slope. Once he stopped, he turned quickly and readied himself to fight. The young girl had stopped just inside the cave where he had first seen her. She was beautiful again and giggled with all the innocence of a play-yard child.

Corey sat up in bed. The sheets were wet from layers of perspiration that seeped from every pore in his skin. He breathed heavily, trying to catch his breath after the chase. He glanced at the clock. It was 6:10, nearly time to get up for school, which he felt thankful for as fear lingered from the vividness of the dream and he did not want to go back to sleep.

That afternoon, when he returned from school, he found UPS had left a package at his doorstep. Corey did not have to read the return address. He knew it was from Hank, and he knew what was in the package. He sat it on the table where he stared at it for several minutes before opening it. Inside was a large Indian blanket woven from thick wool. There was an envelope containing a large sewing needle, the kind used for mending canvas sails. Inside, with the blanket, was several yards of leather binding. There was also a letter that he unfolded and read with dread.

Dear Corey,

By the time you receive this package, I should be arriving at the path that begins my final destination. I've never felt comfortable with how modern medicine strives to keep you alive when it is truly your time to go. You know where my burial spot is, and you must see to it that my body is never found. Do not betray me as my father was betrayed. I'm sorry to burden you with this responsibility, but you and Millie are the only ones who understand why I must do this final act. Millie is a spry old gal who was the best thing that ever happened to me, but she is too old to carry out this, my final task.

Besides, she would not be able to find the secret spot.

You were the son I would have wanted if we could have had children, but you already know that. As difficult as everything seems to be for you right now, trust an old man's wisdom. You will be just fine, for you are closer to discovering the secret to life than you think. Everything you will ever need you already have; you just need to learn to recognize what is before you. You will never cease in your awakenings. That is what makes life interesting.

When you find my body, do not mourn, but think about and celebrate the time we shared.

Love, Hank

CHAPTER THIRTY-ONE

HE CALLED HANK'S HOME BEFORE HE LEFT, BUT THERE WAS no answer. It would take at least seven hours to drive to the trailhead, and that would not account for rush hour traffic or gas stops. And although he felt no hunger, he knew he would have to eat something for nourishment to carry out his dreaded task. Realistically, he wouldn't get there until close to midnight. He had hoped Millie had answered the phone and said that she had talked Hank out of his crazy idea, but he knew that wouldn't happen.

He called a second time after he had been on the road for a couple of hours. Still no answer.

He was about to hang up when he heard Millie whisper, "Hello." "I'm well on my way," he said.

"Good. I just got back from dropping him off." "Millie, I'm so sorry. I was hoping you'd say —"

She cut him off. "Everything is okay, and I'm fine with it. Drop by on your way back. We'll talk then."

He didn't want to make another stop. He drove a little faster, thinking maybe Hank would spend the night at the trailhead and start his hike in the morning. Corey thought that maybe he could reach him there and talk him out of it. By the time he reached the town of Lone Pine, he knew that Hank was probably already at the spot, and already dead.

There was one cafe still open in the small town. Although it was just a little past nine, he knew he had to eat, so he stopped. There was a local newspaper someone had left at the table. He pushed it aside thinking the headlines would be about the war, which was not something he wanted to read about at the present, but as he pushed the *Mono-Inyo Gazette* aside, he happened to glance at the front page, which surprisingly was absent of any headline concerning Vietnam. What caught his eye was the title to the feature article: "Wildflowers: Your Sierra Calendar."

The article was written by a local woman who explained the color of the flowers and their elevation on the mountains, along with the time of the month they bloomed. The article also revealed not only the current season, but also what you could expect as to the weather in the up and coming months. The article further informed the reader how long the season would last by the width of the bloom of each genus. She wrote how the aspen leaves were an excellent indicator not only of the time of year, but whether there would be an early or late summer and whether to expect it to be mild or hot. She explained if the leaves facing the sun were a dark green and their underside was a lighter, almost lime green, then the summer would come early and be hotter than normal. As he read the piece, he couldn't help but think this was the kind of article Hank would have enjoyed. He hoped he had read it before starting his final journey.

Corey finished his food, paid the cashier, tucked the paper under his arm, and left. He reached his destination around eleven. He thought about hiking that night since there was a full moon and the trail was visible, but then he reconsidered in case the path grew steep and was covered with slippery slate. If Hank had fallen into some ravine, he would not be able to spot him at night.

He got out of his car and found the mountain air quite chilly despite Ruth, the author of the article, saying it would be an early and warm summer. Since it was too dark to search for firewood, he stretched out his sleeping bag in the back of his station wagon and tried to go to sleep.

He couldn't sleep. He kept recalling good times with Hank on their many trips into the Sierras. Finally, about an hour before dawn, he decided to begin his hike. The trail would be flat, only a gradual incline for the first mile. If Hank had collapsed early, he would be on the trail. Besides, he had thought to pack a flashlight and could cover a small radius around the path. He reached the incline just as the first light of dawn leaked over the mountains east of him. The yellow light reflected on the sage, creating a deep purple haze among the shrubs. The red bark of the mesquite plants glowed orange-pink. Corey wondered if Ruth would write a follow-up piece on how you could tell the time of day by the color of the sun's reflection on the mountain rocks and plants. He hiked the next mile, stopping frequently to look down the slopes in case Hank had fallen.

When he reached the cutoff from the marked trail, the one that led to their secret lake and Hank's chosen spot, Corey found several rocks stacked upon each other. He knew they had been placed there by the old man in case Corey had forgotten the turnoff. He kicked them down as he headed toward where he knew he would find Hank.

The first time they had hiked this trail, Corey was ten. They had a map, which showed a lake at about nine thousand feet elevation. When they got to the point where Corey now stood, he remembered how tired he was as a boy, and when he looked at how far and high they had yet to climb, he felt discouraged.

"You got any adventuresome spirit in you?" Hank asked, sensing the boy's dampened spirits.

Hank pointed south of the trail. "See the way the mountain slopes there? The granite mountainside has a funnel where water from the melting snow once cascaded into the basin. The rock looks green and still moist. There are hundreds of unmapped lakes in these mountains. I wouldn't be surprised if there isn't a small lake at the base of that peak. If I'm right, it would be a lot shorter hike. I don't know about you, but I'm kind of tired and that would be a lot shorter."

"There's no trail," Corey said.

"I think you're wrong," Hank said. He pointed toward what looked like a narrow path about twenty-five yards from where they stood. "Looks like maybe a bighorn sheep or deer trail. I bet it leads to a lake."

They slowly made their way over rocks and slate until they reached where Hank had pointed. There was a narrow ledge that wound along the mountain. They even found dried sheep scat.

Corey quit looking for Hank's body as he reached the barely visible trail. He knew that Hank's will was greater than any doctor's prognosis. He knew Hank would be at the lake. He hiked another two and half miles, having to go slow because of the loose shale. He reached the lake just as the sun fully shone in the eastern sky.

The lake lay right at timberline. It was lined with aspens and a few old scarred and ragged pines. The lake was surrounded by steep granite rock mountains except where the sheep trail ended. There, at the lake's mouth, was a small rocky beach. Corey looked north to one small pine that grew from a flat-out crop along the west side of the lake. The pine was about fifty feet higher than where he stood. From there, you had a panoramic view of the lake and parts of Owen's Valley to the east. But Corey was in no hurry now.

He slid his day pack off and walked to the water's edge. There was no wind, so the glassy water reflected perfectly the jagged peaks of the mountain and the thin line of aspens that grew among the rocks.

Corey searched for a flat rock. Seeing the one he wanted,

he picked it up and skipped it over the water. He counted ten skips.

"Finally beat you, old man," Corey said, looking up at the solitary pine on the ledge.

As a boy, he had several rock-skipping contests with Hank, and Hank always won. The most Corey could get was six. Hank had held the record with nine skips.

"First try," he said, then went back for his pack and headed for the ledge.

Hank's body was there. His pants were pulled down and the plastic vein in his leg was partially pulled out. A pocketknife lay near the moist dirt between his legs. He had not been dead long, for the mountain critters hadn't found the body yet.

Corey closed the old man's eyes then turned away. He shouted at the lake, "Goddamn."

goddamn ...
goddamn ...
goddamn ...

His voice echoed around the lake.

The lake wasn't on any map, they called it Echo Lake after they discovered how pure sound resonated off the canyon walls.

It was during their second of what would become an annual trip to the hidden lake when they discovered the echo. They packed in a two-man raft the next time, because on their first encounter with the lake they saw trout but caught none. Hank said he didn't think the lake was stocked with hatchery fish. He reasoned they needed natural bait and would have better luck in the deeper water at the center of the lake. On the way up, Hank found a red ant mound and dug into it until he reached the larva, which he scooped into a jar. They also brought live crickets.

Out on the lake, Corey stuck his finger while trying to bait some ant larva on his hook.

"Fuck," he said, and immediately panicked. He was at the age where he and his friends started swearing just to be grown-up, but he never had sworn in front of an adult. Any hope that Hank had not heard it was immediately dashed as his high-pitched "fuck" reverberated in stereo around the lake.

"I'm sorry," Corey quickly said.

"Sorry for what?" Hank asked. "I'd be pretty pissed off myself if I stuck myself with a fucking fishhook. Know any other swear words?"

Corey looked at the old man suspiciously and said nothing.

"To use a good swear word for something trivial or just as part of your vocabulary is vulgar. It might even be a blasphemy to profanity; but there's a place for it, like now. Let's hear what 'shit' sounds like."

Corey hesitated, then shouted, "Shit."

They both laughed as they listened to the echo.

Corey turned back to Hank's body. He pulled the old

man's pants back up then lifted him onto the blanket. He folded the blanket over him, then he took the leather string and began to sew the edges together. He had forgotten gloves, so soon his hands blistered, then the blister broke and his hands began bleeding.

Once he finished the sewing, he began to dig the grave with an army shovel he had brought.

He got the hole maybe two feet deep when he found the rocky soil still frozen. He went back to the lake and gathered as much dead aspen, shrub, and pine limbs as he could find. He built a fire and surrounded it with rocks.

When the rocks got hot, Corey shoveled them into the hole. The frozen soil sizzled as the ice melted. He shoveled out the rocks and another six inches of soil. He repeated the process for several hours, constantly rebuilding the fire and shoveling the stones.

As he dug the hole nearly five feet deep, he noticed how bloody the shovel handle was. He looked at his hands, and although they looked as if they had been skinned, he felt little pain.

He placed a thin layer of small rocks on the bed of the grave, then lowered Hank's body onto the rocks. He then covered the blanket with more rocks before shoveling back the dirt. As he began filling the hole, he started feeling the soreness, a throbbing pain in his hands.

Once filled, he stamped the dirt down the best he could, then scattered the excess around the ledge. He left no sign of a grave. He looked at the blood-covered shovel, picked it up, and hurled it as far out into the lake as he could. When the shovel hit the water's surface, a large trout darted away from the sinking shovel. Corey smiled.

They had discovered bigger trout in the lake than they had ever seen in other lakes they previously visited. The day he had pricked his finger was also the day he caught the biggest trout of his life. Hank estimated it to be close to fifteen pounds. His fishing line was not nearly strong enough for a fish that size, so under Hank's guidance, Corey played the fish for a half hour until the fish gave up in exhaustion.

Hank netted the big fish and removed the hook from its lip.

"Thank him for his noble fight, then release him. He's still strong and will survive," Hank said.

"Can't I keep him? My friends will never believe me."

"So what? You know he's real. He is more food than we can eat and he'd rot if we tried to pack him out. This is his sanctuary and he granted us the pleasure of his company for a while. Thank him and release him."

As Corey obeyed and lowered the fish back into the water, he noticed that his hands were blistered from the long struggle, yet curiously, he never felt the pain until the ordeal was over, and even then, he felt the blistered hands made the struggle with the fish even more rewarding.

Corey looked at his hands again, grabbed his pack, and walked back down to the lake where he washed them. He submerged them in the cold lake water until they turned numb and the water temporarily anesthetized the pain. It was early afternoon, just enough time to make it back to his car before dark if he hurried.

An osprey circled the lake looking for fish. He had seen many hawks and a few eagles before, but osprey were rare. The bird looked as majestic as the rocky enclosure of the lake.

“Good fishing,” he shouted to the bird. The canyon walls repeated his wish. He looked once more at the lone pine, then hurried back to his car.

CHAPTER THIRTY-TWO

THERE WAS BARELY ENOUGH LIGHT TO FIND FIREWOOD. HE found a few chips and a partially burned log left by previous campers, enough to make a small fire. He thought about driving back to Lone Pine and getting a room for the night and a good meal. He had not eaten anything since the night before and he had not slept much the last two nights; still he felt like being alone. He knew if he were around other people he would feel awkward explaining his presence in Lone Pine and even more uncomfortable lying about why he was there. He needed to sleep under the stars as he and Hank had done for many years. He had a can of nuts and he had thought to bring along water. He found a ring of rocks, probably built by park rangers, which he used for his fire pit. He unzipped his sleeping bag and wrapped it around his body and sat cross-legged in front of the dim flames. He wasn't aware of how dehydrated the day's exertion had made him until he started sipping his water. The sips turned to gulps that his parched throat seemed to absorb like a dried-out sponge. He nibbled on the nuts and then drank more water.

Suddenly he was startled. Someone was sitting on the other side of the fire. At first he thought it was his imagination fueled by fatigue and the hunger. Across from the flames sat Hank. He was much too vivid to be an apparition.

Hank's eyes were so bright they reflected the flames of the fire. The old man said nothing. He just smiled at Corey as much with his eyes as his mouth. Hank lowered his eyes toward the fire as if there was something burning in the logs the old man wanted Corey to see. As Corey looked at the flames, they seemed to increase in size but not in heat. Soon the flames became so large that Corey felt as if he were inside the fire looking out rather than watching them from the ring's circumference. That's when the visions began.

In the first one he saw himself in a parking lot in front of some kind of store. To the left of the entrance a woman sat next to a baby carriage. Her back was toward Corey so he could not see the infant with which she was playing. She hummed soft melodies to comfort her child. She began singing a lullaby of notes without comprehensible words. There was something in her tone that expressed the universal love all mothers have for their babies. Corey moved around her to sneak a peek at the child. On clean blankets inside the carriage was a healthy-looking cat of no identifiable breed, but rather a mixture of several. Its luminous green eyes were slanted like those of a Siamese, but its fur was longer and platinum colored. Its coat was clean and neatly combed.

Corey could not recall ever seeing a pet so well-kept. The cat rewarded the woman's care by purring contently. The woman turned and smiled at Corey, who saw her face for the first time. She appeared to be in her fifties and was obviously mentally handicapped. Although her eyes were brown, they were slanted the same as the cat's. As she stroked the cat she looked up at Corey, revealing a proud and friendly smile which seemed elevated by Corey's desire to see her baby. Corey smiled back at her and reached out to pet her cat. Just as suddenly as the vision appeared, it vanished.

Instantly he found himself in a completely different setting. He was in a spacious, elegantly decorated dining room. The room was occupied by several boys and girls, all of whom, including himself, appeared to be in their late teens. They were obviously friends and shared a festive mood. Corey did not recognize any of them, although he felt he had been there before. No one seemed bothered by his presence. It was as if he was invisible to the group, yet he felt he should introduce himself and was about to when a very frail old woman, dressed in an expensive, but old-fashioned dress, the kind he remembered his grandmother used to wear, entered the room.

"Granny, we are having so much fun. We thought we would go out and get some ice cream.

Want to come?"

"Oh no. I'll just wait here," the old lady said.

Corey could see by her expression that she wanted to go,

but insisted they went without her. In the next instant, they were gone, but just as quickly as they vacated the room, they were back sharing laughter as they finished the last bites of their ice cream cones. The old lady eagerly greeted them at the door. Excitedly, almost child-like, she said, "Did you get it? What kind did you get? I like almost anything."

Corey instantly felt a bolt of pity shoot through his mind. The depth of sorrow he felt for her was greater than any he could remember experiencing before as he saw the disappointment on the woman's face. The granddaughter, embarrassed by neglecting to even thinking to offer to bring something back for her grandmother, sympathetically said, "Oh, poor Granny. She thought we were bringing it back. I'm so sorry," then affectionately hugged her grandmother.

"I probably shouldn't be eating ice cream anyway," the grandmother said, still smiling, but her forced smile was a hollow attempt to hide her disappointment. Corey felt as if the empathy he was feeling for the old lady was so powerful that she could feel his thoughts emanating and immediately looked toward him as if she alone was aware of Corey's presence. Her smile became warm and relaxed, as if to say thank you for understanding. He was about to say "What kind do you like? I'll run back and get you some" when, before he could utter one word, that scene too disappeared.

Next, Corey was walking down a main street somewhere. From the decorations on the storefront windows and adornments strung across the street attached to lampposts, it was nearly Christmas and cold enough to snow. A man dressed in well-ragged clothes, with no jacket, walked toward him. Corey did not know the man, yet he felt as though he had seen him before. The man looked to be in his late thirties. The small muscles in his face twitched spasmodically as he shouted meaningless words not aimed at anyone or with any apparent coherence or sense of direction. His words were like imprisoned thought fragments that were only important to the impoverished man.

People looked away from the man as they hurriedly altered their paths to give him plenty of distance as he walked in their direction. Corey could see that eye contact with the man was impossible, for his eyes looked toward another place and time void of any awareness of the present. Corey was warmly dressed but still felt the chill of the night. He glanced at the man's feet. He saw he wore no socks and his shoes were so badly worn that his bare toes protruded. They were white and the skin cracked by the freezing temperature. Corey reached into his pocket to give the poor man money, and again as soon as Corey attempted to enter the scene, it vanished.

More visions came and went, each bringing with them an intensity of emotion Corey had never felt before. All the scenes were short and had no beginning or end. Instead he was thrust into a moment where his feelings were so intense that to try and give them any common definition seemed inadequate. Even with the despairing images — when he was touched by pity or sorrow — disappeared once he tried to somehow remedy or enter in the moment. It was as if he was not to gain wisdom from the visions, but only feel the depth of the empathy they evoked.

Corey surfed the scenes as if there was an infinite number of rides. And like when he rode real waves, regardless of the outcome they summoned an invigorating adrenaline rush from the anticipation of experiencing a perfect ride. Like his best days of surfing, he wished the images he was viewing would never cease.

They did end though. Corey fell asleep. He didn't realize he had fallen asleep until he awoke into a different level of consciousness. He was back in the dream he had the morning before Hank's letter arrived, where once again he chased the Indian girl into the cave. This time, when he reached the end of the cave, he saw her seated next to an old man. They sat behind a campfire and faced Corey. He looked at the old man first. Instead of resembling a snake, his face looked kinder, and although his skin was dry and wrinkled like the skin of a reptile, he appeared to be more like an old desert tortoise. His small dark eyes were filled with the wisdom of having lived a long life. Yet sometimes, when the fire flickered, the expression on the old man's face momentarily changed back to that of the hissing snake.

Corey fixed his gaze on the girl. She was still young, but the childlike innocence he saw before now looked more sensual, even adulterous. Like the old man, her appearance shifted between innocence and wickedness. It was as if he were looking at a holograph that changed depending on the angle viewed or the reflection of light produced by the dancing flames.

Corey was convinced that the purpose for being in the cave, in the dream, was because the two images held some profound truth they were to confide in him. As if they read his mind, they began to speak. They spoke at the same time and very rapidly; often their words ran together so he was not sure which one was saying what. Sometimes what he heard was beautiful and so elegantly phrased they produced images as magnificent as any he had ever seen or heard, yet in an instant their words changed and, in so doing, summoned apparitions so ugly and sinister they produced emotions of unbearable suffering.

Corey shouted at them, demanding they speak separately so he knew who was saying what. They only talked faster and louder, mixing words of profound truths with heinous lies. Because they spoke at the same time, he could not discern who was saying what. It seemed to Corey both spoke lies and truths as frequently as their images changed appearances.

"Please, one at a time!" he shouted again.

The two figures laughed and seemed to intentionally make their words more incomprehensible. Their ever-changing appearance and the mixed messages from their chatter made discerning truths from falsehoods, beauty from the grotesque, impossible. Corey now feared them both, yet he tried to overcome his fear because he felt if he could comprehend what they were trying to tell him, some profound enlightenment would be revealed. Their words began being amplified and echoed throughout the tunnel walls. The pounding in his ears sounded like the screeching of tires braking just before a collision. Fear overcame Corey at last, so he tried to flee but could not move. He knew he had to wake from the dream or be lost in the cave forever.

Suddenly he felt warm and gentle hands grab him. His body shook with involuntary contractions. Corey opened his eyes. He saw a hint of dim, glowing embers in the dying fire. Hank was gone, and the pitch-black of night was being pushed to the west as the rising tide of blue permeated from the eastern horizon. Morning had broken, and with it came a calming blanket of serenity.

He arose and poured some stream water on the coals, then kicked dirt over the hissing, dying fire. He tried to fold his sleeping bag, only to become aware of how sore his hands had become from his ordeal. He threw it unfolded into the back seat of his car. The wind came up as he pulled away from the camp, shaking the car so hard he had to tightly grip the steering wheel, cringing as the pain in his hands shot up into his arms and shoulders and neck.

Just before he reached Lone Pine, the rising sun provided enough light to reveal the Sierra mountain peaks to the west. The taller more distant peaks were still covered with snow. Suddenly he saw a huge white cloud ascend from the valley below one of the steepest peaks. Although the wind howled across the highway, apparently there was no wind up in the mountains, for the cloud finished its ascension and slowly floated directly back from where it had emanated. Corey pulled his car onto the shoulder, stopped, and got out. He watched the snow cloud waft back to the earth. He had just witnessed an avalanche, an occurrence even more obscure than seeing the fishing osprey.

"God bless you, old man," he shouted, but the wind carried away his words as if he had only whispered them.

CHAPTER THIRTY-THREE

He parked his car one block over from the street where his parents and the Victors lived. He no longer thought of the old block as being his street since the confrontation with his father during Christmas break. He was adamant about not wanting his parents to see his car parked in front of the Victor's house, least of all his father who, although he would most likely be at work, sometimes dropped by his house since his office was nearby. It was half past eleven and as usual on weekdays, the neighborhood was quiet. He rang the doorbell and waited for Millie. He expected to find her disheveled and perhaps still crying; instead, her hair was combed, she wore a clean dress, and appeared quite dignified.

"I'm sorry we put you through this," she said upon seeing Corey. "You were the only one Hank trusted. You were the only one who knew where his burial spot was to be."

"I was honored," Corey said, stepping into the house and kissing Millie on the forehead.

"There were no problems?" she asked.

"Not at all. More importantly, how are you holding up?"

"I've shed what tears I need to shed. When you've lived with and loved someone for as long as Hank and I have, your feelings no longer need public display."

"There will be a lot of questions. Are you prepared for that?"

"I've already called the police and told him that Hank went for a hike in the local mountains.

My nephew and his wife will verify that we tried to talk him out of it. By now they will have found his abandoned car and are probably now searching the San Gabriels." She looked at Corey's hands and gasped.

"I forgot my gloves," he said.

"I have antiseptic and bandages in the medicine cabinet. Wash your hands and get them cleaned and covered. I'll fix you something to eat. You must be starving."

"I am, thank you."

Corey walked down the hallway toward the bathroom as Millie went to the kitchen. Just before he got to the bathroom, he stopped and stared at a picture of Hank. It was a picture he had seen many times before. It was taken when Hank was about Corey's age, when Hank had first left the reservation. There was something about the photograph that looked out of place among later pictures of Hank. Hank's hair was black, his face chiseled with the characteristic high cheekbone of the Apaches, but what captivated Corey were the old man's eyes. Ever since Corey had seen him for the first time in the Victors' backyard, Hank's eyes always looked happy and exuded both warmth and understanding. Even in death, despite the obvious pain he had to have been experiencing, they appeared contented and nothing like the piercing and angry eyes in the photo. Hank's long-ago eyes were the same as Corey's when he saw his own reflection in the mirror every morning since he had entered college. Maybe they were the universal eyes of youth, but they definitely were not the same eyes Corey saw when they first met.

Corey stepped back from the picture and peered at each object on both sides of the hallway. As often as he had passed through that corridor, for the first time he realized there was no time sequence to where objects had been displayed, but rather a random collection of pictures and other memorabilia that were significant in Hank's and Millie's lives. There was a story behind each, some of which had been told to him in the past, while others were self-explanatory. Corey saw that their lives were comprised of so many wonderful moments that sequential order was unnecessary. As Corey surveyed the walls, he realized it was all one big picture that when added together was a miracle we call life itself.

He went into the bathroom and washed his hands, and the hot soapy water made them burn again. He was careful not to look in the medicine cabinet mirror as he washed. Even when he finished and dried his hands, he avoided looking at himself. He swabbed the antiseptic on his hands and bandaged the worst wounds. As he closed the medicine cabinet, he inadvertently caught a glimpse of his image. He quickly looked away, then paused and slowly looked back at his reflection, which caused him to smile. He returned to the front room where Millie had a sandwich and glass of lemonade waiting.

"You said you knew Hank was going to do this even before he did?"

"Yes, he had let me read the article about his father's death a long time ago. Although we never spoke much about it. I knew my Hank disagreed with his father's views, but he still loved him, although he never admitted it. I knew he was sorry for their estrangement so much so he longed to find some redemption."

"What makes you think that?" Corey asked.

"Because he knew his father loved him not despite his defiance, but because of it. Leaving the reservation was a brave act that only a true warrior could do. I think his father was too proud to admit that he respected Hank's decision. Hank inherited his father's stubborn pride, so the two would never show their true feelings for each other." Corey nodded.

"You need to reconcile with your father, even if it's just for your mother's sake. She wasn't always the way she is now," Millie said.

"I know. I hope to someday, but today is not the right time or the right place."

Millie nodded, then asked, "I have one more favor to ask of you. Your girlfriend, Karen, she's a photographer, isn't she?

Corey nodded a yes.

"I peeked by the hallway to see if you were all right. I noticed you staring at our collection of photos and other things. Would you take Karen to Hank's spot and take a picture?

Not of the grave, but looking out from where he's buried? I want to share that place with him by adding that picture to our wall."

"Of course. I didn't get a chance to tell you yet, but Karen and I are getting married this summer. I had already decided to take her to Hank's grave the moment I shoveled the last bit of dirt on his grave. The place is so beautiful I have to share it with the people I love the most." Corey paused. "When you see it, you'll be moved in a way you can only describe as spiritual. I knew you would want the picture to help give you closure."

Millie smiled as if Corey said something funny, like when a child tries to impress an adult by using a big word, only the child uses the word incorrectly. "I never understood why people talk about closure. Why, with the love my Hank and I had for each other, would I want closure? I want to keep him alive in my memory just as that hallway will always keep him alive in my mind. I want to look from his grave and imagine he is standing next to me and describing what he was seeing in his own unique way of illustrating things."

Corey stammered, "I didn't mean —" He hesitated.

"I know what you meant. It's okay," she said. "I've said enough, and I know you're about to start finals. I better let you get on your way."

"I don't want to leave until I'm sure you're all right."

"My nephew and his wife are coming over to pick me up. I'll spend a few days with them — I'll be fine."

Corey held her hands and said nothing. He continued to look her in the eye. She sighed, then almost in a whisper she said, "I always wanted to die first, even though I'm younger than Hank. I always looked upon him as being so much stronger than me, so much so that I could not see myself carrying on alone. He sensed that. Before he died, Hank made me travel to places I always wanted to go but could never find the time. He encouraged me to read more and join a book club where I met a lot of new friends, some who have become travel companions. In short, he made me learn how to be independent, just like I suspect your Karen is, which is an improvement your generation is providing for future ones. Hank made sure that I would, and could, enjoy every bit of my remaining life. I'll be just fine; now go."

Corey let go of her hand, but not before kissing her cheek and giving her a gentle hug. "We'll get the picture enlarged and put it in a nice frame. We'll have a dinner party and tell Hank stories late into the night." Corey paused, then hugged her one more time before he left.

As he got to his car he looked up towards his parents' house again. He wanted to drop by and say hello, as if things were the same as they had been when he was in high school, but he knew they were not. As Corey thought to himself, he so much wanted to believe, "Time will heal our differences."

CHAPTER THIRTY-FOUR

COREY WANTED NOTHING MORE THAN A GOOD SLEEP, YET as tired as he was, a residual adrenaline surge pulsated in his blood. He arrived back at Mission Beach before anyone had returned from school. He walked out to the beach, hopped the boardwalk wall, and sat facing the ocean, his back resting against the cement which was warm from absorbing hours of spring sunshine. The heat penetrated the stiff muscles of his body and its warmth soothed them and made needed sleep seem near. Corey closed his eyes and listened to the sound of the waves, which sounded different from the early part of the week. He realized he was hearing the first of the southern swells of approaching summer. The surf too was rising and would produce much better waves than there had been for at least a month, yet he was too tired to think of going into the water. Out of habit, he opened his eyes to see if the surf was coming up or if it was just his imagination. From the corner of his eye he noticed someone hop over the wall carrying a surfboard.

It was a young surfer, probably just back from school. The surfer quickly walked toward the shoreline. At first, he thought it was Joey from the profile, but from the back the young surfer's body looked muscular and too well-defined to be Joey. He watched the surfer go down to the water's edge to study the break. The young man had most of his weight on his left leg; the thumb of his right hand rested on his right hip. He shaded his eyes with his left hand. That pose was exactly the way Corey stood when he studied the break. The young man turned to wax his board when he noticed Corey watching him.

"You're back," he shouted.

Corey realized it *was* Joey, and although he had just seen him a few days ago, he looked so much more mature.

Joey came running up. "Hot told me about the death of your friend. It was that old guy you always talked about, wasn't it? I'm so sorry," Joey said. "I know you felt real close to him."

"Thank you. It was his time to go — and it was a nice service." Corey paused, then added, "Let's change the subject. How's the team doing?"

"Great," Joey answered. "We play tomorrow afternoon if you want to come to the game."

"I might do one better than that. Do you think if I get my

hair cut in the morning, Coach Thompson would still want me to coach?"

Joey beamed. "Of course, but I wouldn't want you to do that just for me."

"I was thinking. I can still oppose the war with short hair, maybe even be more effective, but friends like you are more important than both hair and wars. Besides, the reality is there is such a narrow window in which I can still coach you. I'd be a fool to let it pass."

"If you want to do that, I'd —"

"I definitely want to," Corey said, not letting the boy finish.

"All right! Let's celebrate with some surfing!" Joey exclaimed

"Not today, I'm too tired now. The waves look great. You go ahead enjoy yourself. If you hurry, you can have these waves all to yourself for a while."

It was then that Joey noticed Corey's hands. "What happened to your hands?"

"That's a story for another day. I need to go in and get some sleep now. I'll see you tomorrow, hopefully as your coach. I promise."

Joey started to return to his board when he turned back toward Corey. He wanted to look Corey directly in the eye, but the boy inside his changing body was still present and the boy was too embarrassed to do so. Joey's eyes cast upon the sand before Corey's feet. Finally, he made brief eye contact and said, "I think I know how much that old man meant to you." Joey looked as if he wanted to say more but didn't know how.

"You said just the right thing. It means more to me now than you could possibly know. Now hit the water before it gets crowded."

Corey returned to his apartment, where he found the front door ajar. Karen stood inside waiting for him.

"I saw you on the beach. You looked like you needed to be alone. You okay?"

Corey looked as if he didn't understand the question. He blankly stared at her for a few seconds before saying, "Hank's dead and I haven't been able to cry."

"Oh, honey, it's okay."

"No, you don't understand. I've cried over lesser things in the past, none of which meant as much to me as Hank. How can I cry those same tears now?"

"They're not the same tears. The ones you need to cry now come from a much deeper place in the heart."

His body felt limp. It was like a wave had just knocked him over and held him helplessly underwater. He was powerless and disoriented. He wasn't sure which direction the surface. He felt unable to breathe. His lips quivered and his body shook. Suddenly he felt rescuing arms reach around him, pulling him to the surface. He gasped, then began crying.

"Everything is going to be fine, babe," she said as she held him. "You need to know that everything is going to be fine so you can let it go and cry as long and hard as it takes to get it all out," she whispered and stroked her hand through the back of his hair.

Corey didn't know how he could still stand as he felt so weak. It was Karen who kept him from falling. She was silent as he continued to sob, but she remained, holding him tight and gently stroking his hair.

"Everything is all right, babe — Everything is all right," she whispered once again as she faced the picture window in the front room. As she looked out toward the ocean she saw a lone surfer enter the water.

Joey paddled out as a new set rolled in. He had learned that the seventh wave of each set was always the biggest, and usually the best shape. He kept paddling and counting waves, letting swells pass he would have caught if he was competing with other surfers, but now he was alone and had his pick of any wave. He positioned himself for the seventh wave, and true to surf lore, it was the largest.

Joey paddled hard, thinking maybe he had started too late. Instantly, his senses were heightened as the wave caught him. His stomach stayed at the top of the crest while his heart raced downward with his board. Joey picked up speed as he leaped to his feet and banked off the bottom, extending his body almost prone to the wave's face. He then twisted hard to the right, lifting the outer rail completely out of the water. He turned one hundred and eighty degrees back up the wave's churning face. Then, at the top, instead of banking off the lip and straightening out for a long ride across its wall, he twisted right again, doing a complete three hundred sixty-degree turn.

Again, he picked up speed at the bottom of the turn and raced to get in front of the curl, which he did at maximum speed, allowing another right twist and executing a second three sixty on the same wave. He followed with a re-entry into the curl, where he was buried in the tube and thought the wave would crash over him, but the trapped air in the tunnel blew him forward and freed both body and board from the crashing wall of water. Although he was completely covered for just a few brief seconds, it seemed an eternity. He kicked out of the curl, landing on the backside of the wave. He faced the open sea.

"Yes!" he shouted, and thrust his fist toward the heavens as he bowed his head to the waters.

THE END

maybe ...

CRAIG WALLENBROCK

Craig has always been passionate about baseball from when he first started playing as an eight-year old in Little League baseball in Pasadena, California. He eventually found himself playing at Pasadena City College, the alma mater of Jackie Robinson and several other future major league players. He earned a small scholarship invitation to play for San Diego State University where he began to question his own ability to play at a higher level. While living off-campus at Mission Beach, California, he developed an alternative passion for surfing. The carefree lifestyle of a surfer during the turbulent sixties and the Vietnam war, pushed baseball aside as he not only doubted his baseball abilities, but began questioning the values of his parents' generation.

Craig finished college and the surfing/hippie world Craig had embraced became his surrogate for baseball. He realized the alternate life-style, although enjoyable, almost to the point of hedonistic, was impractical. Craig's younger brother by eleven years, Judd, begged his older brother to help him with baseball, which had also become Judd's passion. Although Craig was reluctant at first, his own fire and love for the game was rekindled. Craig fully committed himself to his beloved game working seven years coaching college baseball, thirteen years as a professional baseball scout, eight years working for a baseball agent, then working his private batting lesson business and occasionally consulting hitting for various major league affiliates. In 2016 he accepted a position with the Los Angeles Dodgers as a hitting consultant and roving instructor for their minor leagues, a position he still enjoys.

One other spark or smoldering ember still burned deep in Craig's mind. As an English major at San Diego State, and ever an avid reader, he had always thought about being a writer. The anguish and passion of his college years led to a metamorphosis of his value system which he never satisfactorily understood. He wrote Sun and Water in an attempt to not only put his own life's journey in perspective, but to explain his generation's cultural revolution of the sixties.

Made in the USA
Columbia, SC
03 August 2020

14617504R00204